THE

MIDDLE

PLACE

THE MIDDLE PLACE

KEALAN RYAN

MERCIER PRESS

MERCIER PRESS
Cork
www.mercierpress.ie

© Kealan Ryan, 2019

ISBN: 978 1 78117 607 8

A CIP record for this title is available from the British Library

Printed and bound in the EU.

For my Carol

PROLOGUE

I'm still here. I know I am because I can see them. But how come I can see them all at once when they're in different places? That doesn't make any sense.

I'm not …? Stop thinking that.

Can you hear me? Can you see me? I can't see myself. I can't breathe, I can't scream. I want to scream. I must be dreaming, but I can't wake up.

You're not dreaming.

I can't do anything. Yes, I can. Get a hold of yourself. At least I'm still with her. With Pamela.

No you're not.

Yes I fucking am! But she can't see me.

Hold on. It's okay. It's a dream.

Long fucking dream.

Of course it's a dream! It's definitely a dream. Okay. Thank God for that. What a crazy messed-up dream. Okay. Time to wake up now. I can always wake myself up from my dreams. Wake up now like a good man. Christ, that was scary. Wake up. Wake up, you bollocks! Wake the fuck up. Why am I not awake? And why am I still seeing him? I don't want to look at him. Look at her instead. Look at my Pamela. He's still here. Or I'm there. Look at someone else. Not him. My parents. No, they're too sad. Back to Pamela. Oh Christ, please stop crying.

You can hear me, Pamela, can't you? Except I know you can't. Stop crying, baby.

My baby. My Robbie. My angel. My son. My life.

This isn't a dream, is it?

It must be. The alternative is not meant to happen like this. Everything is supposed to just go black, right? Oblivion.

How do you know?

If not black, then heaven. God, angels and all that craic.

Hell?

Jesus, I wasn't that bad! Don't tell me I've landed in hell. No, if it was hell, she wouldn't be here. It's not hell, Pamela is here. And my baby boy, my Robbie. I'm with you, buddy. Don't worry, I'm with you.

But I'm not, am I? So what? What the fuck happened? Don't say it. Don't admit it.

It will be okay. Focus. Get through to her.

She can't hear you.

Someone else then.

None of them can hear you, you stupid dead bastard.

There. I said it.

Dead.

No, it's not true; it can't be.

So what then – you just obtained mystical powers?

Stranger things have happened.

They really haven't.

So that's it then?

That's it, alright. Admit it.

No.

Just admit it.

I'm dead.

You're dead.

Am I still me? I still feel like me. I still think like me. I'm alone, I know that much. But I'm still here. That's got to be something, right? Not really – I don't want to be here, not like this. But I am. I've got to deal with this somehow.

But how? Why?

You know how. You know why. Think about it.

I don't want to think about it.

Admit it again then.

I don't want to.

You have to.

I have to.

It's the only thing you know for certain.

I'm dead.

Okay. I've admitted it. Now what?

Now it's time to figure this whole thing out.

No, fuck that. I'm dreaming. Time to wake up.

THREE
MONTHS
DEAD

1

The funny thing about being dead is that you start to think about stuff you never thought of when you were alive. I mean, you'd think you wouldn't have a care in the world after you die, but the truth – for me, anyway – is that I started caring about things a lot more.

Take those ads on TV, the ones for Concern or whatever. I watched those ads hundreds of times when I was alive but never cared enough to pick up the phone and make my seven euro a month donation. Seven euro, for fuck's sake. 'Earthquake in China' – *That's a pity*. '10,000 people homeless across Ireland' – *They really should do something about that*. But did I really give a shit? Not really.

I don't know if that makes me a bad guy. When I was alive I thought I was great – it's only now I'm starting to re-evaluate things. A bit late, I guess.

Just to clear something up – the life flashing before your eyes thing is a load of bollocks. Truth is, you haven't a clue what's going on when it happens and the past thirty-five years, or however long you've lived, is the furthest thing from your mind. I was thinking of Clint Eastwood, for fuck's sake. I thought I was going to be fine. Even after you've died you still assume that you're going to be all right. Believe me, it takes a while for the realisation to land, but when it hits, it hits harder than anything you can possibly imagine. Try to think of the worst sinking feeling you've ever had. I bet you could see a way through, no matter how bad it was, whether it's by throwing money at the problem, or even just waiting it out. But death? What the hell can you do to get out of that one? Your life starts passing before your eyes over the next few hours, weeks, months – but it doesn't flash. It crawls.

***

Since my death I've been trying to think of one defining moment that proves I was a great person in life and I can't come up with any. I've come up with plenty that, on paper, make me sound like a bad bastard, though. If I were in a romantic comedy I'd definitely be the asshole that everyone hopes doesn't get the girl. Any time I watched those movies I'd even be rooting for the nerd guy, not realising that I was much more like the dickhead character.

I did do some nice things, of course. I loved my wife very much and was a good father. Was good to my parents and brothers. I participated in the odd fun run, did Movember each year. If any of my mates needed help moving house or anything like that I was always Johnny-on-the-spot to lend a hand. I had no problem making airport runs. If anyone needed a lift anywhere, for that matter, I was your man.

But I also cheated on my wife shortly after I proposed to her, broke my best friend's nose for no reason, and when I was in school I bullied a kid named Simon so badly that he had to leave. I brushed thoughts of these acts aside when I was alive and focused instead on the kind, but relatively minor deeds that I'd done that gave me some sort of reward – never fully admitting that I only did them so people would think I was wonderful. In life, your regrets are things like missing a night out or never finishing college or some shit. When you're dead the only regrets you have are the times where you let someone you care about down.

So, as if being dead isn't depressing enough, I'm also beginning to see now that I was a bit of an asshole when I was alive. Tough to come to terms with, that one, because I can't make it right. Not now. All I can do instead is wish that I could change things, wish I had been a better man, wish I had committed one truly selfless act. Wish that I hadn't been so full of shit all the time.

2

I miss chilling out and watching movies. It's weird, but that's one of the things I miss the most. Sounds kind of stupid, I guess. I miss my wife and family too, obviously, but I don't want to think about that right now. It's the small things that are getting to me at the moment. I can't relax and stick on a film. I can't have a pint. I'd love a pint.

Oh yeah, the other thing about being dead is that you are cold all – and I mean all – the time. It fucking sucks. I never exactly pictured the afterlife as me hanging around my old neighbourhood, freezing my balls off. I've got a chill deep in my body, except, of course, I can't even see my body – I just know I'm here. Existing. It's weird. Kind of hard to explain. All I can say is you're not going to like it.

There's not a lot about being dead that I like, to be honest. Life was so much better, so enjoy it while you can. This whole thing isn't at all how I imagined it. I don't mean to be all gloomy and morbid – you're probably thinking what a miserable bastard I am, but Christ I can't help it. The old me was happy-go-lucky. Well, maybe not happy-go-lucky exactly, but definitely not depressing. I was happyish most of the time. Some things used to piss me off but, by and large, I was pretty upbeat.

Now everything pisses me off. Even the things I used to love the most – in fact, especially the things I used to love the most. The people. Because I can't do anything with them; I can't hold them or talk to them, laugh with them. I can watch them, which is comforting, I guess, but then sometimes that makes me feel like a bit of a weirdo. I mean, they haven't a clue that I'm there. But what the hell else am I supposed to do? I've got no life – literally.

The one positive in this whole shit state of affairs is that I'm kind of like a superhero. A completely useless superhero, but still. I can read minds; I hear people's thoughts and memories, I know what they are feeling. I can go from place to place and time to time depending on what I'm focusing on. I can fly. I can walk through walls. I'm invisible. I can see things no one else can see. I can feel things. Not in the way I once did. Not to touch, but I can feel life grow and thrive everywhere. I can take hold of it and become part of the world around me. I can't see myself but I know I'm here, existing in several places at once. I see what is happening with all the people I love all the time, the people who were affected by me. I'm with them, always.

Maybe this is what I'm supposed to do. When you're dead you're meant to watch over your loved ones, aren't you? But am I watching over them or am I just watching them? I know for a fact that I'm not helping them, so I'm beginning to think this whole guardian angel stuff is a load of crap.

3

Bullying that kid Simon was bad, I totally accept that, but to be perfectly honest with you, he was kind of a knob. He was one of those kids that even the teachers hated. He was on the slow side, always showing off and never knew when to shut up. He just rubbed me the wrong way and whipping the piss out of him was a happy pastime for me back then.

He had this bowler haircut, not the cool Oasis-style bowler, more of a lame *Eight is Enough* type thing. One day, I started chanting, 'Bowler ... bowler ... bowler ...' at him in the classroom and pretty soon my chant had turned into a screaming mantra from the entire class. Simon kept his head down on the table, crying, while we all laid into him. My friend John was the only one who tried to stop it. He'd dished out as much as anyone at the start, but after a while he must have figured that enough was enough, so called out to start slagging one of the other oddballs in the class instead. But I stayed on Simon, like the asshole ringleader that I was. The more insulting I got, the worse language I used, the cooler I felt. I knew it was wrong, but, with the entire class behind me, there was no way I was stopping. When Mrs McGuire walked in we all went mute. She saw that Simon was crying, had heard the roar of the class, but didn't give enough of a shit about him to do anything.

He left about two weeks later, and everyone knew it was down to me. I pretended to act like I didn't give a bollocks, but deep down I felt a bit bad. I was only eleven – I had no big master plan to break this kid's self-esteem and force him out of the school. He was just an annoying boy that I didn't like, so I pushed him around.

I used to see him about from time to time after he left. He still lived in the same area. Every time he saw me he'd give me a big smile and an 'Alright, mate.'

I never understood that.

'Alright, Simon,' I'd respond.

If someone treated me the way I'd treated him I'd sooner spit on them than say hello. What kind of a person was he, to greet me like we were old friends? Did he have such a low opinion of himself that he still wanted to be buds despite everything?

I had hoped that he'd get on better in his new school, but I heard that he ended up being as much of an outcast there as he ever was in Saint Michael's. After a few years, though, I stopped seeing him around and he left my mind completely.

I don't know why he's back in my thoughts after all these years. Like I said, I'm thinking about all sorts of stuff that I never bothered with when I was alive. Life crawling before my eyes. Memory stops for a little while on Simon O'Donnell and then moves on again to something else, someone else.

I can remember things perfectly, not as if they happened yesterday but as if they're happening now, right in front of me. Splashing around in a puddle with my dad when I was four is as clear to me as the day I passed my driving test, or the first time I was allowed to have a shower instead of a bath. There used to always be a fog obstructing these things. But now, for me, that fog has lifted and everything is crisp in my mind, allowing me to look back over my past with perfect clarity.

When I was still alive, I'd forgotten just how good my parents were to me – how much they truly loved me. I was one lucky bastard growing up – and all through my life, really. How well they treated me, how many things they did for me. The look on Dad's face at my funeral, trying to console Mam – they will never be the same again and I can see that in them. The same way I can see it in other faces. They've both been so good to Pamela. Shit, I really let her down. *But I'm going to make it up to you, baby. I'm going to protect you somehow, make sure you and Robbie will be okay, live happy lives.* I'll figure it out. I'm here for something, amn't I? I have to be.

If I'm not here for that, then what am I here for? All the cool things that are supposed to happen after you die haven't happened. I'm not playing hacky sack with Jesus on a bunch of fluffy clouds, or having beautiful angels feed me grapes while fanning me down.

Instead I have to concentrate on the good memories from my life to make the days bearable. Or focus on things I never truly noticed when I was alive. Like the sea. I lived beside the coast for most of my life, but I never really looked at the sea. It's amazing, particularly given how I can watch it now – I can follow the waves as they race towards the strand; I can ride along with them, sense them lifting, struggling, then crashing down on the shore only for the cycle to begin again, the waves rising.

I want to rise again, to live again. I want to hold my wife, breathe air into my lungs, touch the sea – really touch it. I want to feel Robbie's little hand in mine. I want to close my eyes and discover that this is all over; close my eyes and wake up beside Pamela. If I can't do that then let me go; it's too painful. Let me go, let me close my eyes and just disappear.

4

Robbie's my son. He's two and a funny little fucker. I love watching him, that's one thing I can't get tired of. What he gets up to when no one is looking is the stuff I like the most. He enjoys making faces in the mirror; sticking out his tongue and laughing hysterically. Then when he hears Pamela approach he'll stop and pretend he wasn't doing anything. If he gets his hands on a skinny candle he'll snap it in two. Pamela has them all over the gaff – to add atmosphere or something – so it's easy for him to nab one, and when he does, the sound of the soft crack gives him a little rush before he strolls off, leaving shards of wax everywhere. I wish I could spend my whole day with him, but my thoughts are constantly being pulled to darker places – I don't like those places and try to force myself back to sweet things, like Robbie and my Pamela.

Pamela. She looks different now – older. She's only thirty-two but has bags under her eyes that weren't there before. Her walk is different. She used to have such a springy step, bouncing all over the place. You'd hear the clack-clack-clack of her heels coming from halfway up the road. I could never figure out how someone who was only five feet five could generate such a loud noise just by taking a step. Whenever I was waiting for her on a busy street, the sound of her stride as she approached would rise above everything: heavy traffic, horns honking, passers-by. As soon as it reached my ears, my smile would stretch up towards them too, because I knew that the next thing I'd see would be her. Her march had been glorious. Not anymore. Now her walk is silent.

She was a great wife. I never really went out with anyone before her because most girls annoyed me after a short enough time. Or maybe I annoyed them. But not Pamela; I always had great fun with her and she laughed at every damn thing I said. She found me hilarious. Way funnier than I actually am. Was. Although she seemed to find a lot of things funny. She was always so ready to laugh. At her own jokes too. She'd be in stitches at her own gags, way louder than the people she would be cracking them to. When she'd tell a story that she found funny you could never understand the end of it because she'd be laughing so hard. She loved slagging people too and, like most Irish women, she was great with the insulting one-liners.

She's still like that, at times. She's just sadder now. But I love when she can forget about me for a minute and crack one of her gags, or smile at somebody telling a joke or at a funny ad on TV. It's beginning to happen more and more now, though she's still a far cry from her old self. Everyone is sound in the office where she works, but it's still a grind for her to act normal. She's doing her best to get on with things. To bury her grief and her fear of being left alone deep down, where it becomes numb.

Christ, the first month was unbearable. I have to hand it to her friend Orla for being there the whole time. I'd never liked her – not because she was a bad person or anything, just because I thought she was a bit of a muppet. She's one of those people who would say things like, 'I had every intention of walking that path but then life tapped me on the back and pointed me in another direction', or 'Thanks a thousand' instead of 'Thanks a million'. Head wrecking. But she really came up trumps for Pamela, so I'm grateful to her for that. I have no idea how the fuck she put up with all that crying for a full month. I wouldn't have been able for it. Mind you, I wouldn't have been able for Orla for a full month either.

It's good that she has such a close friend. Pam is oblivious to

Orla's shit because she's known her for so long. Same way that I am to John's, I guess, and he is to mine. We've been friends since we were four – our first week at primary school, to be exact. The pair of us were kicked out of class for talking too much. Neither one of us gave a damn; we thought it was great – so much so that when the teacher came to get us we were nowhere to be found. We spent the next hour wandering around the corridors, nattering away, and have been best friends ever since. More like brothers, really.

I think he misses me almost as much as Pamela does. I'm with John a lot. He's getting married in a few months and I was supposed to be the best man, but now that's shot to shit. I feel bad because I've put a dampener on the whole thing; he's lost all interest in it. His soon-to-be missus, Niamh, can't help getting pissed off sometimes at his lack of enthusiasm and then he gets furious at her for being annoyed: 'I just lost my best friend, for fuck's sake. Sorry if I don't give a shit about who sits where!' So they're fighting a fair bit now. I'm trying to send out positive energy in the hope that John will get more into the whole thing, but I'm so damned depressed I don't think it's working.

John's a great guy, though; he'll make it work. The poor bastard's just so down. He works as a landscape gardener. He did our garden, put in mainly stone slates so I wouldn't have to do much with the lawn mower. It looked the business. The part that did have grass was surrounded by flowers and then near the back wall he put in a water fountain. Pam wasn't mad on that bit. She thought an angel pissing into a pond was too tacky, but I reckoned it was ironic or something. Plus, I figured Robbie would think it was gas when he got older.

I watch John at work now, the way he puts his back to anyone who might be around when he's digging a hole or whatever, working hard, and I can see tears running down his face. It happens to him a couple of times a week. He seems to be okay when he's working with someone else; it's when he has to do something by himself that I see him welling up. It's difficult watching the people you love be so upset, but as hard as that can be at least you know that you were loved, and there is a certain warmth in knowing that I am missed.

Still, when this happens with John, I try not to look. My attention moves to his shovel and down to the grass. I can feel the grass grow, which is another unexpected perk of being dead. Sounds boring, but it's not; there's something incredible about being able to feel life growing so slowly and continuously, to feel the wind around it, the moisture in the air grabbing hold of a single blade, forming tiny, almost invisible beads of water that run down till they hit the soil. That journey might take all day, but then, I've got nothing but time. Besides, I like it – to rest on a little drop of water and ride it as if it was the slowest roller coaster known to man. I always go back to my family and friends eventually, of course, but it's nice to be alone too sometimes.

So this is how the day passes for me. Half the day, anyway. Watching Robbie stumble around. Waiting and hoping for Pamela to smile and loving every second that it lasts when she finally does. Checking in on John, or my folks and my two brothers, Tim and Brian.

They're two gas men – I've always loved watching them bounce off one another. I'm nine years older than Brian, the older of the two, so I was never as close to them as they are to each other. That never overly bothered me, though. I loved how close they are and love it even more now. They still joke and laugh together – maybe not as much as they did before my death, but they're still fun to watch. Tim in particular cracks me up; he's a wild fucker, but he's all heart. Total alcoholic, but he's only twenty-four so he gets away with it. He's a happy drunk, though; I saw a guy start on him once outside a pub, but instead of fighting back he wrapped your man in a hug and wouldn't let go until he hugged him back. He's a strong lad too, so it's not like he was afraid – he just didn't want to fight. He's a great knack for sidestepping a fight no matter how imminent it might seem; he'd challenge opponents to blinking competitions, thumb wars, hug-offs. Anything to defuse a dodgy situation, which, to be fair, he often landed himself in in the first place. You just can't stay mad at Tim, even if he vomited on your brand-new suede shoes. Which he actually did to me once, the little bollocks.

Brian's a wonderful older brother to him; he's always looked out for him and never treated him like a younger brother. Never. Even as kids, when a two-year age gap can seem like a lot, Brian included him in everything. He always took his side too, no matter how wrong Tim might have been. He still does, their dynamic hasn't changed in the slightest from when they were four and six.

I was never like that with them. I preferred the idea of being the big brother, so much older and aloof. I tried to cultivate the image of being kind of an enigma who they'd have to look up to. It didn't work. Tim looks up to Brian instead and – as an extra kick in the nuts – Brian actually looks up to Tim in return.

Apart from John, I don't visit my pals as much as you'd think. They're all getting on with their lives. I've sat with them at the pub once or twice but I never stay. They don't talk about me enough and I've never enjoyed watching people get drunk when I wasn't drinking anyway.

Besides, I have more important things to do, someone else to visit. The rest of my time is spent with a man named Danny Murray, a man I only met once.

The man who killed me.

5

Danny Murray wakes every morning at 6.45 a.m. and presses the snooze button for half an hour. Once he reluctantly crawls out from under the covers, he doesn't bother showering, he just suits up, scoffs a big bowl of oatmeal, then rides on the number 37 bus into his workplace in town where he sells mobile phones. What he doesn't know is that I ride along with him. I can't help it; I'm drawn to this bastard whether I like it or not and if it takes me the rest of his life I'm going to get back at him somehow. I'm dead, that makes me a ghost, so I should be able to haunt the person who killed me, right? I'm just not sure how I'm going to do it, exactly.

I do feel a connection with this guy more than anyone else, though; more than my son, even, which only gives me another reason to hate him. He's the only person who might be aware that I'm around – although maybe it's just his conscience at him – but I think it's more than that.

I know he's frightened.

When I say *haunt*, by the way, I don't mean sneak up from behind and spook him with a 'Wooooooo'. I want to really fuck with this guy's head, make him suffer. He took everything from me, all that could ever be – *my whole life, you son of a bitch. You walk into work acting like nothing happened, you know what you did and you're going to pay, you prick.* How can a person take another man's life and then go into work pretending that everything is cool?

The only problem is I still don't know how I'll get back at him. I wish I had someone to help me, like the way Swayze in the movie *Ghost* had that ugly bastard ghost from the subway. But as far as I know I'm alone; I'm sure there are other poor pricks like me out there, but I can't see them.

I have to figure this one out for myself. It's a pain in the ass because I'd love to be slamming doors on him, knocking books off the shelf and all that to freak him out, but I'm a total fucking amateur and haven't a clue where to begin. Although, I think he might sweat more when I focus on him. Also, the other day as I loomed over him, I could feel him shiver. No one else reacts to me like that. Maybe it's the hatred I have for him that carries over – I don't know.

I can't stand the fact that I spend so much time with him. I'd rather spend it focusing entirely on my family, but I need to find out more about him. It helps that I can still keep an eye on them even when I'm with him – I'm always aware of what they're doing the whole time. In the same way that I'm aware of what he's doing all the time when I'm with Pamela or Robbie or John.

That need to know more about him is so strong within me that I won't be ready to let go until we're even. It's funny. I do believe that I'm a better person now than when I was alive – or, at least, I'm starting to become one – but while I was alive I never had the urge to kill anyone.

And now I do.

6

Danny's girlfriend, Michelle, is the only one close to him who knows what he's done and the crazy bitch doesn't seem to mind too much. 'I still love you, Danny ... I'll stick by you no matter what you've done.' Scumbags.

Danny's dad actually seems alright. Wait till he finds out what his shit-bag son is after doing. Danny will have to tell him sooner or later; everyone will have to find out.

You're up in court, aren't you, dipshit – and you're fucking sweating it.

I have to laugh when I listen to Danny and his bird talking in bed, Danny crying like a baby, 'What's my dad going to say, he'll hate me, won't he?' No mention of me, though, is there? What will my wife say? What will my boy say when he grows up? *They'll fucking hate you anyway. But you don't give a shit about that, do you?* All he talks about with Michelle is how is he going to tell his dad and how is he going to get off? Is there any way he can swing this without going to prison? No remorse, he's just pissed off that he's put himself in such a lousy position. He's a big brute of a fucker and doesn't look like the type of guy who'd be afraid of what his dad might say – can't always judge a book by the cover, I suppose.

Danny has a beard. That's another thing that pisses me off about him, because I had always liked a man who wore a beard. Hipsters took from them a bit, of course, but even with those knobs I'd always admired a good beard. When I was a kid my dad had a beard and I grew one when I was nineteen. Well, I grew what I could – which back then meant hairs sprouting in random tufts on my face.

Danny has a good beard, I'll give him that – kept short, the same length as his hair.

He fancies himself as a bit of a fashionista. Wore the skinny jeans before anyone else and got slagged off by his mates for wearing half a wet suit. Of course six months later they all had a pair. Danny's mates are all dicks, just like him; each has a bigger mouth than the next. All talk about how many pints they had the night before, who puked where and who can stay up the latest – that kind of shit. They're from the same middle-of-the-road-type background as me, everyday fools, but these tits act as if they're street – starting fights the whole time and thinking it's great, still acting like they did when they were eighteen. I mean, Danny's twenty-eight now and still acting like a tosser. More than that, he's a bad fucker, and I'm not just saying that because of what he did to me. He sits there with his mates, doesn't shoot his mouth off as much as some of them, but just sits there, grinning. Knowing that no matter how many layers of bullshit they pile on top of each other, he is the toughest of the lot.

Why don't you tell them, Danny? You fucking want to: 'I killed a man.' They'd all think you were the big swinging dick then, wouldn't they? Not the nobody you are now.

He's waking up a lot in the middle of the night. I often wonder if it's because I'm there. I think it is. I hope it is.

I hang over him, willing him to wake, roaring at him, putting all my energy into brightening up the dark room as much as I can. Pitch-black night, but under his little eyelids I imagine it being as bright as the sun until he opens them. Slowly, just enough for me to know that he's awake, just enough for me to believe I've disrupted his sleep. *I can do this all night, Danny. Do you know I'm here looking at you? I think you do. You're scared and you should be.* I'm going to figure out this haunting thing sooner or later.

SIX
MONTHS
DEAD

7

I remember the first time I knew for an absolute fact that Santa Claus was real. I was six years old and beginning to hear on the grapevine that the Santy thing was one big hoax. All I wanted for Christmas that year was a cowboy wagon complete with horses that I had seen in some obscure Spanish magazine my parents had brought home from our summer holidays. I thought it was the most badass thing ever. At about a foot and a half in length, it was a proper replica of an old frontier stagecoach, not a toy at all, but was instead intended for middle-aged nerd enthusiasts of the American Old West. Of course, I didn't know that it wasn't a toy; all I knew was that it had real canvas for the covering, a long stick break for the wheel, a jockey box at the back and – my favourite of all – a holster for keeping the shotgun up front. Savage yoke altogether.

Looking back, I feel sorry for my mother because I was convinced Santy would get it for me. She of course (being Santy) knew for a fact that she could not. It was a real make or break Christmas – John had claimed that he saw his mam putting out the presents the year before. That cast a pretty big doubt in my head, but when I opened up my present on Christmas morning to find the exact – and I mean exact – wagon that I'd asked for, all my doubts went out the window. 'See, Mam? I told you. Brilliant!'

All she did was smile. Turns out she'd been up North one weekend when she happened to walk past a shop window with the wagon on display. She almost started to believe in Santa Claus herself at the sight of it. The silly price to spend on a six-year-old didn't matter – not if it meant keeping her boy believing in magic.

I was the oldest kid I knew who still believed in Santa – right up until I was twelve, for fuck's sake. Granted, I kind of milked it the last year, but still. It was because my folks went all out each year. The best was when, one year, they got a pair of wellies and stuck their soles in the soot from the fire, then made footprints all the way from the fireplace to the Christmas tree – fading with each step. That kind of thing has caught on a bit now, but it was unheard of when I was a kid.

I had planned to continue the tradition by doing little tricks like that for Robbie. He was too young to know what the hell was going on the Christmases I had with him. Pamela's family weren't as into Christmas when she was growing up, so she wouldn't have known about half the shit I was planning. Fuck, now that I think of it, who's going to put up the lights this year? We had the best lights in the estate last year and I'd bought loads more in the January sale to make sure we were the best again this year. Bollocks, I suppose no one will. First Christmas without me, they're probably going to keep it low key.

8

You know the way you hear that Christmas can be a sad time for a lot of people? I never really got that, or at least I'd never experienced it. I get it now, alright, because everyone I'm watching is having a shit time.

Pam had grown to love Christmas almost as much as I did, particularly after Robbie was born – but now she's miserable. I was right about the lights too; the house looks fucking bleak. The only reason she even put up a tree was for Robbie – she would have preferred nothing. My folks are the same. In past years, Mam always went all out with the presents, giving us some from them and different ones from 'Santa'. The first year me and Pam were married the lads gave us an awful slagging because the pair of us stayed over in my parents' house Christmas Eve, and, in the morning, we ran down the stairs as if we were kids, rushing to open the presents under the tree along with my two brothers who were themselves in their twenties. We always got loads of deadly stuff. But this year my mam said, 'Let's just take it easier, okay? I really can't face shopping for everyone.' It's gas because I could see that Tim was a bit disappointed. Obviously he totally understood, but he couldn't help being a bit pissed off that he's getting fuck all pressies this year.

Sorry, buddy.

***

Danny has bought his dad a phone for Christmas – what a crap present; he works in a phone shop. You'd think he'd put a bit of thought into it. Suppose all he can think about is the court case and how he will have to tell his old man what he's done. The idea of prison sickens him. I love watching him get so stressed. I can feel the butterflies in his belly when I focus on him. Feel them weighing him down. He has them all the time, fluttering away, upsetting his stomach. Sometimes he can't eat he's so afraid. He's been so cocky all his life, but now he's shitting it. He knows he's not a real tough guy, so how the hell is he going to manage in prison surrounded by fucking animals? He's decided to hold off until the new year to tell his dad: 'Happy New Year, Pop; I killed a dude.' Should be good.

When his dad finds out he'll be in bits. I can't help feeling sorry for him. Like I said, he seems alright, he just raised an asshole. Danny's mam died of cancer when he was seven, so it was only the pair of them in the house. They always got on very well, but Danny still acts like he resents his dad sometimes for turning into an alco after the wife died. He pulled himself out of it, though; he hasn't drunk in, like, fifteen years.

Danny likes bitching to his girlfriend about his 'tough upbringing' whenever he's in the bad books. It's pathetic. He totally hams it all up. I think it was understandable – his dad losing it. If Pamela had died instead of me there is no way in hell I wouldn't have drowned myself in whiskey. I wish I could hit the bottle now.

I always really liked getting pissed. I could be a stupid drunk, but I was a happy drunk too. I hadn't been aggressive on the drink since I was a young lad – the time I broke John's nose. We were at a twenty-first birthday party in a pub and I was basically showing off all night, drinking all sorts of mixers, acting crazy and pretending to be more pissed than I was. I was drinking gin, something I was never able to drink again after that night. If someone just said the word 'gin' for a good year after it I'd get goosebumps. It ended up getting me as locked as I had pretended to be earlier.

I was slagging John all night about not scoring with that many girls and stuff, telling him he should 'come out'. I'd only really say things like that when other people were around. I thought I was being gas, but now thanks to my perfect memory I can see that everyone thought I was being a shithead.

Eventually John just told me to fuck off. He happened to say it in front of a girl I fancied, so I got all embarrassed and stormed out like a knob. Twenty minutes later, he found me half-asleep on a bus-stop bench up the road from the pub. He kept nudging and shaking me to get me up. With each prod, my anger grew. Finally, I just saw red, stood up and walloped him as hard as I could in the face. I didn't floor him; he just took a little step backwards, though I felt his nose crack under my knuckles. I expected him to lunge at me. He should have at least punched me back. But he just looked at me. We were both in shock, at all the blood more than anything.

After a moment, I turned around and lay back down on the bench, a flood of guilt mixing with the drink in my stomach. I had to get away from it – from John and all the blood on his nice, chequered going-out top. I closed my eyes and pretended to fall asleep, waiting until I heard John leave before I stood up and staggered home.

I talked to him the next day on the phone and he was cool about what had happened; he just put it down to me being locked. Sound bastard. That made me feel even worse. His folks had to fork out for a cap on his tooth, but they never bothered straightening his nose. It wasn't all wonky or anything, it just wasn't quite as straight as it used to be.

He still looks good, though; he's a handsome guy, John. He's going to look great in his tuxedo.

9

I'm glad Pamela is going to John's wedding. I wasn't super-pals with his bride-to-be, Niamh, but I liked her a lot. She's extremely down to earth, could have a laugh with anybody. Her default facial expression is a smile and she never seems to have a bad word to say about anybody. Pam gets on well with her too, though she'd also be closer to John. At first, I wasn't sure if Pam would go, but now she's half-looking forward to it. Niamh made a special phone call, asking her to do her best to come and said that Pam could leave whenever she wanted. She probably would have gone, anyway, but it was nice of Niamh to make the call.

I'm raging that I'm missing it. When John asked me to be best man I'd been honoured. I mean, I'd expected it, but I was still honoured. I wanted to be the best best man ever, so I started on the speech straight away. I actually had the entire thing written, can you believe that? Spent ages on it too, getting it all worked out – when I'd be funny, when I'd be sincere. It was perfect. I'd even practised it in front of Pamela. I was so damned prepared. What a complete waste of time that turned out to be. I wouldn't mind, but I'd been a last-minute man my whole life and the one time I got something done early I ended up dead before I got to use it.

I would have been deadly at it. I had never been a best man before and was really looking forward to it. I wasn't going to get too pissed either – not before the speeches, anyway. The last wedding I attended the best man made a balls of the speech because the poor bastard had been so nervous he'd downed a few too many drinks to calm himself. It was kind of funny to watch. He never said the bridesmaids looked well or even the bride, for that matter. He just kept going on about how much himself and the groom, Peter, were best mates and the bride Liz was tearing them apart. I don't think he really meant it – the dumb shit just thought it was funny so kept going on in the same vein until the whole room felt awkward. Then, to break the embarrassing silence he'd created, he broke into an impromptu little song of 'Me and Pee and the devil makes three, don't want no other lover baaaby.' A tumbleweed practically smacked him in the head after that.

I learned from this eejit. I wasn't going to make any mistakes like that. I'd say nice things about Niamh and I had funny stories from when me and John were kids, but mainly I wanted the whole room to know how much I loved him – or maybe not the whole room; I wanted him to know.

There'd been so many things I wanted to do for his wedding, like I was planning to get a pocket-watch to give him on the morning of the ceremony as we were all getting ready. I even knew what I'd have inscribed on it: *To my best friend John on his wedding day, with love from Chris.*

10

'I'm so proud of you, John.'

'Thanks, Dad.'

John smiles as the two of them stand facing one another. They're in John's old room and it hasn't changed since he lived there; still has the Guns N' Roses posters on the walls. Of course he only moved out a couple of years ago, but still.

'No I mean it, you've really turned into a wonderful young man. Me and your mother are both so proud of you.'

'I know you are, Dad, thanks.'

John's face reddens. His dad doesn't usually talk like this.

'Here, let me fix your dicky bow.'

John looks straight into his dad's eyes as they glaze over. Jarlath's one of those guys who seems a lot bigger than he actually is; everyone always says he's over six foot but he's barely five ten. It's just that he's wide – not fat but strong wide: broad shoulders that would fill a doorway, spades for hands, long arms. His whole appearance is like a stereotype of a big thick Paddy with his fine red nose, white curly hair, smiley face; all he's short is a pair of wellies. He has a large scar down the right side of his jawline that he got in a farming accident as a child but which everyone always assumes is from his days as a garda. Tough-looking, but a lovely fella. He looks funny in the tux now. I can't quite put my finger on what's wrong. It just doesn't sit right on his frame – tight around the chest or something. It looks kind of lopsided. It's a nice picture, though: the two of them all dressed up, smiling at each other while Jarlath straightens John's dicky bow. His big hands look clumsy around John's neck but he does a nice job of it.

'And we love Niamh, too.'

John nods as the two of them sit down on the edge of the bed.

'Here, I want you to have something,' Jarlath says as he hands him a little box. 'They're the cufflinks that my father gave to me when I joined the guards. The two of us have the same initials so ...'

'Jesus, Dad, thanks a million,' John says as he opens the box. 'I love these.'

Jarlath's dad's name was John Duggan and he was the first man to own the cufflinks. 'My father used to say he'd only ever put them on for special occasions. I don't know what in the hell he meant by special occasion because he didn't even wear them at any of your aunts or uncles' weddings. He figured they were too nice,' says Jarlath with a grin.

They do look lovely – eighteen-carat gold with the initials *J. D.* etched in letters so fancy you almost can't tell what it says.

I feel a bit intrusive, being here, but I'm not visiting Danny Murray today. I'm aware that he's watching the telly in his flat, but I refuse to waste any time focusing on him. Besides, I doubt John and Jarlath would mind my being here.

'You know today is going to go great. How're you feeling?' Jesus, I've never seen Jarlath look so serious.

'I feel good; great, I mean – I'm not a bit nervous or anything. I kind of can't wait to be married, you know?'

Jarlath smiles. 'I was the same when I married your mother. It was a lovely day, just like this, except it was in the summer.'

It is a lovely day, actually – there is a low sun, the sparkle of which adds a glitter to everything that lies beneath it. I'm glad they lucked out on that front. I just wish I could feel a bit of the heat off that sun myself. Despite his words, John doesn't look as happy as he should, nor as I wish he was. When he smiles it's more of a sad smile. Jarlath puts one of those bear arms around his son's shoulders. 'Are you sure you're not nervous? Because you won't get a better girl than that, you know.'

'Ah God, I know. No, I'm not nervous. It's just I remember all the craic me and Chris had at his wedding getting ready. Then the pint and a whiskey with his dad and his brothers before the church. I was just kind of looking forward to that, I guess, for my own wedding. I suppose I just miss him being here for this, you know?'

'Of course he's here,' says Jarlath. 'Do you think he'd miss this day? He's looking down from a better place, enjoying every minute along with you.'

John just fiddles with the cufflinks, not looking convinced. So Jarlath tries another angle. 'You know, today is going to go great and Chris would want you to enjoy yourself. He'd be happy for you. Do you think he'd want to see you moping around on your wedding day?'

It's not that I like seeing him moping around, but I must admit that I am glad I'm being thought of and talked about. Can't help but feel good about myself.

I also feel sorry for Jarlath because I can tell that he just wants to cheer up his son. 'Today you're marrying the woman you love, surrounded by people who love you. You're a great lad and you're going to have a great life. I'm so proud of you, John.'

'Thanks, Dad,' John says as he turns his head to look out the window. He sees his own reflection and starts to feel better. He looks good in the tux and having his dad next to him is comforting. He thinks about Niamh, looking forward to their life together.

'Can you believe how sunny it is out there?' Jarlath says. 'It doesn't feel like winter. Chris must have something to do with that.'

Thanks, Jarlath, I wish I had.

'Yeah.'

John doesn't like returning to thoughts of me; he wants to think of the good things in his life. He hasn't turned around yet because now there are tears in his eyes.

'Shining down on you for your special day.'

What Jarlath's saying isn't comforting to John – he doesn't believe in any of that and Jarlath knows it. I wish I could help him. I can see him searching for something to say that will make John's pain go away. He hates to see his boy upset, especially on what's supposed to be the happiest day of his life. Jarlath shifts, searching for something that a smarter man might come up with. 'John ...' There's nothing to say, not that I could think of, anyway. But Jarlath's smarter than he thinks. 'Here, let me help you with those cufflinks.'

11

The wedding reception is in the countryside, about an hour outside Dublin. There's nothing but breathtaking castles all around Ireland's countryside that are perfect for weddings, but they chose none of them. Instead they went for a fairly bog-standard hotel. Niamh liked it because it's near where she is originally from in County Meath. John liked it because it was the first place that Niamh suggested.

One good call they made, though, was deciding that no kids were allowed at the wedding, which means more fun for the adults. It also means it's Pam's first night away from Robbie since my death. I'd say it will do her good. A bright-orange knee-length dress hugs every inch of her body. God, she looks great, albeit slightly reserved, as she sits at the table, fiddling with her empty dessert bowl. I always loved when she straightened her hair. She's lost a little weight these past few months but she's still nice and curvy. Beautiful, big golden eyes. Man, I was so lucky. She's been put at the same table as my mam and dad, which I'm not sure was a good idea. Stinger for everyone else at the table – stuck with three gloomy people with big sad faces through the entire meal. Can't see why they couldn't at least have put her with my brothers. Tim and Brian seem to be enjoying themselves, as usual, mainly discussing which girls they're going to try and score with. There's not a whole lot to pick from, most have boyfriends or husbands. Fair play to Brian, he's gone over to Pam and the folks' table a few times to see how they're all getting on, 'What did you guys have, the beef or the salmon? Yeah, me too, stuffed now. Can I get anyone a drink? Pam?'

'Gin and tonic, thanks, Brian.'

All fogeys at her table, she's beginning to feel old herself. What the hell was John thinking putting her here? She sees enough of my folks. She can't wait till the tables are cleared and she can hang out with someone else. She needs to be having a good time. The poor thing is beginning to regret coming. She loves my parents, but my mam in particular hasn't been the same person at all in the past six months, not half as much fun.

The speeches are pretty good. Our friend Davey ended up being best man. He's alright at it but nothing special. A lot of his gags he got from a best-man speeches book; I know because I'd read the same one and decided not to use any of them. He opens up with, 'Hello, I'm Davey and I'm here to tell you all about John and how thoughtful, handsome and ...' Then he looks up from his piece of paper. 'Sorry, mate,' he says, looking at John, 'I can't read your writing.' It pretty much stays on that level throughout. Davey's a naturally funny guy, he's just too nervous to carry it through on the mic. Jarlath's speech is deadly. He even mentions me. Actually I'm mentioned four times through all the speeches – by Jarlath, Davey, John and even Niamh, which I wasn't expecting. What she said turned out to be the best: 'I want you all to raise your glasses to Chris, who I know is raising one right back at us from some wonderful place even sunnier than this one. We love and miss you very much.' I got all choked up when she said that.

⁕⁕

My mam and dad head off to bed early, which is unusual for them – or at least it used to be. Once the dancing starts Pamela really lets her hair down. The DJ is typical, lashing out all the wedding classics like 'Come on Eileen' and 'Greased Lightnin''; all the shit you would never listen to at home but go mental for at weddings.

The 'afters' were always my favourite bit of the day – everyone's all liquored up and going crazy on the dance floor. So many weddings I made a total tit of myself dancing. I used to look forward to it and ruined countless suits by skidding on my knees or attempting to do the splits. Pam never danced half as much as me, but she's going all out tonight. She really seems to be having fun – herself and Brian are hanging out a lot, going for smokes and stuff in between the bouts of dancing. I haven't been mentioned for a couple of hours, but the more drunk everyone gets the more I'm on their minds.

It's also looking like Tim is going to score with one of Niamh's cousins. They sit next to each other at one of the tables, his hand on her lap. Then he starts telling her all about me – partly because he wants to talk about me, but mainly so she'll see how well he's dealing with the tragedy, feel sorry for him – then hopefully, well, then hopefully bang him.

Brian and Pam start talking about me out in the courtyard. 'He would have loved today, wouldn't he?' Brian says as he searches for his lighter in his pocket.

'He sure would,' says Pam, 'He'd be in his element. You should have heard his speech. It was gas.'

'He would have been better than poor auld Davey,' Brian grins, lighting Pam's cigarette first and then his own. 'Talk about a Nervous Fergus.'

'I know, the poor guy. It was total shite.'

'Ah Jesus, that's a bit strong,' Brian says, laughing.

'Oh, I'm sorry, but it was. That joke about wiping his arse with his speech went down like a lead balloon – you don't talk about taking a dump in a wedding speech.'

Brian shakes his head. 'The poor bastard. He had such a redner.'

'I know,' says Pam, 'and Davey's usually so funny. He should have had a couple of whiskeys or something before going on. Apparently he didn't have one drink before the speech 'cause he was so afraid of messing things up.'

'Not even a pint?'

'No.'

'Ah that's just stupid – you need a little bit of Dutch courage – Christ, it's no wonder he was shitting himself.'

They both start laughing. I love Pamela's laugh, it almost sounds dastardly, kind of like Muttley the dog's laugh.

Pam wrinkles her nose. 'Speaking of shitting yourself, did you fart?'

'No, Jesus – you think that's me? It's the fucking cows, for fuck's sake!' Brian declares. There's a fierce bang in the air from a nearby farm. Brian starts coughing and laughing at the same time. 'Jesus, I wish I could fart like that.'

'Me too.'

'Ah here.'

Pam smiles at the look of disgust on Brian's face and takes a drag of her cigarette. 'How do people live here?' she wonders. 'How do you open your door to the smell of shit every morning?'

***

Tim's after overdoing it on the whiskey. His tongue is protruding slightly past his lips, as though it has outgrown his mouth. The slurring doesn't help his cause and Niamh's cousin, Mairead, is losing interest in him fast. Jesus, I love watching Tim – he's a funny little bastard; I mean, he had this bird sewn up. She had been laughing at all his jokes, thinking he was cute, and now there's no way he's getting anywhere because he's after getting too locked. It's like watching a car crash; he spills his drink all over himself, and her, by accident. It's clear that Mairead doesn't know what to make of this guy, especially since almost immediately after drenching her he throws the head in for a kiss.

'I think maybe you're a bit too drunk,' she says, pulling her head away from his sticky face.

'How dare you, madam!' he yells, then storms off to the dance floor.

Ten minutes of dancing later, however, Mairead walks past him and he jumps in her way. 'Have you forgiven me yet?' he asks.

'Piss off,' she says.

'Ah come on, it's a wedding after all. Let's just let bygones be bygones. Come on, we both said some things we didn't mean and now it's time to make up.' This couldn't possibly work. 'You like what you see and I like what I see, so let's stop playing these silly games,' Tim perseveres. The dancing has sobered him up; there's hardly any slurring from him at all. Mairead can't help but laugh at his bullshit. Tim has a cheeky grin on his face as he goes in for the kiss again – and this time she accepts it. *You little bollocks, how the hell did you pull that one out of the fire?*

***

I'm really enjoying the whole event. Tim's been kissing that Mairead bird ever since – lucky bastard's probably going to get laid. Very happy for John and Niamh too, they're obviously made for each other and both seemed to have a blast all day. It's 2.30 a.m. and they're all still up in the residents' bar. Now that I think about it, this was actually my favourite part of a wedding. Everyone relaxing, jackets off, ties missing or being used as headbands – pints of Guinness and a bit of a sing-song. I'd love to be joining in; I knew loads of songs and loved singing when I was drunk. Davey and Tim are talking about just that: 'It's a pity he's not here for this one,' Davey says.

'He was a divil for a sing-song alright,' Tim nods. I can't

understand why Mairead is still hanging around Tim; he's more langered now than ever. Every once in a while Tim belts out the start of one song or another, the whole place quietens down for him and then he forgets it after the first line. The latest is: 'A hungry feeling, came over me … Came …' Then he just takes a sip of his pint as if he has done nothing, leaving everyone else wondering if they should wait for the next line.

Pamela's talking to some guy I don't know. Or rather, he's talking to her. He's a bit annoying, but she's putting up with him because she's in a good mood. Plus she's pretty drunk. I haven't been mentioned yet, but I know it's just a matter of time considering this dummy's going to try and score with her and Pam's clearly not into him. I can't blame him for trying to chat her up – she looks amazing and there's no me there with my arm around her.

Still, it's annoying to watch. If I was there I would have bounced this asshole ages ago. Have you ever listened to a drunk person try to chat someone up when you're sober? The waffle they come out with is ridiculous. This guy's been talking about his job for the last ten minutes. Nobody wants to hear about your job, unless you're a race-car driver or astronaut or something.

Graham – that's his name – is just an engineer and he's been going on about some fucking generator up in Derry that he's supposedly in charge of. I mean, Jesus, who gives a shit? Pam clearly doesn't, anyway. 'The generator bearing overheated because of problems with dirt ingress in the lube oil pumps.' What the fuck is he on about? 'So they send me up, it's a pretty common problem but they rely on me too much so …' The blank face on Pam is priceless. This guy's really reaching, you can tell the poor fucker knows he's being boring but what can he do? He has nothing else to give.

Looking back, I wasn't a million miles away from this clown when I first talked to Pam. I was twenty-six when I met her. I was in Australia on a year's working holiday visa and she was a friend of this girl Karen who I hung out with over there. Pam was just over for the summer. The first time I met her I was after smoking a bunch of weed. I was sitting in this Irish bar called The Fiddlehead, which was the mangiest shithole of a pub in all of Perth, yet somehow the best craic as well. She sat down beside me so I had no choice but to talk to her. I've always been useless chatting up girls – unless I'm drunk, anyway – but being stoned and with someone out of my league? I hadn't a hope. It was horrible, I don't ever remember being so boring – I even wanted to get away from my own company by the end of the conversation. She hooked up with one or two other lads before I scored with her about a month into her stay, and when I finally did we ended up going out. After we spent the rest of the summer together, she decided to apply for a visa herself in order to stay for longer, and I was only delighted as I'd already fallen in love with her.

'So have you a boyfriend or anything?' Graham asks. *Yep, only a matter of time.*

'No, I'm married.' *Good girl, Pam.*

Graham frowns, looks around the bar. 'Oh, right, where's your husband?'

'He's not here.'

'Really, how come?' Ah shit, Pam doesn't want to talk about it, not with this guy anyway.

She looks at her drink, near empty. 'Well, actually he died. He's dead.'

'Oh my God – that's terrible. Is he dead long?'

'About six months.'

I'm not buying this guy's concerned face and neither is Pam. He has the sad expression on for two reasons:

1) He thinks with a sad face he still has an outside chance of scoring.

2) He's pissed off the hot girl he's been talking to is actually some
   lonely heart with a dead husband.

He slides closer to her on the couch. 'That must be very hard. You
poor thing.'

Pam sighs. 'To be honest, I don't want to talk about it if you
don't mind, okay?'

'Sure, sure. Of course – let's talk about anything you want.'
Graham the tosser then starts singing 'Let's Talk about Sex, Baby'.
I know he didn't mean any harm – he's just nervous, but Christ,
what an idiot. He knows it too. 'Sorry, bad joke.'

Pam has had enough. She stands and hurries out of the residents'
bar before the tears fall. Brian and Tim notice her leave and follow
her out to the elevators.

'Shit, Pam, are you alright?'

'I just want to go to bed,' she says, wiping her eyes. The elevator
button is lit up; the electronic screen above the steel doors has an
arrow on it, pointing downwards.

I wish to God I could hug her. I could never bear to see her cry,
no matter how mad I was at her, or even if I was the cause of it – in
fact, especially if I was the cause of it. The sight of her crying melts
my heart, pure and simple. I'd always give her such a hug any time
I saw her like this. Brian hugs her now, but I wish it was me. Jesus,
now Tim's half-crying, rubbing at his eyes.

'What the fuck happened?' he asks.

'Nothing, just that eejit in there, talking about Chris and stuff.'

'What fucking eejit?' Brian asks. He looks fit to burst someone.

Pam shakes her head. 'Nobody, it's nothing. I just want to go to
bed. He's just some fool.'

'Who the fuck did it?' Brian demands. Part of me wants her to
tell him, but she's beginning to calm down.

The elevator door pings open. Pam steps inside. 'Nobody did anything, Brian. I just got a little upset. Seriously, I just want to go to bed. Sorry for ruining everything.'

This line seems to devastate Tim. 'Pam, please, please now – you didn't ruin anything, that's the last thing you should be thinking of. You didn't ruin anything, okay?'

'Okay,' Pam says as the elevator door closes, shutting her away from my brothers.

I follow Pam in the elevator. A constant flow of tears is running down her face. She steps out when it reaches her floor and proceeds down the corridor in her new, subdued walk. Outside her room the little red flashing LED tells her that her electronic keycard doesn't work. Her first impulse it to fling it away, but she gathers herself and tries again. Green.

She steps inside and exhales a breath as if she has just been holding it for a long time underwater. I watch her undress – she is so beautiful it hurts; part of me wishes I could look away. She gets under the blankets naked. The last time she stayed in a room like this, I was naked beside her. It had also been for a wedding and we had snuck away early to go to bed. Given that it was a rare night away from the house and Robbie, we wanted to have big, loud, noisy, drunk sex. It was fantastic. Now, she's curled into a little ball. I used to curl up behind her and cup one of her breasts till I fell asleep. She misses my hand, misses my body warming her back. She was always cold when she first hopped into bed – no matter how warm the room, she'd say she was freezing until I warmed her up. Now she has no one to rub her ice-cold feet against. I used to give out about it, but in truth I always loved it. She's cold now. The big blanket won't warm her. *I'll stay with you, Pam, till you stop crying. Till you fall asleep.*

***

Back down to the residents' bar, Tim's getting the spinnies. Brian's riled up for a fight but doesn't know who to take it out on. He wants to be the big man – to kick the shit out of someone for Pam. It's mainly the whiskey that's given him an angry brain, but I think he wouldn't mind venting some anger anyway. He has a puffy-looking head on him, which John spots on his way back from the jacks.

'What's up with you?'

The sight of John's smiley red face calms Brian down and gives him the cop on not to go ruining the night on everyone.

'Ah nothing,' he mutters. 'I'm just looking for my drink.'

John nudges him. 'Would you look at the state of your little brother, he's bollocksed!' The two of them start laughing at Tim, slouched on the couch while Mairead tries to talk to him.

'Are you listening to me, Tim?'

'Huh?'

'Are you alright?'

'I'm grand, thanks.'

As soon as he says this he's up on his feet and heading for the door. The air out in the courtyard is much better than the stuffy bar. Tim takes a deep breath and looks up at the sky.

'I miss you,' he whispers.

I miss you too, Tim.

The crisp air begins to wake him up. The grass is damp, but this doesn't stop him from sitting down – there is no one else outside and Tim likes the fact that he's alone. He sparks up a smoke and looks out at the darkness. Sooner or later, he'll have to go back inside, but for now it's just the two of us out here together, enjoying the cold.

MY DEATH

12

12

The day I died all I wanted to do was watch *Unforgiven*. It's my favourite Clint Eastwood movie and Pamela had just gotten it for me on Blu-ray, a nice surprise as mostly we just streamed shit for free, but this was the special edition with loads of cool features. I was delighted when she gave it to me because I'd wanted this edition for ages but couldn't justify paying €30 for it. I knew if I bought it at that price, the following week I'd see it for a fiver – that's happened to me too many times before.

'Ah fuck it, let's just stay in and watch *Unforgiven*,' I'd suggested.

Pam shook her head. 'No, we're going out.'

She had already told Orla that we'd meet her in town, but I wasn't too on for it because none of my mates were going and, as I said before, Orla wrecks my head. I suppose I was always going to go – Pam had already sorted a babysitter and there was no way I'd stay in by myself. Besides, I knew from experience that as the night went on I'd end up enjoying Orla in spite of myself – but for some reason I always felt I had to put up some form of protest when it was just the three of us going out.

As it happened the night went pretty well, at first. I hadn't been in town in a good while and was enjoying the buzz of the city. Dublin can be great for that, all the people milling about in the streets. There's always so many people outside, especially if the weather's nice, which it was. We did a bit of a pub crawl and ended up in a real Orla-type pub – huge, fancy, darkly lit, jam-packed, standing-room only, playing gammy chart-type music on full blast and full of wankers.

One of those wankers was Danny Murray.

He was at the other end of the bar having an argument with Michelle when we first walked in. Since I've been living in Danny's head I now know what they were arguing about – nothing. Completely pointless. Just arguing about arguing, the way couples can do when they have a good few drinks in them. Michelle had started making a scene by raising her voice at him, causing Danny to get all embarrassed. 'Shut the fuck up, you stupid cunt,' he shouted. He used the word 'cunt' on purpose because he knew how much she hated it – he wanted to get at her like she was getting at him. The only problem was she stormed off when he said it.

'Michelle!'

Danny caught up with her at the door where we were standing and told her to calm the fuck down and not to be running off like that. I always got a kick out of watching another couple fighting on a night out – plenty of times it had been me in that position and it's kind of funny watching the expressions on the two faces.

Danny saw me laughing at the pair of them and got even madder at Michelle. He's a striking-looking fella when you first see him. Kind of an ugly bastard, but he's so unusual-looking I'd say girls could find him attractive. Dark skin, dark eyes. He's very tall and wide, built like a fucking wrestler. Most Irish guys, even if they're big and strong, aren't that well cut – but you can tell that this guy is all pumped-up even through his shirt. It looks a bit much; you just think *gym knob*.

The pair were causing such a big scene that we were thinking of moving further inside. Then Michelle gave Danny-boy a push and the ignorant fucker fell back against me, spilling half my pint. 'Here, watch what you're doing, will ya?' I gave him a little shove off me and the big thick bastard didn't even look around or apologise or anything. He just followed her outside to continue their domestic.

I forgot all about him then and went about enjoying my night. Pam was in great form – as fun as Robbie is, we were delighted to have a night off – and I was even managing to get a kick out of Orla. 'Men just find me too intimidating,' she declared at one point. The Why Don't I Have a Boyfriend Speech was a regular occurrence on a night out with Orla.

'Why's that, because of your spiky haircut?'

'Oh fack off, Chris.' When Orla would say fuck, she wouldn't say it like normal people – she has this makie-up conceited Dublin accent. It's like she's going for a mix between 'feck' and 'fuck', but it comes out as 'fack'. 'No, it's because I know what I want and I go out and get it.'

'Well then, why don't you go out and get a boyfriend?'

'Oh fack off.'

I asked Orla once why she uses the word 'fack' instead of 'fuck'.

'That's just the way I talk,' she said.

'Well why not use "a" for all your vowels then? – "Fack aff ya stapad cant!"' It ended up becoming a joke language for me and Pam for a while – 'Wat tha fack ar ya cakan ma far danar ya batch?'

'Ap yars.'

That kind of thing.

'Would any of your mates be interested in taking Orla out?' Pam asked with a grin as she sipped at her G&T. She only says this to put me on the spot; she knows full well there wouldn't be a fucking hope of it.

'Em. Yeah maybe,' I stuttered.

Thank God Orla butted in. 'Oh please, as if I'd go out with one of those Neanderthals.' Herself and Pam burst out laughing. Christ, Neanderthals – what a stupid thing to say.

'Who's a Neanderthal?' I asked.

'Fred for one.'

'Why Fred?'

'His name is spot on for a start – he even looks like Fred Flintstone, for fack's sake.'

I had to laugh at that one. He does look a little like Fred Flintstone.

Last orders had been served and I was thinking about *Unforgiven* again. The two girls were talking about trying to get into some club, but I convinced them to come back to our gaff, smoke a spliff and watch Clint Eastwood be a cowboy – I used the old 'It's not fair on the babysitter' routine.

The girls suggested going for one more smoke outside before catching a taxi home. I shrugged. One more couldn't hurt, right? Wrong. When they say smoking kills you I don't think that they have my scenario in mind, but still that's exactly what happened.

Danny and the girlfriend were outside in the smoking area too, looking solemn – as if they were sick of arguing but had still not made up. I had literally just pointed him out to Pam saying, 'There's that fucking eejit that bumped into me' when he came strutting over.

'Can I get a light?' he asked.

'Sure,' I said a little grudgingly.

Danny sparked his smoke and then just walked off without saying thanks. That's a real pet hate of mine, fucking height of bad manners. Between that and bumping into me, I felt I had to say something.

'You're welcome by the way.'

Danny turned. 'What?'

'I said you're welcome.'

He strode towards me, cheeks red. 'Have you got a problem?'

I started getting a little nervous then because he's such a big cunt, but I tried not to show it with Pam and Orla standing there.

'You're my problem, shithead – what the hell is wrong with you? You don't say thanks when someone gives you something?'

'Fuck you, asshole!'

I saw the look on Pam's face, so thought twice about slagging him again. 'Look, just forget it,' I said. Michelle called out to him to just come on.

'Not until this dickhead apologises,' Danny said.

As soon as he said that I burst out laughing – as soon as I burst out laughing he swung for me. The punch hit me on the left side of the neck, my head spun around sharply to the right and I collapsed to the ground never to recover. The blow caused a haemorrhage in the main artery of my neck and I died minutes later.

I knew it was serious when I hit the ground. I wanted to stand up, wanted to tell Pam to stop crying – that I was fine. But my body wouldn't respond. She knelt down beside me and Danny was standing behind her looking proud that he'd just floored a guy with one punch. I didn't want to look at him anymore; there was no way I was getting up to fight and I was afraid if I kept looking at him he'd kick me in the head or something.

Stop crying, Pam, I'm grand – if I could just say the words. Everything started going dark; even though I had never fainted before, I knew I was about to pass out. *I wish I'd got at least one dig in, I'm out for the count here, hope it's not too serious. Shit, I hope we still get to watch* Unforgiven.

13

One punch – that's so fucking humiliating. What's my boy going to think when he grows up and finds out that his dad was killed with only one punch? It's so embarrassing – he's going to think I was a pussy. Everyone likely does. My folks, friends – whether they'd admit it to themselves or not.

When I came to there were loads of people around me. I thought it was a dream. Pam was screaming her head off while Orla was trying to calm her down. Danny was still there – he was sitting on a bench with his head in his hands, crying. Michelle stood a few feet away from him, her hand over her mouth. She looked fit to vomit. There were a couple of paramedics hovering over me, along with some guards and a bunch of gawkers just hanging around.

I tried to tell Pam to calm down but realised that I couldn't speak, that I wasn't actually there. I was apart from it all, including myself. I'd had some weird nightmares before but they'd been nothing quite like this.

Looking at myself lying on the ground was what really freaked me out. For some reason, I still didn't think I was dead; I just kept thinking about how funny I looked – how I didn't quite look like me. I'd never seen myself how other people see me, after all; I'd only ever seen myself in the mirror. True, I'd seen photos and videos, but I always thought I looked weird on camera and never realised why until those moments hovering over my lifeless body. Me in a mirror is the reverse of what everyone else sees. Seeing my face as it actually is made me think that my features looked all out of proportion. I had always thought I was pretty good-looking, but in that moment

I started to doubt it. So about the same time that I was figuring out that I might be dead, I was also realising that I had gone my whole life thinking I was better-looking than I actually was. It sucked.

I finally dragged my focus away from my body to all the faces around me. It was only then that reality struck –

Holy shit, this is fucked, am I dead or what? Pam! Pam! – I can't be. I'm not fucking dead! No. Pam, Pamela! – Orla. No, please God, no, Pam! Oh God, please, please don't let me be dead.

I fell apart.

One minute I had been having a smoke, talking to my wife; the next I was fucking dead. Just another poor bastard who had gotten killed on a Saturday night out – some small note on page 33 of *The Herald*, a fucking statistic. *What am I going to do now – what's Pam going to do? Oh shit, Robbie.*

My whole world spun as, bit by bit, the weight of what had just happened began to crush me. Thinking then of my poor folks and brothers. I wished Pam would stop crying.

The guards had taken Danny away, at least. I was relieved that I didn't have to look at him anymore – but then, for the first time, I realised that I could still see him. All I wanted was to stay with Pam – why was a part of me going with him? Following him to the back of the squad car, sitting with him all the way to the station. Listening to every little sound he made – every panicked breath, every sob.

14

Everybody wants to see their own funeral. Well, the good news is that you'll get to. The bad news is that you'll feel so damn sorry for yourself that you're not going to be able to enjoy any of it. It happens so close to your death that you're still freaked out and not used to the idea at all. (I was in shock for weeks, still half-hoping that it was some horrible dream.) I can look back on the day now and see the nice aspects of it, but at the time I was too devastated to give a shit.

One thing I didn't like – and still don't – was the priest. It just came across like he didn't know me from Adam, which, to be fair, he didn't. There was a fierce amount of padding during the ceremony and a lot of talk about God and how I'm in a better place and stuff. Even the holiest of Joes didn't find any of it comforting, listening to the priest hunched over and mumbling into his cheap mic with crackly speakers: 'The death of Chris is not the end of his life, but rather a transformation in an outward journey towards eternal life with God. His call to eternal life began in the waters of baptism. There is of course sadness for the bereaved in his parting and a sense of shock. But with this sadness we find consolation that he is with Christ, our life and resurrection. We give thanks to God for the life of Chris and we pray that God may forgive whatever sins he may have committed through human weakness.'

Oh, fuck off.

It was a great turnout – including loads of people I didn't even know. I was glad they were there to bring up the numbers; I just wished they had acted a little sadder. I wasn't too into them all chatting nonchalantly outside the church. Still, it was good to have the place packed; I honestly didn't think there would be as many. I didn't have a whole bunch of friends. The lads I hung out with in school were the same guys I hung out with right up until the day I died. Made a few more pals along the way but not a whole lot. But for my funeral everyone turned out. I suppose my being young made it extra sad, so anyone that half knew me or used to be friends with me made the effort. One guy, Jay Loughran, flew all the way from London. Fierce decent of him. I had been mates with him in school but hadn't seen him in years. I know I wouldn't have gone to his funeral if I'd been living in London. I'd be sad about it, sure, but it wouldn't cross my mind to fly in for it. I wasn't really thoughtful like that when I was alive – not that I'd set out to be mean or anything; it just wouldn't have dawned on me to be so considerate. People can be very good. He always got on well with my folks so wanted to lend his support. I'm sorry now that I didn't keep in touch with him.

Robbie cried through most of it, which aggravated my dad a bit. My poor mother was just in a daze. I stayed mainly with Brian and Tim for the funeral – it was too much for me to be beside Pam. For some reason I got strength off them. They're the only two who weren't in floods of tears the whole time. Well, my dad wasn't either. Everyone was all impressed with how well he was dealing with things, but I could barely look at him.

He's like a different person now. He'd always been a quiet man, but very happy and content. He'd never really get in a bad mood. I rarely saw him sulking or angry. I never saw him look vulnerable either – he always seemed so strong to me. Any time something bad happened he'd see a positive in it – or at least a way out. When I was alive I only ever saw him cry once and that was at his mother's funeral. It wasn't much of a cry either, a single tear running down his face. But now, when he's alone, he'll let go. It's Danny that has

done this to him – changed my dad, taken the life out of him. He
was so pale at the funeral, his heart broken.

***

I always liked the idea of having a big Irish wake – one where
everyone could get drunk, sing songs, maybe cry a bit but mainly
have a good time. Do that whole 'celebrate the life' thing instead of
mourning. I was a bit pissed off that my funeral wasn't like that. I
was glad everyone was sad, but I figured there would be plenty of
time for that after the wake. Brian and Tim would have preferred
a bit of a piss-up, but they understood that no one else was in the
mood. Well, John would have been up for it too, but there was no
way any of them were going to push for it. It ended up being just
family and close friends that went back to my parents' house.

'What should we do about that cunt who killed him?'

I was wondering how long it would be till that came up and I
wasn't surprised that it was Tim who said it. He'd waited until they
were alone sitting around the kitchen table, nursing the few bottles
of beer that were in the house.

'What do you mean?' asked Brian.

'You know what I mean.'

'Let me guess. You want to show up at his house with balaclavas
on and beat the shit out of the fucker.' Brian looked agitated and
John just kept his mouth shut.

'Don't talk to me like I'm an asshole – and I want to do more
than just beat the shit out of him.'

'Oh right, kill him is it? Sure why not? Let's kill this guy and we
can all go to jail.'

'We have to do something, don't we? What do you think, John?'
Tim knew he was getting nowhere with Brian, so figured John would
be a better bet. I knew Tim had no real desire to go through with

his crazy idea, but I couldn't blame him for at least wanting to talk about it. In truth, it had crossed all their minds, but they're not really the type of lads who could carry anything like that out. They're just normal guys, not scumbags or hard bastards. Still, on some level, it would be nice to think that you're the type of guy who would avenge your brother or best friend's death, so I guess talking about it was, weirdly, the first step in forgiving themselves for doing nothing.

'We can't let him get away with it.'

I was surprised when John said that, as he's always been kind of a pacifist. Still, it was obvious that he didn't mean it. The lads knew he didn't mean it too, but Tim latched on to it anyway.

'Right, thank you. Are you with us, Brian?'

'Am I with you? Fine, if you guys really want to do something, then I'll go along with it. I mean, what is it you want to do?'

Tim hesitated. 'I suppose we follow him one night and jump him – not kill him, but we have to at least give him a beating.'

'Christ – that's really going to solve a lot, isn't it?'

'He was our brother for fuck's sake!'

'I know – do you not think I want to do something too? But Jesus, what good will it do? His bruises will heal and Chris will still be dead. Unless we kill him, which I fucking know no one here will do, then we'll never get back at him – never.'

'We have to do something, Brian,' John pleaded.

Brian shook his head. 'Okay, John – you do something. Let me know what you come up with.' Brian left the kitchen then, walked into the living room and sat down beside my mam. He smiled at her and placed his hand on her knee.

That night, Brian stayed away from everyone for the most part. He was pissed off at Tim and John because he knew they were full of shit. If any of them would do anything it would most likely be him, and he wondered if he had it in him.

15

The next few weeks were tough. Actually they were downright horrific. If I wasn't already dead I would have killed myself for sure – which of course makes no fucking sense at all. When I look back on it I still feel nauseous. Everyone crying, including me, especially me. The first time I stopped crying was in the pub with the lads. Literally the first time in three weeks. Think about that for a second before you brush past it – crying solidly for three weeks.

The lads were out for pints in the local. Every time my name was mentioned I'd lose it, but bit by bit I started to come around. It was actually Davey who made me smile first. He's such a flakey guy you can't help but enjoy the fucker. There were four of them out: Davey, John, Fred and Fanny. May as well explain Fanny's stupid name first – simple really – his name's Niall, but when he went to Florida at thirteen he came back with one of those bum-bags. Stupid-looking things, anyway, but he made the mistake of calling it a fanny pack. 'They're handy yokes, and it's not a bum-bag – it's a fanny pack.' Jesus, the laughter – he couldn't get a word in edgeways after that. So the poor bastard has been lumbered with the name ever since. Even his mother calls him Fanny.

There's a local lottery in the pub that we never really do, but this particular night it was up to four grand so John reckoned they should give it a shot, 'Come on, lads, 50 cent each only.' The other three threw their money on the table while John picked out the numbers. 'How's fifteen, three, one, nineteen and twenty-nine sound to ye?' Everyone seemed happy enough with them so John continued, 'Grand so, I've a good feeling about this one.'

Just as he was saying that he saw Davey stopping the lounge boy again, 'Sorry, mate, give me another one of those tickets will you – double me chances what?'

The lads thought nothing of it, but then John noticed the numbers Davey ticked off: fifteen, three, one, nineteen and twenty-nine. 'What the fuck are you doing?'

'What?'

'Are you putting down the same numbers that we all did?'

'Yeah, so what?'

'Jesus – you can't do that.'

At this point I started to smile. The other lads did too, but John was getting pissed off. Davey was only doing this to get a rise out of him; we could all see that – except for John himself, of course.

'Why not?'

'You just can't – what if we win?'

'Well that's great if we win. That's why we're playing isn't it?'

'Yeah but what happens, are we still getting €1,000 each?'

'Of course not, don't be stupid.' Davey handed the lottery ticket back to the lounge boy and took a sip out of his pint.

John's face had turned puce. 'So, what? You get two grand and we have to split the other two between the three of us? That's bollocks.'

'No, we split the other two between the four of us,' Davey replied as he wiped the Guinness moustache from his face.

'Ah fuck that, don't be such a dickhead.'

'Hey come on now, I'm taking the biggest risk here – I deserve the biggest reward.' Fred and Fanny were laughing by now, and so was I. 'You can buy another ticket as well if you want – I don't mind.'

'I don't want another fucking ticket!'

'Well what are you complaining about then?'

'It's just not in the spirit of things, we're supposed to win it all together, not you get €2,500 and we only get €500.'

'Don't be so greedy, €500 is nothing to be sneezed at.'

'They're my numbers, you prick.'

'They're more mine than they are yours; I paid €2.50 for them whereas you only paid 50 cent.' Davey had a point.

'Yeah, but I picked them for all of us to win.'

At this point Fanny had enough. 'We're not going to win, you fucking eejit.'

Davey stepped in again. 'If someone else picked those same numbers, someone you didn't know, would you mind then?'

'No, but it's not the same thing.'

'Oh, I get it, you don't mind sharing with some stranger, but you'd begrudge me, your friend, a little bit of the action?'

'It's all the action, you wanker – I'm not the bad guy here, you are.'

'Would you listen to yourself, for God's sake – stop being such a pus – "Ooh, I picked them for everyone."'

That was enough to shut John up. He was still pissed off but copped on that chances of them winning were pretty slim at best and he was starting to make a fool out of himself.

I wish to God I had some power from beyond the grave that could have made them win that money the following week. I'd have given anything to see John's face as Davey collected his winnings. I've seen Davey do that type of thing to piss John off a million times before and I've always enjoyed it – but this time it actually helped me. To finally be able to laugh – even if it was just at Davey acting like a prick. I don't know, I guess the whole thing just gave me a little bit of hope.

16

Night-times can be particularly hard. No one is doing anything so it can be boring as hell. That's why I spend most nights at Danny's. At least I'm doing something there – trying to wake him, to get through to him somehow. And it seems to work. He always wakes up. He hasn't had a full night's sleep since I've been with him. And the longer I've been around the more I'm managing to wake him. I like to think that he can feel my presence breathing down his neck, my soul burning a hole in him. That he's scared for the first time in his life.

Wake up, Danny-boy, time for another lovely day – open your eyes, you fucking prick, come on, Danny – wake up.

His eyes are open now. I'm positive he knows I'm with him in his dreams, but what about now that he's awake? He can never quite remember what he dreamt of, he just senses that the dreams were terrifying. His sheets are drenched with sweat and the blankets thrown off. It's amazing Michelle doesn't wake up with all his tossing and turning. She did, at first. I guess she's just gotten used to it.

I like watching Danny after he's been woken up – eyes open, breathing heavily. He often looks around the room as if expecting someone to be there. The first time he wakes he'll usually get back to sleep. It's the second and third times that cause him such trouble. It can take anywhere from ten minutes to two hours before he's asleep again – if he returns to sleep at all. And if he does manage it, I do everything I can to force him awake again.

It's not just messing with his head that I like about the night. I enjoy the darkness, or, more particularly, I like that I can see everything even though it's pitch black. I had always wanted a pair of night-vision goggles when I was alive, but a decent pair cost around six or seven hundred quid and I was never able to justify spending that much on what would basically just be a toy. Now it's like I have night vision, except much better. You know the way it is in movies when the army guy puts on the goggles and everything turns green – it's not like that for me – there are just as many colours at night as there are in the day – more maybe. And, if anything, the colours look richer.

Sometimes, I let myself drift off and leave Danny's house for a while. Leave all the streetlights behind, the lights from houses as I aim for the darkest spot I know – drifting out to sea or to the woods near my parents' house. I used to cycle my bike there when I was a kid, and drink cans there with the lads as a teenager, concealed by oak and birch. I also kissed my first girl in those woods when I was twelve – it was a terrible shift. The amount of drool I left on the poor girl. I can still see her face, the disappointed look she gave me for ruining her first kiss nearly turned me off kissing altogether.

I first came here after my death, as the woods were the darkest place I could think of and I wanted to check out my new night eyes. But now it's something more.

I never realised how many memories I have here – I think that's part of why I'm drawn to the place. I had forgotten about how much time I spent here as a kid. Me and John were down here all the time when the weather was nice. It's the place where we had our first drink together. We were thirteen and it was Halloween so our parents let us stay out extra late. Three cans of Budweiser each. We both thought we were so cool until I puked on our way down to a bonfire. Then I felt like a bit of a lightweight. John laughed at me as he patted my back. I was well impressed with him because he seemed grand while my stomach was in knots.

The tree stump that we sat on while having our cans is still there. I sit here alone now, listening to the wind and the rustling of the trees. I love the way they sound and can feel myself swaying with them, even as the wind rushes through me. I can hear John's voice, telling me about the girl in our class, Helen, that he fancied.

'I hope she'll be at the bonfire tonight.'

'I'd say she will be.'

'Do you think we should save one of our cans to drink down there?'

'Yeah maybe – although what if one of our parents' friends is down there or something?'

'Ah they won't be – we should save one for down there. Or at least half of one anyway.'

'Yeah okay … like show up drinking one?'

'Yeah … God, I hope Helen will be down there.'

I like the feeling that I'm talking to John again. For a few moments I can almost believe that it's actually happening, that we're starting all over again. Except this time I'd make sure that he talked to Helen instead of just waving at her. Instead of me putting him off, 'Let's just play it cool, you don't want to look all needy.' How many times did I make that same mistake? Holding myself back – even with Pamela. My whole life I'd played it 'cool' with girls I liked and never got anywhere with them. How did I not see that this was a terrible method of attracting women? Women don't like it when you're all aloof and they don't know what the hell you're thinking – that's just annoying; nobody likes that. They like confident guys who can talk to them – not just wave at them and then ignore them for the night. Helen had liked John, but instead she'd ended up shifting Barry Lynch, who was a tosser – but a tosser who'd actually gone over and talked to her. This time it would be different:

'Go over to her, John.'

'What about Barry?'

'Barry's a knob, you're way cooler than that fool – go over to her.'

'Are you sure?'

'Fucking right I'm sure – you're the man.'

'You'll be by yourself.'

'So what? You go and make Helen's night. Go over to her, pal – go get her!'

Ah yeah, this time it would be different, I think, but then Danny makes a gargling noise in his sleep and I'm right back in his house, just like that, remembering all that he took away from me.

SEVEN
MONTHS
DEAD

17

The thing that worries me the most since I died is that when Pam dies she could find out that I cheated on her. Maybe it's a slim chance, but if any of my friends are still alive who knew about it she could easily find out. If she's still in contact with them that is. I presume she'll have the same crap powers as me where she could read their minds and if they think of it at all that will be that. And it's not like your perspective on that kind of thing changes after you die – she's going to feel just as betrayed dead as she would alive. Maybe if she lives for many years she won't care about me as much and it won't really bother her – although that thought is almost as upsetting as her finding out just how much I'd let her down.

I don't know why I did the dirt. If I was alive I'd tell you it was because I was drunk or I was getting cold feet with our wedding on the horizon – but the truth is I simply wanted to. I went out that night hoping to pick up some young one. I mean, I was drunk as well, but I didn't have cold feet. I loved Pam and couldn't wait to marry her. I just wanted one last fling before I did.

It wasn't a good shag or anything, just a drunk night with someone I hooked up with in a bar and would never see again. The thing was, I didn't feel hugely guilty after it. I felt a bit bad, alright, like the whole thing was kind of unnecessary, but my conscience was relatively clear. It's only now that I feel like a scumbag.

It took me ages to blow my beans; I kept losing my stiffy. I wasn't used to having sex with anyone but Pam, so it freaked me out a little. When it was over all I wanted to do was get out of there – instead I fell asleep. I even had sex with her again in the morning.

Cold light of day and no, 'My God what have I done?' No getting out of there as fast as I could, but instead hanging around for some more.

Looking back now, one was as bad as the other – I knew just as much what I was doing drunk as I did sober. I felt like a bit of a snake afterwards, alright, ringing Fred to tell him that if Pam asked he was to say that I stayed in his apartment. I knew he didn't give a shit, but I didn't want the other lads finding out, especially John. He would never do it to Niamh and I figured he'd be disappointed in me if he found out.

I figured right. Fred the fucking eejit went and told everyone before the day was out. John never said anything to me about it, but I could tell that he didn't like it. When I filled the lads in the next week with all the dirty details, it was just a slight look he gave me. It wasn't a high up on his horse kind of look – just an involuntary reflex, like a grimace.

When I told Pam that I'd stayed in Fred's she accepted it without a second's doubt. The more I talked to her, the more the reality of what I'd done faded from me; all the anxiety of seeing her, the worry that she'd somehow know. She was just herself. Happy, beautiful Pam – and I was glad I still had her. Bit by bit the worry left me and pretty soon my feeling like a snake left me too, as I knew I had gotten away with it. I started feeling happy that I'd gotten laid but still felt like it was a little unnecessary, which I was glad of too, because it made me think that I would probably never do anything like that again.

I wonder if I would have.

I look at Pam now and wonder what the hell must have been going through my mind to risk losing her. I wish I had never done it. Not so much for the act itself, because it meant nothing (sounds like a cliché, but it did mean nothing – to me, anyway). It has more to do with the fact that I let her down – and that she could eventually find that out. That the man she loved, trusted and mourned for wasn't the person she thought he was. The man she missed and cried herself to sleep over time and time again turned out to be just another cheating asshole who couldn't be trusted.

18

Danny has never done the dirt on his bird. He's not been going out with her for as long as I was with Pam, but they've still been together a fair while. He's crazy about Michelle and I can see why – even though she's a bit of a dose, she's a little lash, way out of his league. How could a big oaf like Danny get a cutie like that? It's ridiculous. Not only is he a weird-looking fucker – I guess she's into that – but he's a moron as well. He says stupid things all the time. Tells crap stories. Honestly, I'm surprised that he's been able to keep this small matter of killing me to himself.

He was locked up for two days before he was released. Two days. If it was in America or somewhere they'd throw away the key on the bastard until his trial began – but not here. No, the poor fella has endured enough for now, let's let him run free for the next few months. Really make the dead man's family suffer. He got away with it in work because he rang them to say he'd crashed his motorbike; the asshole doesn't have a motorbike. He'd even put on a limp for the first few days back.

I was kind of impressed, I guess, that he pretty much dealt with it all himself. If it had been me I'd have gone straight to my dad and John, got help sorting out a lawyer and stuff. He confided in no one apart from Michelle and I think he would have even kept it from her, except that she'd witnessed the whole thing.

These past months have been hard on him, not so much because of the act itself, but because of all the shit that has come with it. The horrible feeling in his stomach when he realised I wasn't getting up – *one punch, you bastard* – being dragged off to jail by big thick garda boggers and held there for two days. Longest days of his life, trying to understand how this could have happened to him, trying to figure out how in the hell he could get out of it.

Mad time for him. He's been fighting with Michelle a lot. They had always fought, anyway, but now it's all the time. Inwardly, he's shitting himself that she's going to dump him.

When he's not fighting with Michelle, he worries about what his dad is going to say when he finds out. He's tired all the time, not sleeping. Staying up late watching crap on TV, hoping that it will make him tired enough to get a full night, but all it does is make things worse. He's not selling anything in work and keeps getting shit off his boss because his head's not in it. The man is in a total daze all day. Looking over his shoulder. Wondering if there is a hell and is he going to it. Thinking of his hearing that's just around the corner, wondering will it be put off again, hoping it will. How is he even going to bring it up with his old man? This has been the worst Christmas of his life. All the while thinking how it could be his last proper Christmas for quite some time.

The past several months have been tough for Danny Murray, alright, but now Christmas is over and here comes the New Year. And with each new year comes new responsibilities and challenges. *You've got two, Danny – tell Dad and go to prison.*

19

I was never a big fan of New Year's; I always felt it was a bit of an anticlimax of a night. Mind you, I would like to be around for this year's. Everyone, whatever they are going through, is with someone who loves them for the countdown. Whereas I am alone with everyone I care about. And one person I don't.

10

The festival buzz in the city is electrifying and although the club they are in is jam-packed, the atmosphere is pure deadly. Fanny and Davey hug like mad in the middle of a hundred others all jumping up and down. Fred has Bulmers all over his T-shirt as he shouts out:

9

Michelle looks for Danny in their local – no sign of the prick and she worries that he's off scoring with some bird outside. Even with all the commotion a lot of guys are checking her out. She doesn't notice it – accustomed to it by now – she doesn't notice the next count either.

8

I have to laugh at Orla. She's standing in our living room and has been trying to come up with something profound to say to Pam all night. She wants to say something insightful for when the hugs are over. She's looking at Pam now, thinking about it; so far the best she's come up with is, 'If anyone can take the hard knocks it's Pam Cosgrave – and you took the hardest, right in the gut. You've been on autopilot for over half a year and it's time to take yourself off it. When you want to cry, cry; when you want to laugh, laugh. Just say goodbye to that horrendous year, and hello to a new beginning.'

Christ that's weak.

7

Jarlath's countdown roar is louder than anyone else's in the golf club. Himself and John's mam, Cathy, go there every year. They always have a good time and tonight is no exception, even though two of the people who usually sit at their table aren't with them – my folks used to love going there too.

6

Nobody shouts out the numbers in my parents' house. My mam and dad hold hands, watching the countdown on TV. It hurts so much to see them like this – I wish they were enjoying themselves like John's folks. If I could only turn back the clock and keep my big mouth shut after Danny had used my lighter. If I'd only kept my big mouth shut, then my parents would be happy now – down at the golf club with all their friends instead of watching some tosser on the telly calling out:

5

Tim and Brian seem alright, at least – hopping about the place in a stuffy rocker bar down in Galway. I never actually celebrated a New

Year with them as adults. I should have; they are just like my own mates. My two little brothers – not little anymore, of course. Tim even grew to be taller than me. Their bodies are locked together as if they are the only two people in the place. I'd love to be wrapped in their arms with them.

4

Niamh and John are kissing already, loving every second – Niamh doesn't even notice Fred's sweaty hairy back rubbing up against her on the dance floor as the clumsy fucker keeps backing into them. He has his stained T-shirt ripped off and his horrible naked back keeps touching her bare arms. Ordinarily this would freak Niamh out; she's kind of pernickety at the best of times and she finds Fred revolting. Right now, though, all she's noticing is Johnny-boy.

3

Danny walks off the dance floor, his eyes filling up. He's trying to get away from all the happiness. All he wants to do is avoid his asshole friends and I don't blame him. One of them just slipped off a table before getting the chance to call out:

2

Pam smiles at Orla. She could have gone to any number of parties, but she came to our house, as she knew that Pam would want to stay at home this year, mind Robbie and keep it low-key. I love Pam's smile. It changes her entire face. Even when she's just smiling normally it looks as if she's giddy. You can almost see every tooth in her head. She doesn't do it often enough anymore, but having Orla there in this moment brings one out in her.

She has slight butterflies in her stomach, though; I'm on her mind but she's trying to avoid letting it upset her too much. She is holding the memory of our last New Year's together in this same room. We hadn't been able to go out with everyone else because we had no babysitter, but we ended up having a wonderful night anyway. Drank about five bottles of wine, chatted and laughed all night – just the two of us – until we nipped upstairs and made the mistake of waking up poor little Robbie. We hugged him till he stopped crying – then couldn't get him back to sleep for ages.

Finally, once Robbie was asleep, we went back downstairs to put on some tunes. We wanted to play something deadly for the first song of the new year; after much debate we settled on Led Zeppelin's 'Gallows Pole'. Cracking song, not a bit romantic but we'd kissed to it anyway.

She wishes I was there to kiss her tonight.

1

Robbie is fast asleep. I hope he dreams of beautiful, happy things, oblivious to the terrible burden that surrounds him. His life is going to be different to most other boys, but there will be plenty of time for that.

For now sleep tight, don't let the bedbugs bite. Wake up happy, Robbie, I love you so much. You are the one and only reason why I am glad I was born at all. If I didn't have you my whole life would have been for nothing. You are the only thing that keeps me from insanity. Because of you my life had a point. You're going to grow up to be a wonderful person – you already are – much better than I was. The gentle kindness in you already shines out through your big, beautiful brown eyes. I'm so proud of you. You're going to do great things and I'm going to be with you always. *Thank you for being my son – thank you for being so perfect. I love you more than anything. Sleep well, my darling little boy – Happy New Year.*

20

Every New Year's Day my dad goes swimming with a bunch of his mates in the freezing cold water off Velvet Strand Beach. He's been doing it for years – not for charity or anything, just for the craic. Mad bastards. Hilarious to watch: fifteen out-of-shape, pasty-skinned old dudes running flat out into sub-zero temperature water. About half of them always turn back at the knees – these are always the new guys who are doing it for the first time. But the core group – the guys like my dad who have been doing it since I was a kid – never flinch. In head first and coming out smiling.

I went down last year to watch, something I hadn't done since I was seventeen. It brought back loads of great memories from when I was a kid. It was a nice feeling, bringing my own son to watch his granddad. I remember thinking that I might give it a shot next year or maybe the year after, when Robbie was old enough to take it in.

My dad's the only one out of all his mates who doesn't look woeful with his shirt off. I thought that last year too – all his pals look ten years older than him, skinny arms and legs with flabby bellies. Tough men, though. I think I would have been one of the run up to your knees, come to your senses and turn back guys.

It's cool looking at the wives watching the husbands. No matter how bald they are, no matter how white their legs are or how fat their guts – the wives watching them run into the sea look as proud as if they were watching David Hasselhoff in his prime hurdling the waves. Honestly, I doubt Hasselhoff would be able for it. Freezing. We used to go down in woolly hats and gloves – I can't imagine how it must feel when the water hits your nuts for the first time.

It's tradition that my mam would have everyone back to the gaff afterwards for mulled wine. We'd all come in shivering, but I swear to God the people who didn't hop in the water needed heating the most. My dad always seemed grand.

He wasn't going to do it this year, but I'm glad my mam convinced him to.

His flip-flops are the last thing he takes off and as soon as they are, he runs like hell over the sharp pebbles with me running right beside him. The two of us reach the water and it's the first time I ever notice my dad flinch. Not a whole lot, his shoulders just tighten slightly on his second leap. He probably does it every year, but I was too far away or cold to notice. I am right beside him this time. Martin, his mate, is just in front of us and my dad wants to catch up and dive under before him. The splashes from Martin strike him square in the face and for the first time since my death I can see that my dad is happy. He has smiled and stuff in the past few months, but not once have I seen this grin. This grin is different: curled up slightly to one side and gritting his teeth with excitement.

Martin stubs his toe on one of the underwater rocks so starts the worst-looking dive I've ever seen. It almost appears like he's dancing. If a wave hits it won't look so bad – they usually dive into a wave – but, unfortunately for Martin, he plunges when the water is shallow and calm.

This gives my dad his chance to skip past and hurl himself into a foaming wave with me right behind him. His smile is in overdrive as he holds his breath – everything seems as though it is in slow motion. He can feel each tiny drop of icy water touch down on his neck, run along his back until he is totally submerged. The cold feels good, invigorating. Immersed, he shuts his eyes as the salty water closes in around his mouth and ears, but he doesn't want to come up just yet. Holding on to his breath a little longer, he skims his chest off the seabed – the same little ritual he does each year. I stay with him. He's still strong and handsome, especially for a guy in his sixties, and looks the image of an older Val Kilmer, although I suppose Val Kilmer must be pretty old by now too. The water is dark and murky, but I can see him perfectly – making a face like he's blowing into a trumpet.

In a way I wish I could stay down here forever with him – only a few feet underwater but a million miles away from all his troubles. For a second he just drifts along – enjoying the sounds of the ocean and the distant muffling of people shouting and splashing. Everything is so peaceful for these few seconds. He slowly starts rising till his head feels the wind whip past it, but before any more of himself hits air he takes a deep breath and dives in again. My mam goes to wave at him but he is back underwater before she has raised an arm.

When he comes back up the second time, Martin is standing beside him, spitting and blowing snot out his nose. The Baltic weather doesn't seem to bother him, just the fact that too much saltwater has gone into his gob. 'That's it, Marty, get it out – just try not to get too much more on me like a good man.'

Martin can barely speak he is coughing so much. 'Feckin, ugh – swallowed the water the wrong way.'

'The wrong way? Jesus, Marty, you're not supposed to drink the stuff – people piss in it, you know.'

'Ugh – don't say that. Jesus, I took a mouthful there.' Martin's eyes are watering up so much it looks like he is crying. My dad, on the other hand, looks like he is having a ball.

'Jesus, Marty, pull yourself together – your wife's watching, for God's sake.'

'Piss off, Frank.'

'Well you don't want her to see you crying, do you?'

Martin starts smiling, 'Piss off will you.'

'Here, let me help you.'

Before Martin has a chance to say piss off a third time, my dad is on top of him pushing him back under the water. Too weak from all the coughing to fight him off, he gives up almost straight away. He shouldn't scream though, that's his biggest mistake – mouth wide open once again to take in another fresh batch of piss-filled saltwater.

The women laugh their asses off at Martin's face when he comes back up. None more so than his own wife. He looks around to give my dad a thump, but he's disappeared like a flash, smiling away to himself as he heads out to sea. He swims out further this year than he ever has before. Usually they just kind of swim about in a circle for a few minutes, then head back. It's not so much swimming but splashing about and sticking your head underwater – this year though my dad is going for a proper swim, so much so that my mam starts to get a little anxious about how far out he is. He just keeps swimming straight, swimming so hard the water isn't even cold anymore. My dad has always been a strong swimmer, so this is the first time I can keep up with him. It's great, the two of us cutting through the water as if we are racing for gold in the Olympics.

Eventually my dad stops – he is getting tired and the shore is a fair distance away. He can't even hear the voices of the people on the beach anymore, just his own heavy panting. It's funny, but this is around the spot where I sometimes come at night – when I'm not in Danny's or down in the woods, I like to drift out to sea and look back at the shore.

Treading water, he tries to decipher which figure on the beach is my mam. When he can't spot her he half thinks of swimming further out still, but instead allows himself to lay back and float here for a while, looking up at the cold, grey sky. He closes his eyes as his breathing becomes more regular – the sweat from all his exercise washes away and goosebumps begin to rise on his arms and chest.

Small drops of rain begin to fall and lightly sprinkle his face. I can see right up to the cloud where the first drop originated and know there are plenty more where that came from. I think my dad knows too – he starts smiling seconds before the bucketload comes down; he always loves swimming in the rain. He takes one more look to the shore and spots my mam – knows it's her by the way she is standing. Knows she'll be waiting for him and won't be able to stop herself from worrying. Time to go back so. He puts his head down and swims even harder than he did on the way out and doesn't stop until being welcomed with a warm towel underneath my mam's umbrella.

21

Orla wakes up on the same couch I had woken up on countless times before. At first she doesn't know where the hell she is, but after a second of focusing in on the fireplace and the pictures on the walls she gets her bearings. A horrible noise woke her. When she raises her head she notices Robbie pressing the buttons on a toy telephone. I always hated that thing. All those noisy toys used to drive me crazy. I always said I'd never have them in the house when I had kids, but the problem is that other people buy all that shit for him. I always figured he'd be as happy building bricks or bouncing a ball as he would be pushing a head-wrecking button or playing with so-called learning toys that make the noise of a cow mooing.

The great thing here is that it was actually Orla who got him that particular toy. The face on her is priceless. Groggy head, messy hair, dry lips and last night's caked-in make-up are making her feel even worse than she looks.

'Robbie, honey, turn that off; you're waking Orla,' Pam says.

'No, it's okay. I'm awake,' she says, stirring.

'Oh sorry, Orla, I hate that damn thing.'

'Hey! I got that for him.'

'Oh really?' Pam laughs. 'In that case, Robbie, keep playing with it.'

'Oh fack off,' Orla says, then shoots her hand to her mouth for swearing in front of the boy.

Rising up on her elbows she takes another look around the room. Christ, it's not too bad; she figured it should be a total pigsty after the night. Even though it had just been the pair of them they sure managed to raise the roof – brought in the new year in style. Orla had even sourced a bit of weed off her brother. Pam hadn't smoked any in ages, but she loved it last night. The party had everything except for people. Wine, vodka, weed, singing, dancing – basically trashing the place and going wild.

'Jesus, did you clean all that mess up?'

'Sure did, sleepy head – or is it fake sleeper?'

'No, I swear, I was asleep.'

'I know you were; I'm only messing. Sure you couldn't fake that snoring.'

Orla's cheeks blaze. 'God, I wasn't, was I?' Pam starts laughing at her. 'What time is it?'

'Half eleven.'

'Agh, what time are you up since?'

'I'm up with Master over there since about eight.'

'Wow. You're some woman. You're not cleaning since then, are you?'

'Not at all, I was pure mush the first couple of hours. The mess wasn't actually that bad once I got started.' The *buzz buzz* off Robbie's phone makes Orla wince and sit up completely. He presses it again and Orla gives the little man a dirty look that neither he nor Pam notice. *Buzz buzz.*

'Christ, I see what you mean about that thing.'

'Robbie, honey, stop playing with that. Poor Orla is not feeling too good.'

'Yes, Rob – Orla must be coming down with something.'

Robbie looks up at Orla and then presses the button again. *Buzz buzz.*

'Oh Christ.' The two of them start laughing.

'Here, do you want a cup of tea?' Pam offers.

'Love one.'

Orla follows Pam into the kitchen. She doesn't look too sure-footed when she first stands up, but with each step seems a little steadier. Looking at herself in the small mirror above the landline gives her a shock. 'Oh God. I look like Medusa.'

The pair of them sit down at the table with their mugs of tea. Orla has a pint of water and two fig rolls before the kettle is even boiled. Her stomach is in knots, but she's one of those people who don't like to admit to getting hangovers. Pam's biting her lip, trying not to laugh. She hasn't seen Orla this bad in a while.

'How's the head?'

'Fine, yeah,' Orla says as she holds her forehead and looks outside at the frosty day. 'It was some night, though, God almighty.'

'It sure was.'

'Are we party girls or what?' Orla says, then her expression turns more reflective. 'It was just what we needed. You have to let loose once in a while or else what's the point?'

'You're telling me.'

'You needed that. To get drunk and have a good cry.'

Pam smiles. 'I sure did – well the drunk part, anyway. Thanks again for coming over.'

'I wouldn't have missed it. Besides any other party wouldn't be the same without Pammy at it.'

'Well that's true.'

Pam looks happy. She has the type of hangover where, even though you feel sick, you don't mind because the night was so good and you're hanging out with someone who's in the same boat as you. 'Do you want to watch a movie or something?' she asks, eager to keep things going.

'No, I better be heading off.'

'Stick around, sure – we'll have a fry-up.'

'Ooh, tempting. And it does look particularly Arctic out there.'

Arctic. Who says that?

Pam nods, her hands wrapped around the mug, drawing in its warmth. 'Sure does. You know Chris's dad went swimming in that this morning.'

'Tell me you're kidding.'

'He does it every year.'

Orla looks a little sicker at the very thought of it.

'I was just on to Chris's mam, Kate, there,' Pam continues. 'She said he did great. Swam miles out, the rain didn't bother him a bit.' Pam cracks another one of her smiles. 'It must have been freezing.'

'Well, I really admire that,' Orla says. 'Throwing caution to the wind and saying what the hell?' She still annoys the hell out of me, but I have to say I am warming to her more since I died. 'I'm a bit like that in business, and you can tell the rest of the staff appreciates it.'

Strike that.

'You are?'

'Oh sure – you have to take chances in this life, sweetheart, otherwise why get out of bed?'

She works in a post office.

'I get out for this little fella.' Pam picks up Robbie and tickles his belly. 'Don't I, Mister Early Bird.' Robbie giggles. God almighty, I love that sound. It's about the only thing I loved in life that doesn't cause me pain in death. It just sounds that sweet.

'That's right, and that's the biggest chance of all – raising a son.'

I don't even know what she means by that.

'Stay for a movie,' Pam persists. 'We'll hang out.'

She ends up staying for the fry, alright, but hightails it after that. It doesn't do her any favours – the grease off the rashers disagrees with her and she knows she'll have to spend the rest of the afternoon with her head down the toilet. I wish she hadn't headed off so soon. Pam looks sadder now that she's left. Not mad miserable or anything

– it's just the happy glow she had when she woke up is gone.

Robbie is annoying her a bit too, saying repetitive stuff the whole time. 'Da ba', referring to the next-door neighbours' dog barking. 'Yes, sweetie, the dog is barking,' Pam responds patiently.

'Wha da?' – where is the dog.

'He's outside,' Pam tells him.

Robbie sits on this information a while and then says, 'Da ba.'

I find it cute as all hell, but Pam is in no mood. 'Robbie, darling, play with your car,' she says, handing him the red race-car that Pam's mam got him for Christmas. That only occupies him for a few minutes, until he breaks off one of the wheels. Now he keeps repeating over and over again, 'Ca boken … ca boken.'

Poor Pam's head is wrecked.

I allow myself to drift off for a while out into the rain. It's a miserable day for a New Year's, but I feel pretty good. Usually when I try and feel the world around me I get a bad vibe. But today is different. Maybe it has to do with everyone celebrating or maybe because this time of year is a family time – either way the horrible depression that has been with me since I died has lessened. I don't exactly feel good, but I don't feel all that bad either.

22

Sure enough, as expected, it's those who avoided the water who are trying to heat themselves up back in my parents' house. Most of the swimmers are fine. My mam has a bunch of finger food out: chicken goujons, cocktail sausages, sausage rolls. She always puts on such a great spread. Her dad had been this amazing woodturner and a few years back he made her a beautiful big bowl out of bog oak. It's perfect for her mulled wine and she takes it out each year after the swim for that reason. Everyone always oohs and aahs over it as they ladle out the wine and get slowly pissed.

My mam is in her element serving all the grub and keeping herself busy. Dad is more subdued; he has said little since leaving the beach. Marty starts slagging him about swimming halfway to England, saying that he had swum that far out because he was afraid of what Marty would do to him in response to being dunked. My dad just laughs and takes another sip of his Heineken. Ordinarily he would take the piss back, but today he just seems happy to sit there smiling.

'Who the hell were you trying to impress anyway, swimming all the way out there?' Marty presses.

'No one, Marty. I was just going to the toilet.'

'Haha, good man.'

They all seem to be having a lovely day. Most are hungover from the night before but, in the same vein as Pam, they all feel as if it adds to the whole thing, everyone buzzing off the fact that they are all wrecked.

I used to like hangovers. Not when you had to go into work or anything – then I'd hate them – but I used to love hangovers when you had nothing to do. Like a day spent lying in bed with Pam, watching a movie or something; just the two of us arsing about the place, a bit of alcohol still in our system, not yet fully sober. Chatting and laughing about the night before, guzzling back the water and trying to decide whether to eat French toast or have a fry-up. I'd always get a giddy feeling in my belly on those mornings – knowing that I just had a deadly night. Even after Robbie was born and hangovers became less frequent, I still didn't mind them. A headache was no match for the sight of his two outstretched arms as he asked to be picked up.

Ah well, no more piss-ups or hangovers for me. Danny, the prick, took care of that.

Speaking of which. Sleeping beauty – *get up, you lazy shit, it's fucking five o'clock.* Jesus, I'm all on for sleeping in late but this is ridiculous – it's not like he had a super late night or anything. How the hell does Michelle stand him? Drooling on himself and snoring, fucking pig. He looks like your man Brutus out of *Popeye.* A bit of consolation – for me, at least – is that he had a crappy night last night. That pub they always go to is shit. It looks like something out of *The Commitments* – no windows, stained brown carpet, shit wallpaper, the jacks stink, or at least they look like they should stink – mad slippy floor. People pissing wherever the hell they damn well please and nobody cleaning it up. Why pick this place as your local?

Just after midnight Danny went into those manky jacks. There was no one in the toilets – everyone was on the dance floor hugging each other, so Danny had his pick of cubicle. He always goes for the cubicle whether it's a number two or not. He never goes in the urinal, even if the cubicle stinks of stranger dump and he has to wait to get in there. It's weird. He's afraid of getting splash-back off either himself or someone else. It happened to him once, years ago, when he went for a piss wearing shorts and felt nothing but little sprinkles ricocheting off the urinal and hitting his shins. He was getting it from all angles because it was one of those wall urinals instead of a bowl. But Christ, not to use them ever again is a bit much. Besides, he was wearing jeans this time.

As he was standing over the bowl he saw an empty pint glass on the floor beside the toilet. He thought: *If I can fill the glass, I'm getting off.* Not only did he fill it, but it overflowed and the dumb bastard even looked happy. No, not happy, relieved. He left the toilets smiling, as if everything was going to be okay. As if being able to fill a pint glass full of piss was going to get him off his punishment for what he did to me. I had to laugh at the stupid fucker.

His smile lasted about as long as it took him to see Michelle coming towards him. Then reality hit – shit night, pissed-off bird and one hell of a crappy year ahead.

'Where the hell were you?'

'Take it easy, I was just in the jacks.'

'You missed the whole countdown.'

'I didn't, I heard it from the jacks.' Danny thought this would make her smile, but all it did was piss her off more.

Michelle stabbed him in the chest with her index finger. 'Prick – we were supposed to bring in the new year together and instead I'm stuck with your asshole friends. This could be our last New Year's for a while ...'

Danny looked away. 'Jesus, don't say that shit. I'm trying to enjoy myself tonight and you have to mention all that shit – shut the fuck up about it.'

'Yeah, you look like you're having a lot of fun, Danny,' she sneered.

'I am having fun – at least I was until you started bitching at me.'

'Fine.'

Michelle headed for the door. At first Danny felt glad that she was leaving, but in the space of about thirty seconds he calmed down and chased after her. He caught up with her outside.

'Michelle, would you wait!'

'Fuck off,' she said, shrugging off his outstretched hand.

A couple of people outside sniggered at them – Danny noticed it out of the corner of his eye and it reminded him of me. He had noticed me do the same thing a couple of hours before he killed me. The thought of this nearly floored him – it felt as if someone had kicked the back of his knees.

'Michelle, wait.'

If she had looked around, I think she would have gone back. His face had turned pale in those few seconds, his eyes red with about-to-burst tears. The thought of how quickly everything happened that night made him want to vomit. How his life had been destroyed by a stupid, throwaway act. A sudden burst of anger and now he's fucked.

Michelle was storming off and he had no energy to run after her; he made it as far as the curb and sat down. The further she walked the more pissed off she became. She kept thinking that he would catch up with her – to try and make up with her. When he failed to appear, she was furious. She's stormed off millions of times and he'd always caught up with her. She decided to go back to her mother's house; it was closer than their flat and she didn't want to see Danny anyway. New Year's night and she was going home at ten past twelve – classic.

Once Danny's head stopped spinning he went back inside and drank a bunch of sambucas with his idiot friends. He rang Michelle but got no answer. The worst New Year's Eve for him in recent memory. *Ah well, I'm sure next year will be even worse.*

Looking at him now, I'm surprised that he's slept so well; I usually have him up long before now. It's 5.04 p.m. before his eyes begin to open. *Morning, pal, I wonder if you still have a girlfriend?*

***

The last of my parents' mates leave just as Danny opens his eyes. My mam looks tired and my dad notices as soon as he closes the front door.

'You want another glass of wine, love?'

My mam shakes her head. 'No, thanks. Although you know what? I'd go for a gin and tonic.'

'Coming up.'

In the kitchen, he pops the last cocktail sausage into his mouth and pours himself a brandy and Mam a G&T. 'That was a grand day, wasn't it?'

'Sure was. I'm tired now, though,' she says, trying – and failing – to hold in a yawn.

'I'm not surprised, you've been going all day.'

'Yeah.'

They move into the sitting room; Mam takes a sip of her drink and sits back on the couch as my dad goes for his recliner.

'You must be tired yourself – after that swim and everything.'

'Suppose so, although I think it's more the afternoon drinks than anything else.'

'Go for a snooze, sure.'

'I might do.'

'Do, put your feet up there,' Mam insists.

'Ah, I'm alright for now – maybe in a bit,' my dad says as he takes another little sip from his brandy. 'Is there any turkey left?'

'Of course.' The two of them smile at each other. 'Jaysus, you'll turn into a turkey one of these days.'

My mam rises from the couch, makes for the kitchen.

'Ah thanks, love.'

The sound of the fridge opening and clashing cutlery reaches my dad from the kitchen. 'Do you want it on brown or white bread?' she calls out.

'Brown, but with just a bit of butter and no mayonnaise,' he answers.

'I know.'

My mam smiles as she prepares the sandwich. He always feels he has to tell her how to make his sandwiches, even though she's been making them for nearly forty years.

By the time she's back from the kitchen my dad has the TV on. 'There you are, Mr Cosgrave.'

'Lovely, thanks a million, hon – Mrs Cosgrave. Look it, *Back to the Future* is on.'

'Oh very good – one of Chris's favourites.'

'I know, can you believe it?'

'Well, it is on every Christmas.'

My dad takes a big bite out of his sandwich. 'Um, lovely.'

I did love *Back to the Future*, superb film. Although it's the second one that's on the telly. My dad wouldn't know the difference. Mind you, I loved all three of them.

'He used to watch this every day as a kid.'

'I think this is the second one,' Mam says.

Dad frowns. 'Is it? This one isn't as good, is it?'

'No. I hated that stuff with him playing all the different parts.'

'Yeah, that was dumb. The western one was good, though.'

'Chris loved this one too – he adored all three of them.'

They both settle down to watch it and pretty soon my dad falls asleep with his brandy in his hand and the empty plate on his lap. My mam watches him nearly more than the movie. Each little sound he makes, she'll crack a little smile. Every now and again he opens his eyes and takes another sip from his drink – which makes Mam smile even more. A couple of times she half-laughs at his slight stirrings, causing him to look around like a badger sticking its head out of its den. For a moment, he'll wonder what the noise is; then he'll take another sip and nod off again.

This goes on for the whole movie. Like I said, Mam isn't really watching it; her head's in a different place. Looking at my dad makes her happy, but thinking of me – which she does during the entire film – makes her sad.

It's weird knowing that the very thought of you saddens people. Especially when it's the people you love. They never talk about me in a positive sense; it hasn't reached that point yet. They never tell funny stories about me or mention funny or cool things that I did. It's always just sorrow that they feel when they think of me. It sucks. I keep waiting for the time that they'll all be able to sit around telling Chris stories and laugh their asses off, saying what a great bloke I was. Instead whenever I get mentioned it's *poor Chris this, poor Chris that. Oh if poor auld Chris was here he'd love this.* I am here and I don't love it – in fact, I think it's shit. I'm worried it will never get to the point where they tell funny Chris stories because by the time they all get over their grief they'll have forgotten all the good ones. Me dying has put a dampener on everything I ever did. There are no funny Chris stories anymore because they all end in ... *and then the poor prick got killed while having a smoke.*

My dad is still asleep while the credits roll. Mam is crying. When she notices him waking she rubs her eyes and takes a sip of her drink.

Dad looks over, notices her damp cheeks. 'You okay, Kate?'

'Yeah, I'm fine,' she says, attempting a smile. 'It's just watching that movie got me thinking.'

'Ah Jesus.' My dad gets out of his seat and moves in beside Mam on the couch. 'Come here, hon.' He puts his arm around her and she cries into his chest.

Neither one of them says anything – they've been over it all a million times. All he can do is hug her till the crying passes.

'What are we going to do in two weeks, Frank?' she asks once the tears subside.

'Nothing we can do,' he says, kissing her forehead.

'I don't think I can handle seeing him.'

'Well, you don't have to come, you know. Myself and the lads will be there and I know John is coming as well.'

Mam wipes at her nose. 'Don't be stupid – of course I have to come.'

'Well, if you can't handle it, honey, then you shouldn't go.'

'Jesus, I'm just thinking out loud – you could be more supportive. Of course I have to go, it's just the thought of seeing that bastard has me so wound up.'

Dad nods. 'I know, me too.'

The two of them sit in silence for a while. Both wondering how they'll react when they see Danny Murray for the first time.

Mam is the first to speak. 'Poor Pam, she must be dreading it. Having to get up on that dock or whatever you call it.'

'Yeah.'

'How the hell is she going to face him again?'

'I don't know, we'll just have to be there for her.'

Mam hopes she will be able to suppress her own grief so that she can be strong enough for Pam. She's glad, too, that there will be a few other people there for support.

'Did you say John was going to be there?'

'Yeah.'

'Will he not be on his honeymoon?'

'No, he's back just before – the day before, I think.'

'That's decent of him to come; it will be the last thing he feels like doing.'

Dad mutters, 'No shit.'

Mam starts chuckling.

'What?' my dad asks, smiling.

'Just the way you said that.'

'What, "no shit"?'

'Yeah. Oh God, I shouldn't be laughing.'

My dad begins to chuckle with her. 'Well, the poor prick's only back, like.'

'Oh Jesus.'

The two of them crack up.

23

John's flight is a long one. A little brat in front of him keeps standing up on his seat, playing with his younger brother and making a whole bunch of noise. You'd give that a pass normally, except every few minutes he screams 'No!' in John's face. What the hell does that mean? Poor John doesn't know where to look. Their useless mother makes no effort to shut him up either, or even give John an apologetic nod, as if to say, don't worry, screaming in strangers' faces is just his thing. But that is nothing compared to the ignoramus behind him – a big, long-legged bastard who is constantly kneeing the back of his seat. He's also up to the jacks every ten minutes, leaning on John's chair each time he stands or sits, forcing it to tilt further back. As a result, John hasn't slept a wink.

His ears are going red with anger. Why does that cockhead refuse to acknowledge me once? Just once would make some difference. Why does that woman not do something about her weird child? Ask him to stop shouting 'No' at the nice man sitting behind him, maybe? Would that be so hard? At least give it a shot.

People can be such scum. What the hell is wrong with that guy who keeps knocking into John's seat? He knows he's keeping him awake yet he still chooses not to care. What brings someone to act like that? To have total disregard for those around them. I'd say he was just like the brat when he was young; wrecking everyone's heads while his mother looked on with pride, not seeing what a little bollocks she was raising.

Maybe it's airports and planes that bring out the worst in people. I mean, people are bad, anyway, but they always seem to be worse when travelling. That's when I used to find myself giving strangers dirty looks, or being disgusted by a sweaty person eating, or something.

Pretty much everyone I'd come into contact with when flying would annoy me; the sulky moron at the check-in desk, the jerk who stands up before the fasten seat belts sign has been turned off, the stewardesses who used to kiss your ass before 9/11 but now act as if they're your boss laying down the law. I hated that. The last time I was on a plane I pressed that little buzzer thing with the picture of the waiter on it. It took your woman forever to get to me and when I asked her for another Heineken I thought she was going to slap me. Is that not what the button is for? That's what it used to be for – then she tells me it's just for emergencies. What kind of emergency is going to happen that I feel the solution is to press the little stewardess button, then hang around for twenty minutes till she finally gets to me? The worst part was the next time I wanted a beer I went up behind the curtains to where they all hang out and asked for one – then was told I wasn't allowed back there. What the hell are you supposed to do if you want another drink?

Bin Laden screwed it up for the lot of us, the prick. At least they caught up with him. I loved how, on the news, they kept saying he was 'buried at sea'; translated, this means they just fucked him overboard.

John's not thinking about any of that, of course. The honeymoon went well – wining and dining in New York. Niamh had always wanted to go there and it didn't disappoint her one bit. She thought that the lights on the Rockefeller Center Christmas tree were mesmerising. They went ice-skating on the Wollman Rink in Central Park and Niamh felt it was the most romantic moment of her life. Despite the fact that John kept falling on his ass, it still seemed as though she was the lead actress in a movie. That the world was a perfect place and her new husband the perfect leading man.

John had a great couple of weeks too, but now his mind is on tomorrow. The thought of seeing Danny scares the shit out of him. He wonders what he is going to look like. Will he be able to look him in the eye? I feel bad that all this is on his mind; that he has to think about it right after his honeymoon. The asshole behind him isn't helping matters either – John tells himself that if your man hits his chair one more time he'll have to say something.

Thump!

Christ, that was a fierce knock – more than just him leaning. He resigns himself to taking it on the chin. Fair play to you, John, be the bigger man.

'Stop leaning your chair back,' the dickhead pipes up.

Shocked, John twists his neck around and asks, 'Excuse me?'

'Stop leaning your chair back, you keep hitting into my knees.'

John peers through the tiny gap between the seats, 'I'm allowed to lean this chair back.'

The man snorts. 'You're rocking back and forth the whole flight.' He gives John's seat another shove forward.

John's ears redden further. 'Excuse me, I'm allowed to lean back – you see this button on everyone's chairs? That means you're allowed lean your chair back.' Niamh tells John to calm down as he gestures towards the man. 'Can you believe this idiot?'

Niamh shakes her head, 'I know.'

Poor John is livid – the worst part is that he had just been about to pull his seat forward so he could see his little TV better, but now there is no way he can. 'Am I out of line here? Was I going back and forth the whole time?' he asks Niamh, who shakes her head and throws her eyes up.

He determines to stay seated like that for the whole flight –

even when the dinner comes. He's practically lying down eating the damn stuff. Every now and again he whispers to Niamh, 'What I wouldn't give to sit forward.' And the pair of them giggle at the eejit behind them.

Niamh eventually falls asleep and John's thoughts drift back to what he will have to face tomorrow. He wishes he had just one more day to kick back. Pity Niamh has to go straight back to work too – it would be nice to have her there supporting him tomorrow. Although he senses that she is getting sick of talking about me. And that's because she is. Not in a bad way. It's something she can't help feeling. She'd never say it outright and she still comforts him whenever John brings me up. She's just started changing the subject sooner. Or not quite looking him in the eye when he mentions my death.

It's only natural, I suppose. She liked me, but I was John's mate and John has been acting differently since this whole thing happened. He's not as happy or friendly as he used to be. That's one of the things she loved most about him. How many friends he had and how many people liked him. Everyone liked John – they still do, it's just that he doesn't really make as much of an effort with people anymore.

He's actually made a conscious effort not to talk to Niamh about me as much. Over the honeymoon I wasn't really mentioned at all. The thought that she finds him less attractive because of how he's been unable to deal with my death has wormed its way into his head, along with some accompanying resentment that she would feel like that. This isn't the case, though. Niamh's a good person and really only feels sorry for him over what happened. She doesn't love him any less or anything; she just wishes he wasn't so melancholic all the time. She wants her old John back. So do I, come to think of it.

When their plane touches down in Dublin Airport at 10.25 a.m., John's back is aching from sitting in the one position for the entire flight. Niamh isn't in great form either – mainly because her honeymoon is over and she has to face the rain outside. It also doesn't help that she hates mornings at the best of times.

At the baggage reclaim area, they wait for their bags to appear. Most of the other passengers have already claimed theirs and left by the time Niamh finally says, 'That's our bag there, babes.'

'Where?' John asks.

'Right in front of you, grab it!' she says, wondering how he can fail to see it – it's a big, bright-yellow yoke; not like it blends in.

'Which one?' he asks again.

'Jesus.' Niamh steps forward and grabs the yellow bag, but it weighs a ton so ends up landing on her foot, causing her to yelp in pain and call John an eejit.

**

As John gets grief for being an idiot, Danny is sitting in a room full of them. I'm surprised he's worked right up to the day before the hearing. I guess he just wanted to bury his head in the sand about the whole thing and keep his daily routine as normal as possible. He didn't even tell his boss that he might not be working there anymore. He just took a week's holiday and figured he'd deal with it when the time came. It's worked out for him too, because his last day isn't quite work at all but a half-day sales seminar his boss sent him on. 'You'll be able to digest it all while you're in Portugal,' his boss, Aidan, said. 'Then you can come back and enlighten us all.'

'Sure thing, Aido,' said Danny. 'No problem.'

'Spot on.'

Poor trusting fool.

As always with these courses, it's pretty obvious stuff that everyone seems mad into – except for Danny. He keeps wondering if they are all simply stupid or is he somehow not reading between the lines of the 'dress nice, be positive' bullshit that he already fucking knows?

Three hours in and he doesn't think he can take much more. The chubby blonde girl beside him is driving him crazy with her dumbass questions and her need to vocalise her take on absolutely everything. There's a person like this at every one of these things. A know-it-all teacher's pet who talks more than the actual speaker. The guy giving the course is actually alright, but this chick is wrecking his head.

'I find that the best approach is to let the customer come to you, let them think you're almost too busy to take on their job. We have seven sales staff and that's what I tell every one of them.'

Her smug face sickens him, yet he still finds himself fantasising about her. Following her into the toilets and fucking her hard over the sink, doggy style: 'Take that you know-it-all slut!' He feels his dick move in his trousers and thinks, I've got to get the fuck out of here. One more word out of her and he'll snap.

He isn't waiting long for that one more word. She chimes in again, interrupting the speaker. 'Well, you see some of my clients won't respond to a barrage of phone calls because they might consider us too small.'

That's it. Danny turns towards her and says loud enough for the whole class to hear, 'Sorry – what colour is the building that you work in?' His face looks more sincere than I've ever seen it.

'Red,' she says, unsure what he's getting at.

'Great! Now I know everything about your fucking job!'

Three hours of this is enough. Out the door he goes, leaving the girl speechless for the first time since she sat down. The rest of the class are left half-smiling, half-shocked – all with mouths open.

Good man, Danny.

The fresh air hits his face hard when he leaves the building. He's furious, mostly with himself – what the hell is he doing wasting what could be his last day of freedom sitting in some room listening to that crap? He has more important things to think about. Michelle is still pissed off at him about New Year's, but she's beginning to come around after having endured Danny's incessant begging. 'Please baby, I need you, I can't live without you, you're the best thing that's ever happened to me, I love you, I'm nothing without you ...'

That kind of thing. Suppose we've all been there.

It's gas the different man you are when you're alone with your bird – the shit you say, the way you act. If your mates could only hear half of it. I used to act like such a baby sometimes with Pam, especially when I was in an all loved-up mood. Crawling on her, doing baby talk, singing songs, half-crying even. It's gas when you bust your mate acting like that – if they let their guard down by accident or if they don't know you're there. Although I've been stung a few times myself. One time, years ago, I was strolling down the road with Pamela. I don't know what came over me, but for whatever reason I did like a little ballerina dance step around her. Just one move, that was it, but my timing couldn't have been worse. Fucking Fred was at the end of the road coming towards us and I hadn't seen him. All I heard as I was skipping around was a big loud drawn out 'Chrrrristoooopherrrr.'

My fucking heart – of all my friends Fred is definitely the worst one to catch you doing something like that. I could see how delighted he was when he saw me – the little grin on the bastard. First thing he did of course was run home and ring all the lads. I still got slagged about that up until recently. Every now and again Fred would bring it up with a big happy smile: 'Do you remember Chris dancing around like a little princess?' It would always get the same laugh as if he was telling it for the first time.

I must say I get a buzz out of watching Danny when he's acting like a bitch with Michelle. When he thinks he's completely alone and opens up. For a guy his size he cries an awful lot. He's so fucking sensitive. I don't blame him for being scared, but how Michelle takes all his whining I'll never know.

He's filling up again now as he reaches the bus stop. Thinking about his dad this time. He still hasn't told him. Fucking eejit. He's left it so late now it's even worse than if he'd just got it off his chest straight away.

Jesus, if he's crying just thinking about it, what he's going to be like when he's actually telling him? He can't put it off any longer now, he's already arranged to meet up with him later, so tonight's the night.

By the time he gets home Michelle is already in the apartment. 'What are you doing here, babe?'

'I was off today.'

'Oh great – good to see you.' He gives her an awkward kiss.

'How come you're home so early?'

'Ah I just had that course thing, sure.'

'Oh yeah – how did it go?'

'Yeah, it was pretty good.'

'How you feeling?'

'I'm okay. Glad you're here … I'm just dreading talking to my dad.' Here come the waterworks. 'He's going to be so disappointed in me.'

Yes, he will, Danny.

Michelle's hugging him like she's done so many times before. It's funny how it's never dawned on her that every time she is comforting him it's always to do with him telling his dad or him going to prison – it's never about me. She's never had to comfort him because he's so upset about killing a man. Not once has he said how bad he feels or anything. She's under the impression that he's all broken up about the tragedy of the whole situation – he's not; it's just how the situation he's found himself in affects him personally that has him so upset.

***

It's five past eight when he gets to his dad's house, but he doesn't go straight in. He stands outside for a while, having a smoke and looking in the window. He can just see his dad's feet – two odd socks stretched out on the couch with the telly on. The socks make him smile. Danny's the same when it comes to socks – he never bothers pairing them up. Doesn't see the point; nobody sees them, anyway. Michelle used to slag him about it, but now he's converted her so that she never wears matching socks either – unless it's by chance.

A cigarette usually takes about seven minutes to smoke, but Danny finishes his in three. He's not ready to go in yet. One more smoke and then he'll be ready. His dad is a good man, he thinks – a good father. He's going to be understanding. Helpful. But he knows his dad isn't in the best of health. What if he can't take it? *I've already killed one man – please, dear Lord, don't let me kill another.*

24

Danny focuses on his dad's odd socks as he tries to fight back the tears. He knows if he looks up at his face he'll lose it. The two of them sit side by side on the old leather couch in the living room, their knees almost touching until Senior moves himself a little further away.

'How old was he?'

'Thirty-five.'

'Jesus, Danny.'

'I know.'

'Why didn't you tell me sooner?' The hurt is evident in his dad's voice.

'I couldn't, Dad. I just couldn't.' He moves his eyes from his dad's socks to the fireplace and the swirls of light at its centre.

'You should have told me, maybe I could have helped you.'

'I'm sorry.'

Danny can barely speak. All his concentration is focused on trying to keep that ball of emotion in his gut from rising upwards.

'You couldn't … Jesus Christ, Danny, what have you done?'

'It was an accident.'

'An accident? You punch people by accident?'

The flames of the fire are reflected in Danny's eyes. 'I didn't mean to kill him.'

'Great – you meant to punch him, though. You go around punching people, what the hell do you expect?' That gets him. Danny holds one last breath and a bubble of wet snot bursts out of his nose along with floods of tears. 'You've done it now, Danny –

you've destroyed your own life, not to mention that poor man and his ... did he have a family?

'A wife and kid.'

'Oh God help you – what have you done?' Danny Senior says, standing up and pacing the length of the room.

'I'm sorry.'

At least, I think that's what he says. He's breathing so heavily that I can barely understand him.

'Don't say sorry to me, it's not my life you've destroyed.'

Damn right, Senior.

'Jesus Christ, Dad.' Danny manages to catch his breath, bringing the tears a little bit under control. 'You think I wanted this? You think I wanted this to happen? I don't need you to tell me what a bad person I am – I know.'

'I didn't say that but you ...'

'I know what I did, so don't get all fucking righteous on me; it was an accident. I meant to punch him, not to kill him. Don't tell me you've never gotten into a drunken bar fight – who the fuck hasn't?' He's panting again – rocking back and forth, crying the way you might cry if you were alone. 'It was an accident, I didn't want to kill anyone, Dad, please Dad, I'm sorry – I'm so sorry.'

Senior's heart is broken – how the hell has this landed at his door? He stops pacing and sits back down beside Danny. 'Come here, son – I know you didn't.' Both in tears, they hold on to each other. 'We'll get through this.'

'We won't, Dad – I'm fucked.' Senior can think of nothing to say. His son is right. 'I've really done it this time. And I deserve whatever I get too.'

'We'll get through this, Danny, I promise you,' his dad repeats.

Danny sniffles. 'How?'

'Together – we'll do whatever needs to be done.'

'I'm so sorry, Dad.'

'I know you are, son.' He holds Danny a while longer. 'Please stop crying.' Danny sits up and wipes his face with the palms of his hands.

'Will you come with me tomorrow?'

'Of course I will.'

'I'm sorry I didn't tell you sooner.'

'That's okay – don't worry about that now,' he says, patting Danny gently on the knee.

They sit in silence for a while, Senior trying to take it all in.

'I'm going to prison, amn't I?' Danny eventually says.

'I don't know.'

'How the hell am I going to get out of this? I have to say it was self-defence.'

'Well, was it self-defence?'

'Kind of. Your man was getting all agro at me – I hit him first, yeah, but I thought he might hit me.'

Lying prick.

Senior shakes his head. 'That's not self-defence, son.'

'Well, maybe I should say he shoved me or something.' He knows that's going to be hard for his dad to take. Senior says nothing and when Danny glances up at him his expression is exactly what he expects – heartbreak, disappointment, shame. He can read his dad's face like a book. 'I have to say something, Dad.'

'I know you're scared, son. But no matter how scared you are you can't say something about the dead man that isn't true. You can't dishonour him any more than you already have.'

Junior lets out another whimper, 'But he was mouthing off at me – all squaring up …'

Senior looks straight into his son's eyes. His voice is forceful, insistent. 'That doesn't give you the right, son. What he might have done doesn't matter.'

Danny's got nothing. He knows his dad is right. It's just that the thought of prison terrifies him so much, he feels desperate to find some way out. Talking with his dad now is the first time that he truly realises there is no way out. There is nothing he can do about it except throw himself to the wolves and hope they don't savage him too much.

Losing all hope is in some way slightly comforting. The anxiety of trying to figure out an angle – praying that he will somehow get away with it – has all left him now. He's still terrified but he knows for the first time what he will do.

'You're right, Dad.'

He wipes his tears and decides that he's not going to cry anymore about it. I'll believe that when I see it.

'I'm going to just apologise. There's nothing I can do. Plead guilty and pray that I don't have to go to prison for too long.'

'Oh Jesus,' Senior says, as if he's only now thought of the reality of his only son being put away.

'Well, I'm going to prison, Dad; that's one thing that's certain.'

'Christ … what does your barrister say?'

Danny hesitates. 'He was kind of pushing the self-defence angle as well. That's pretty much what he is planning on saying tomorrow.'

'That's not an option, son.'

Danny nods. 'I know – don't worry, I'm not going to say that anymore.'

Senior stands up and walks over to the liquor cabinet. He had got in a bottle or two for visitors over Christmas. Danny watches him take out two glasses; he considers saying something but holds his tongue.

'Do you want ice?'

'Yeah, thanks.'

Senior notices his hands shaking as he puts ice in his son's glass and just a drop of water in his own. He hasn't drunk alcohol in over fifteen years, hasn't wanted one in ten but knows there is no way he'll get through this night without the taste of whiskey. When he used to go on benders, Paddy's was his drink. He thinks about that as he pours – glad it's a nice bottle of ten-year-old Laphroaig that he's pouring instead. He'd sworn that he'd never drink another Paddy's. Then again, he'd sworn that he'd never drink another anything, period.

'Here you go,' he says, handing his son a glass.

'Thanks. Are you sure you want one, Dad?'

'Yes, I'm sure.'

Neither one takes a sip right away. Senior plays with the glass in his hand a while, watches the oily liquid swirl around, mixing with the water. His eyes fill up. Danny wants to say something – he's never seen pain like it in his dad's face, not even when his mam died.

'I'm so sorry, Dad.'

The cold glass in Senior's hand and the smell of the drink seem so familiar and comforting. Part of him recoils from its allure and he considers standing up, walking to the kitchen and throwing it down the sink, but instead finds himself saying, 'We'll just have the one.'

'Okay.'

Taking his eyes off the glass, he asks, 'Will you stay over tonight?'

'Sure, Dad, I'll just have to ring Michelle.'

'Good,' he whispers.

He gives one last look into the glass, then takes a sip. He doesn't knock it back, just savours it. It feels good. He can smell the smoke, the oak casks it had been resting in, feels the coldness of the whiskey followed by the explosion of heat in his chest. The two of them sit there together in silence as the whiskey touches their lips.

They don't just have the one, though. They stay sitting until they finish the whole bottle.

25

Apart from New Year's Day, it is the first decent night's sleep Danny has had since this whole thing started. Being so drunk helps, telling his dad is a load off and I decide to leave him alone as well. He sleeps like a fucking baby. I should try to wake him, I suppose, but instead I go off to the woods to play with my night-vision eyes and listen to John's voice from past conversations and memories.

I watch a commune of crows sleeping high in the branches. I don't know why everyone hates crows, I always thought they were cool. Is it just because they can't sing? That's a bit harsh. My dad can't sing either, but we still love him. For a guy who literally hasn't a note in his head, it's strange that he still likes sing-songs. He can't even sing *olé, olé* in tune. But every time I'd sing a song I'd look over at him and he'd be quietly enjoying it. He'd look at me proudly with the slightest of smiles on his face. It's not like I had this great voice or anything, but I'd be doing something that he was unable to do – maybe the only thing. That look he gave me always made me feel warm inside. He was like that with Brian and Tim too. Come to think about it, he didn't overly like sing-songs – he only used to like it when me, my mam or one of my brothers would sing. If an aunty or one of my mam's mates sang, I'd see him throwing his eyes up to heaven or looking completely uninterested. Not uninterested, actually – irritated.

My dad is sleeping surprisingly well this night too. My poor mother is barely getting a wink; just looking at her almost makes me go back to Danny to start stirring the bastard. But I stay with her, until she finally succumbs to exhaustion.

I go back to my new friends, the crows. I never saw a sleeping bird when I was alive; I suppose why would I have? There must be about twenty of them, snoozing away. One little thing, though, is wide awake, looking about the place and down on two smaller crows I figure are her young. I sit watching her head dart back and forth, when out of nowhere what seems like a giant bird swoops in from behind and scares the crap out of me. The big crow stands for a long while at the edge of the tree, looking in over his family. It's the kind of thing you would never see unless you're watching a David Attenborough programme (and I never watched them).

I'd stay longer, but I have my own family to watch over. Pam isn't asleep either; she's in Robbie's room, standing over his cot. I swoop in behind her just like the giant crow did with his family and she smiles. I know it's because little Robbie has a funny expression on his face, but I also like to think it's because, somewhere deep down in her soul, she knows I am with her now; the two of us looking down over our son together.

I won't leave her. I won't go to Danny's. All things considered, she doesn't seem as sad as I thought she would; instead, she looks determined. Watching her turn off the lights and set the alarm before getting under the blankets makes me proud.

She used to hate staying in the house alone; she'd get frightened that someone might break in or something. Another thing she's had to get used to since my death. That was probably the hardest thing for her, apart from missing me – being alone at night. She would never go to bed by herself if I was out and she wasn't. I'd come home in the middle of the night and she'd be fast asleep on the couch. I used to love it – she'd be so adorable when I'd wake her up, asking me if I had a nice night, baby, and then stumbling with me into bed. I'd often say that she should have gone to bed and she'd tell me she'd been too scared.

'But what are you afraid of?'

'What if someone breaks in?'

'Well, what difference does it make whether you're on the couch or up in bed?'

'There's more escape routes downstairs. I'd run to get help.'

I'd always tickle her during these conversations – halfway through most of our conversations actually.

'My little hero.'

'Ah, haha, stop it! Stop it!' It would always take at least two yelps before I would.

'But if someone really wants to attack you, they're going to get you no matter where you are in the house.'

'Chris!'

'Sorry, baby – I'm only messing, no one is going to break in.'

'You don't know that, you have no idea how hard it is being a girl.'

'It sounds shit.'

'Totally.'

I'd put my arms around her then and give her a big hug.

If I had known then just how alone at night she would soon be I never would have teased her about it, but I always thought she was cute when she was scared. It's amazing how much she has recovered from that – the first few nights were hell for her. And I don't mean the first few nights after my death; she was too full of grief then and there were a lot of people around anyway. I mean, once the dust settled and people started getting back to their own lives. She was pure terrified at first – looking under the bed, in the hot press – and the sad part was that she knew how stupid she was being. She just couldn't help it. After looking behind all the doors, she'd finally get under the covers and literally cry herself to sleep.

All this was hell for me too. You can't imagine how hard it is, watching the person you love most in the world in pure agony, unable to do anything but watch. That's it, no rub of the shoulder, no kiss on the lips. Just watch.

But she has gotten so strong since those nights. Deep down, she's still afraid, but she doesn't go through the same ritual before going to bed. She simply makes sure the door is locked, the windows are closed, looks in on our son and goes to bed. Sometimes the house noises wake her up. Our house can make fierce noises – floorboards creaking for no reason, pipes going nuts. We were so used to them we stopped hearing them, but when you suddenly find yourself alone and terrified it's the last thing you want to be hearing in the middle of the night.

This time, it's the floorboards that wake her up – they make a sound like someone is walking on the landing and it startles her out of her sleep. Her forehead is sweating and I wish I could rub it for her, but instead I just look. I stay with her though – till she closes her eyes once more, till she drifts off into a deep sleep, till she wakes up to the day in which she'll have to see my killer's face again.

26

Everybody looks a million bucks. My dad's in his dark-green suit that he wears to every occasion he's invited to. The same suit he wore to my funeral. The two lads look like twins – both wearing grey suits. Pam looks lovely in her woollen coat, as does my mam, but they both seem tired too. Orla's dressed smart as well, to be fair. When they all walk up to the towering columns of the Four Courts my mam notices that the River Liffey running past them seems uncharacteristically choppy. She's usually not one for superstitions but still can't help feeling that it's a bad omen. Nobody is particularly ready to go in yet. They just make small talk, while trying not to discuss what the day is actually about.

Brian sparks up a smoke and gives one to Pam.

'Have you got a spare one?' Tim asks. He never has his own smokes. Brian has to take them back out of his pocket to give one to him.

'Cheers.'

As Pam takes her first drag, she notices John and Fanny walking up the road towards them, which puts a smile on her face, 'Look it – here come the lads.'

Brian looks around. 'I didn't know Fanny was coming, jeez, fair play to him.'

Pam gives the pair of them a big hug before they go over to say hi to my folks. My mam looks around and is surprised to see them.

'Ah hello, Fanny.'

Everyone smiles as Fanny goes red; we always got a kick out of when an old person would call Fanny by his nickname. It's strange

– we would never notice ourselves calling him that, but as soon as someone like my mam said it, with such a polite voice, the stupidity of his name would make us laugh. Plus, Fanny is a relatively shy person, so that makes it all the better.

Tim's actually laughing, 'You're looking well, Fanny.'

'Thanks, Tim,' he starts smiling back. 'You're looking well yourself.'

'Thanks very much, I haven't been working out or anything.'

'Yeah, I can tell.'

John goes over and shakes my dad's hand. 'Hiya, Frank.'

'How're you doing, John – how was the honeymoon?'

John shrugs. 'Yeah, yeah – we had a great time, thanks … The Big Apple, some spot.'

'Why do they call it the Big Apple anyway?' Tim wants to know.

'Beats me,' John says.

'Jaysus man, you were just there,' says Tim, disappointed.

'So what?'

'Were you not curious to find out?'

'Nope.'

Fanny's head is full of useless information, so he opens his mouth. 'It comes from black stable boys in the twenties who were used to touring around shitty quarter-mile race tracks in the middle of nowhere. They were so happy going to New York where all the money was – it was so big to them that they referred to it as … "The Big Apple".'

Tim's mouth is open. 'Wow – I'm impressed.'

'Where the hell do you come up with this stuff?' John smiles.

'It's ridiculous. Who knows crap like that?' Pam says as she takes another drag.

My mam seems impressed too. 'Where did you hear that, Fanny?'

They all start smiling again.

Fanny manages not to blush this time. 'Just picked it up, Kate. There is actually another school of thought that it comes from all the sidewalk apple vendors of the depression era.'

'Ah here, that's enough,' my dad says.

'No, no,' says Orla. 'I want to hear something else that will go in one ear and out the other.'

Pam's laughing her Muttley laugh. 'Yeah, Fanny, tell us why The Windy City is called The Windy City.'

Tim jumps in. 'It's because Dad used to live there.'

'Hey – very funny,' Dad says as he swings out a mess punch at Tim.

Pam starts laughing even more – she loves fart jokes for some reason.

I remember when I first started going out with her I used to hold in my farts all the time. It was terrible because I was one of those blokes who was prone to farting. I know all guys are, but I seemed to be even worse. On two separate occasions I was given a present of *A Farter's Pocketbook* by Jan Velden. Once by Pam on my birthday and once by a girl in work for a Kris Kindle. The second time I got it I was kind of embarrassed.

The first time I farted in front of Pam I made a big production out of it. I felt one coming on and just hadn't the energy to hold it in any longer, so I did a kind of dance. The final move was getting into a sumo wrestler-style stance and roaring out a big loud bang. She fucking cracked up. That was her mistake, because from that moment on I never held in a fart again. For the first year or so I'd always do some sort of move before the fart, but bit by bit the moves/dances would get shorter until it was just a question of cocking my arse.

It became so natural a thing that in the end nothing would even be said. We'd be sitting there watching TV, I'd fart and neither one of us would blink. We used to joke about it – that if ever we'd break up where the hell would I get another girl that would put up with it?

When I was younger I remember visiting my grand-aunt and uncle. My Uncle Tommy would be sitting on his chair and let off a stinker, and me and my brothers would be disgusted. Not so much at the fart but more at the total disrespect of doing it in front of my Aunt Kay. I realise now that it wasn't disrespect – he just felt comfortable doing it. She'd just smile and say nothing and I'd put it down to him being old and hoped I'd never get like that. Funny how history repeats itself.

Pam used to love Dutch ovens – when you fart under the blanket and hold your partner's head under there. Everyone else on the planet hates them, but Pamela used to find them so funny that it outweighed the horribleness of them. Once the sick bitch even asked for one for her birthday.

The only person I knew who enjoyed other people's farts more than Pam was Davey. Two years ago a few of us were out on his porch having a smoke and he ran upstairs to go to the toilet. I farted and heard him laughing from upstairs – he held on to his piss and came all the way downstairs just to see who did it, 'Who did it, who did it?'

'Me.'

The guy was in floods of tears as he walked back up to the jacks.

Davey was originally going to come with Fanny and John to the courthouse, but as always with him he waited till the last minute to sort out a day off, so in the end he was unable to get it. I'm glad Fanny has made it, though; he always puts me in a good mood.

'Contrary to widespread belief, The Windy City is not so called because of Mr Cosgrave's flatulence problem,' Fanny says.

'Hey!'

'No, it comes from a reference made about Chicago politicians who were full of "hot air".'

'That's not it either – it's because of all the wind that blows through the town because of the big lake it's next to,' Brian argues.

Fanny shakes his head. 'No, that's what most people think ...'

'Most people think it because it's true,' Tim interrupts.

Fanny's about to come up with some other lame argument but notices Pam's face. All the blood has drained from it and to Fanny it looks like she's aged about ten years in thirty seconds. 'You okay?' he asks. She just stares ahead. 'Pam – you okay?' They all look at her and then turn in the direction that she's facing – to see a big, strapping lad walking towards them.

John freezes. He can't speak – tries to say, 'Are you okay?' or 'Is that him?' All he can muster up instead in the tiniest of whispers is 'Jesus.'

They all stare at the big lad walking with his head down beside a smaller, older man. Pam starts shaking till my dad takes control. 'Come here, love.' He puts a comforting arm around her and turns her to walk the other way. She's still shaking and he keeps his arm tight around her shoulder, rubbing his hand softly up and down. He glances back at Danny and then to the rest of them. 'Come on,' he says, 'let's get a coffee before going inside.'

They all follow, except for Brian. He remains there, glaring – praying that this big prick will look up.

Danny notices them from a distance but keeps his head down as he approaches; he just can't bring himself to meet their eyes. Danny's dad sees Brian, too – it would be hard to miss him. He guesses who he must be by his demeanour and feels sorry for Brian, wants for him to see it in his eyes, but Brian has no interest in him. Doesn't even see him. Danny's dad looks back to his son and tightens his grip around him. He feels sorry for Brian, sure, but he is here for his child. This is the most traumatic thing he'll ever go through; there is no way he is going to let him down.

27

Pam and Orla are the only two Danny has seen before. Until now he wasn't sure if he'd recognise them. All it takes is a split second, though. It's actually Orla that he sees first – well, her shock of red hair to be exact. She wears it short and bright but it's not just that – it's too high at the crown or something so it really stands out.

Anyway, he sees her and looks at the ground. It's the first time since I've been living in Danny's pocket that I can feel real guilt in him. Proper guilt. With my parents and friends there he can see firsthand who he has fucked. He stays looking at the ground, but still he knows they're all staring. Thank Christ his dad is there, he thinks.

He's still trying to decide whether or not to look up when he notices that they are all walking away. All but one. The closer he gets to Brian the more frightened he becomes. It's intimidating, having him standing there, glaring; no way in hell is he looking up now. His legs start to feel weak and, as if sensing this, his dad tightens his grip around him. Makes him stand up straight and walk right past the man he assumes is my brother. A part of Danny wants to stop, wants to say something to Brian – try to apologise – but he is unable to look at him, let alone stop for a quick chat. 'Hey you must be a Cosgrave, sorry about the whole killing a loved one and all – my bad.' He's better off keeping the head down.

I'd almost feel half sorry for Danny, if not for the expression on poor Brian's face; pain, anger, hurt, disgust, fear all swirled together – it's a face I've never seen him wear before. He didn't know how he'd react when coming face to face with Murray. He wants to do something – to say something. I kind of want him to as well, but I don't know what and neither does he. Shouting or hitting him – they both seem kind of futile.

Tim has no such problem. 'You, you fucking wanker!'

On his way to the coffee shop he'd gone to say something to Brian and noticed that he hadn't followed them. He started back towards where Brian was standing and held his tongue until Danny was within ear reach – he didn't want to be roaring for everyone to hear.

Danny doesn't look up, but Tim notices him wince so smiles, 'You juiced-up prick, you're going down, you cunt.'

Senior looks up at Tim with a pained expression, but Tim hardly notices. 'Keep walking, slim – enjoy the fresh air while you can.'

'Leave it, Tim.' Brian turns around and puts a hand on his shoulder. 'Let's go.'

***

My family and friends are hardly speaking by the time my case is called. None of them can take their eyes off Danny, except for Fanny and Tim, who both notice what a great ass Michelle has – but that only makes them hate him more. When she first showed up they were checking her out and couldn't believe it when she went over and gave Danny a kiss.

'Fuck,' Fanny said, shocked.

Tim wasn't happy either. 'The bastard – look at the bird he's going out with.'

'That makes me sick. A prick like him with a girl that hot.'

'She must be a dope.'

'Still.'

Tim got over it soon enough, but for some reason Fanny can't stop looking at her. Sitting down in the courtroom he keeps watching Danny like everyone else, but your one is sitting right behind him, so each time he looks at him he can't help but check her out. I have to laugh at him. Such a serious situation and Fanny the pervert is imagining himself kissing the little freckle on the lower part of her neck.

My dad is burning a hole in Danny's back and he can feel it. He can feel them all looking at him, thinking he is the baddest bastard in the world. He'd always thought of himself as a good guy. Same as everyone else, I guess – like the hero of his own movie. Except the hero of the movie never kills some innocent dude, then goes to prison for it, and now, with those eyes boring into him, he is beginning to really see that. To think that maybe he's the baddie.

I wonder do the real sick fuckers still think they're the goodies? Up until now Danny certainly did. Until he started thinking of all the people he's fucked over – all the fights he's gotten into, all the people who don't like him, the way he knows his friends aren't all that crazy about him, the way he treats Michelle, the way he talks about his dad being an alcoholic to get sympathy, the way he killed me. He's not a good person but at least he can half-see it. What about the complete psychos, though? I wonder did Jack the Ripper go about his business thinking he was the man?

You don't get these kinds of answers when you die – who the fuck was Jack the Ripper, for instance? I don't know if Marilyn committed suicide or if she was killed. I couldn't tell you if Elvis is alive or dead. Well, I suppose, I could – he's dead, but that's only because I don't believe any of that conspiracy stuff. How could anyone think that the biggest star on the planet would just go into hiding for the rest of his life because he didn't like the limelight? Elvis not like the limelight? He was the limelight; sure just look at him on stage – the guy was born to be famous. There are some awful dummies out there.

It's a pity you don't learn all the hidden mysteries of the world. When you're alive you assume you'll find them out when you die, or at the very least you won't give a shit about them anymore. But you do. I'd still like to know who killed J.F.K., but I'm none the wiser than when I last watched the movie. No big deal or anything, but it would be nice to have complete knowledge of the universe as we are led to believe will happen. I still don't even know if there is a God, for Christ's sake, and I'm dead. If you don't know whether or not God exists when you're dead, then what's the world coming to?

Suppose he doesn't; otherwise I'd probably have met him by now. Although I often heard ghost stories about people who had a chance to walk into the light but turned around last minute because they weren't finished on earth – like the way Swayze turned back in *Ghost* because he wasn't ready to leave Demi Moore behind. Maybe that's the story with me. Although I definitely didn't see any beautiful light that I could have walked into, so I have my doubts.

Once Danny is sent to prison hopefully the light will show up. It might, but I doubt it. I hope I don't have to wait until Pam is happy again or something. I want her to move on with her life, but I don't want to have to hang around and watch her shag some other bloke. Maybe once I get back at Danny I'll be able to get out of here, but I still haven't figured out how the hell to do that. Keep him awake at night, whoop-de-do; he fucking killed me.

Orla is really looking forward to getting up on the dock and giving her version of events. She plans on crying a little but not too much – just enough to show people how upset she is – but then hold it back to show how strong she can be.

Her plan seems to fall apart, at first, when Danny admits to absolutely everything. That it was completely his fault and that he will accept any punishment that the court deems fit. With the guilty plea there's no need for a trial or any of that. Thankfully, though, the judge still wants to hear exactly what happened. Orla smiles. She will get her chance up on the stage. But Pam is called first and that's not easy for anyone – especially me. Well, especially her, I guess, but also for me.

Watching her relive the whole thing is terrible. Danny's prick of a barrister keeps hounding her for some reason. Wonky head on him with glasses frames way too old-fashioned for his baby face, asking her loads of stupid questions that don't mean anything.

'What time was it when you went out to the smoking area?'

'I'm not sure, maybe half twelve or something.'

'You're not sure?'

Tosser.

'No.'

She's about to crack. What difference does it make what time it was? Your man pleaded guilty, so what difference do the minor details make? He's asking her how big the smoking area was – now that makes no fucking sense at all. Who gives a shit how big it was?

'Well how far away were you from the defendant when you first went outside?'

'I don't know.'

'Was it ten feet, twelve?'

Pam hasn't a clue about feet and inches or any of that shit. She bursts out crying. 'Just a normal distance away – I don't know how much,' she splutters. Poor thing, bawling crying, and the barrister just looking at her with his crooked eyes as if she's stupid. My dad wants to get up and smack him.

It seems to me like he's just a crap lawyer and doesn't really know what to ask. He looks ridiculous as well. I don't understand why lawyers in Ireland wear that silly outfit, the white wig and black cape. He looks like he's going to a fancy-dress party. 'What are you dressed up as?' 'I'm a highwayman!' All he's missing is the black mask and maybe a musket. The whole time he's asking his stupid questions I keep picturing him riding into work on a horse – cape flapping in the wind, calling out 'Stand and deliver!'

He hasn't thought of any new questions when Orla gets up. 'Miss Halpin – what size would you say the smoking area was?'

'I haven't the faintest idea.'

'You don't?'

'No.'

'Well roughly.'

Orla sniffs, straightens her back. 'To be honest I was a little preoccupied with watching my friend die to measure the courtyard; besides I left my ruler at home.'

Orla has always wrecked Tim's head, but he cracks a huge grin at that.

The barrister appears flustered. 'Okay, Miss Halpin, I'm just trying to establish how everything happened that night.'

'Fine, then let me sum it up for you. Chris was minding his own business, when that man came over to us and punched him as hard as he could with absolutely no provocation. He has admitted as much, case closed, move on.'

Every question he asks her is met with a snappy answer. She's fuming – she's so mad that she forgets to do her pre-planned bit of crying and then holding back the tears thing. She only realises she never cried as she sits back down in her seat and is slightly annoyed at herself because she figures crying might make the judge act a little harder on Danny. Everyone else is proud of her, though; Fanny even finds himself fancying her a little.

After a brief recess, the judge returns. I kind of liked the judge originally, as he seemed very thorough, but now I'm not so sure because he's not holding off on sentencing. Most times you might have to wait a couple of weeks or a month, but this guy saunters out after fuck-all deliberation, acting all grand. Why's he rushing it?

Mind you, peering down over his glasses at Danny, he does look like he's going to sock it to him. Danny thinks so too. His hands are shaking, but he holds them tight behind his back. As the judge begins to speak, Danny tries to listen to what he is saying, but for some reason all he can think about is how the situation reminds him of being sent to the principal's office in primary school. It's so similar. He's standing up straight just like he did when he was a kid in trouble. He can't even see the judge anymore. All he can see is his old principal, Mr Cronin, glaring at him from behind his desk. The room would move on him – not spin but sway from side to side, as if it was floating on a slow stream. The *tick … tick … tick* of the clock was the loudest thing in the principal's office as is the clock behind the judge. Snap out of it, he tells himself – listen to what the man is saying. *Tick … tick … tick.* He pushes the school memory out of his head and focuses in on the judge, but all he can hear is the damn clock; it's like someone has a speaker attached to it. *Tick … Tick!*

Suddenly, as if from nowhere, the judge's voice booms over it. 'It is a difficult sentencing exercise. I hope the public understands you have to be dealt with for a single blow, one which had dreadful but unintended consequences. It is a very sad case for all involved and although it was accidental you must be punished for what devastation you caused.'

Tick … tick …

'Therefore, I am sentencing you to four years with two and a half years suspended.'

Tick … tick … boom.

Motherfucker! A year and a half. A fucking year and a half – that's nothing. What the hell is that suspended sentence shit, anyway? I never understood that – what's the fucking point of it?

This whole thing isn't right. It's not like on TV. I mean, over in the one day? Come on. I thought it would go on for weeks with loads of evidence and stuff. He finds a conscience at the last minute and saves himself all that, saves himself a jury. Fucker. So because the DPP and court agree to a guilty plea of manslaughter, they reckon a four-year sentence with two and a half suspended is grand. The judge took into account how remorseful Danny supposedly is. How the accused is a young man of conscience and had attempted to cooperate fully with the gardaí. What a load of bollocks.

Beautiful, shining, walk-in-to-light passageway? Any chance?

No?

Didn't think so.

28

The first thing Danny notices in Mountjoy Prison is the smell. It's a mix of a bleached locker room and a warehouse that sells cardboard – wet cardboard. He can't figure it out because as far as he can tell there is fuck all cardboard anywhere, but the smell is unmistakable.

The basement stockroom of the phone shop where he used to work would often let in water from the street when it rained heavily. His boss could never be arsed fixing it, and instead would get them to line up ripped cardboard boxes to stop the water from travelling too far. Danny always had the lovely job of changing the cardboard when it got too soggy or smelly. He hated that fucking job; his boss didn't have any rubber gloves so Danny would have to pick up the nasty cardboard with his bare fingers, grimacing as it ripped when he lifted it, or when his hands touched the brown-purplish stuff that had grown on it.

Of all the things that could have been going through his mind at this point, he's surprised it's this. He had expected terror, but he's more pissed off than terrified. Pissed off that he'll have to spend the next year and a half in a place that smells exactly like something he hates.

He's still sniffing away when he's led through the holding cells where all the newbies are first brought. The cells don't look like how I expected them to – they all have glass walls instead of bars, like the way it is in *Silence of the Lambs* where Anthony Hopkins is kept. As he walks, Danny tries not to look into any of them, but one guy gets up abruptly and starts banging his head against the window.

'Fuck sake,' Danny mutters by accident. Loafing his fucking head, what the hell kind of a place is this?

Headbutters and in particular the wet cardboard smell are the least of his problems when he sees the state of his holding cell. No *Shawshank Redemption*-like, fine big room all to yourself to put up posters and little ornaments to make your stay more pleasant. No, instead it's a room he has to share with four other horrible bastards. All of whom Danny wouldn't be caught dead spending time with on the outside. Three of them he wouldn't even risk sitting beside on a bus. The guard who had taken all his details when he first got to the prison explained that he would have to share for a few days until he got his own cell. Danny nodded, figuring he'd have to bunk in with one other guy. Four was pushing it.

At first he's too busy looking at the mostly unfriendly faces of his new roomies to notice that there's no toilet in the place. What a dump. He had kind of expected the overcrowding thing – it had been in the news a lot – but he'd always assumed there would be a jacks.

None of them really say anything, so he decides to introduce himself. After a brief hesitation, they introduce themselves in return. There's a fat auld lad named Seamus who looks even more out of place than Danny; there are two crackhead-looking blokes called Wacko (yes, Wacko) and Damo. Last but not least is a big, tall, scary-looking bastard named Bogdasha, who is from Russia of all places. At first glance I like the Russian the most. Danny hates them all equally: the auld fella because he's too eager to be his friend, Wacko and Damo because they are exactly the kind of scumbags that he hates, and the Russian, well, because he's a Russian.

A lot of people don't like Russians because they are such cold-blooded bastards, but that's exactly why I like them. They come across as ruthless fuckers and you have to admire that. Hard bastards, nothing seems to get to them – I think it's because they are all so used to death that they just don't give a bollocks. Loads of them perished at the end of the Second World War and their own leader managed to wipe out about twenty million of the fuckers. Speaking of which, I've always wondered why Stalin doesn't get as bad a rap as Hitler. I reckon he was worse. Every time people talk dictators it's always Hitler who's crowned The Most Evil Man Who Ever Lived. Stalin only gets an 'Ah yeah, he was a bit of a bollocks too.' You wouldn't be caught dead with a name like Adolf today, but there are more Josephs than you can shake a stick at. Having that lunatic killing half your family would change your outlook. Even the women seem cold as fuck. This Russian girl used to work in the deli across from where I worked – every day for three years she'd make me a sandwich and not once did she give me a look of recognition. I hated that one.

But most of them I liked – then again, she was the only one I'd personally known. Although John did tell me a story about a Russian bloke he worked with – his girlfriend smooched some other guy when she was drunk. No matter how much she cried and pleaded with him for forgiveness he was having none of it. The last thing he said to her as he was walking out the door in his deep Russian accent was, 'You will never see me again.'

Cool bastard.

Other than that I don't know any of them, so I suppose it's the stereotype that I like. But I've found most stereotypes are true enough to fact. Of course there are loads of exceptions, but often, by and large, it's fairly on the money. The Russians have a good one – ruthless, and they are. The Irish have a good one too – a bunch of drunks. And, let's face it, we are. Suppose that one could be taken two ways, but most Irish are proud to be known as alcoholics – it means you like to party.

The English don't really have a stereotype. I wonder why not. Everyone else has – the tanned Frenchman with a cigarette in his mouth, talking to some lash about making love; the American husband and wife tourists wearing the same red windbreaker and beige trousers. What else? Lazy Spanish, boring Germans. Some Aussie bigot driving a pickup truck and drinking a beer. Sleazy Italians, Asian nerds, coke-dealing Colombians. That sucks for the English, not having one. Suppose the English lout – 'Would you look at that English lout!' Or the posh toffs, maybe.

Wacko and Damo are total stereotypes. They're like cartoon characters of Dublin scangers. Both with names that end in 'o', both are thin and wiry, with shaved heads and mashed-up faces.

After the introductions, Danny decides to keep his mouth shut. There are two double bunks that have feet dangling off them and one floor mattress where Wacko sits. Danny parks himself beside him and stares at the wall. Wacko says something to him, but Danny ignores it, barely even hears him; all he can hear is the anxiety building in his gut, pounding away.

An hour passes before Danny's stomach starts calming down. He looks around the cell again and the same thing comes into his head that must come into all new inmates' heads about their new companions: 'What are you in for?' He thinks about saying it but then stops himself. What's the point? He figures he knows what they're in for, anyway. He sees Wacko talking the ear off Seamus, Damo stretched out on a bottom bunk joining in the odd time, and Bogdasha sitting above him saying nothing to nobody. Damo and Wacko are obvious – they're in for robbing one too many car stereos or something like that. Seamus must have been stung for a white-collar crime – screwed over some little guy – and the Russian probably chopped some other Eastern European's head off and fucked it into the canal. No point in asking.

No point in anything. *Is this my tribe now?* Danny thinks. *Are these the type of people who are on my level – who I should be associated with?* He then thinks of his loving father, battling through the despair of watching his wife wither away to nothing and die. He was strong enough to get out from under that pain. He had struggled, sure, but he never made Danny feel unloved and he did his best to make him want for nothing, save his mother. He doesn't think of her often anymore, but he thinks of her now. What would she make of her 'little superstar' now? That's what she used to call him – superstar. His memories of her have grown dim through the years, but the overriding image he has is the look of pride she wore every time she looked at him. If he kicked a ball straight or painted her a picture she would always give him that look. That over-the-top reaction that he so deeply craved and which made him feel so warm inside. Now the thought of that look makes him shiver. His heart feels frozen – he's let her down too.

He thinks of the monumental screw-up he perpetrated which led him to this hell on earth and decides: *Yes, this is my tribe. These are my people.*

I am home.

29

When my mam and dad get home from the court their main emotion is anger. The grief of my being dead they are getting used to somewhat, but the thought of this Danny Murray only getting eighteen months' prison time infuriates them. They struggle to understand it. He's taken everything from them and all that's being taken from him is eighteen lousy months? Actually that reminds me of one of my favourite lines from *Unforgiven*. Clint Eastwood says towards the end, 'It's a hell of a thing, killing a man. You take away all he's got and all he's ever gonna have.' Classic. I never thought that line would end up reminding me of me.

Anyway, my poor folks call Danny every name under the sun, sitting in the kitchen, giving out about the legal system and wondering if there's anything they can do – the same stuff you'd give out about yourself if you were in this situation.

Tim and Brian arrive. Hopefully the two lads will calm things down.

Nope.

They only add to it. Well, Tim does, anyway – he's giving out stink. Brian says little – he's too busy contemplating what he will do and whether or not he should call John tonight, let him in on what he's thinking.

Get it right in my own head first, he thinks. *Do I really want to go through with anything? If so what? Do I want to kill him? Simple – yes. Could I do it? Be honest now – yes. Do you really believe that or are you just telling yourself that to feel better about yourself? Think long and hard now, don't fuck about. I don't know – I think so. If you think so, talk to*

Tim. Will I ring John? No question, ring him and ask him to call over. What am I telling them? I don't know yet. When this man gets out of prison am I going to be able to confront him and kill him?

Jesus, what am I thinking?

I'll certainly be able to beat him, attack him with a hurl – beat the shit out of the fucker, but is that enough? Will that satisfy me? It's certainly not getting even, just a beating – but at least it's something. Do you really think you have it in you to kill; are you that kind of person? Maybe, when I think of him and what he's done to our family – Pam, Robbie. He got off too lightly. Cripple him? How? Beat him with a stick till he's almost dead; if he lives he lives, if not, then not. Get it right in your head, think long and hard ...

He looks at our dad – who'd certainly never approve of how Brian is thinking. I have mixed feelings myself, to be honest. I would like him to kill Danny, I think, but only if there was no way in hell that he'd get caught. But also I'd feel sorry for Danny's dad – he'd be the one hurt the most and I like him; he's a decent man. Thinking about it, I'm leaning towards not wanting him to do it. Hopefully I'll figure out a way to get my own revenge on Danny, although to be honest I'm kind of getting bored with that idea too – if ghosts were actually able to properly haunt fuckers who'd wronged them, then half the world would be scared shitless and you'd hear way more ghost stories.

The doorbell rings and this time it's John and Pam with John's dad, Jarlath. My dad's happy to see him – it's not that they are best buddies or anything, but they have been friends through the years and it's nice of him to come.

'Hey Jarlath, how are you doing?' Dad says as Jarlath enters the kitchen.

'I'm good, Frank,' Jarlath says, shaking Dad's hand. 'How are you guys holding up?'

'Well you heard the news, obviously,' my dad says.

'I did,' says Jarlath, as he leans, arms crossed, against the kitchen counter.

'We're fierce angry, Jarlath; it's just so unfair,' Mam says.

'I know, Kate; I truly wish there was something I could do.'

'I know you do. Thanks for stopping by, though.'

Jarlath chances a grin. 'Well, it was either this or the wife would have me working on God knows what.'

'Jesus, you'd happily walk into the most depressing house in Dublin in order to get out of a little housework, would you?' Tim says. 'You're one lazy bastard, Jarlath.'

They all laugh.

'Well, when you get to my age, Timmy, any excuse will do,' he says, throwing his eyes upwards.

Tim chuckles. 'Right.'

'Besides, I've only popped in for thirty seconds and then I'm up the road to the driving range – the wife won't suspect a thing.'

'Very shrewd, I like it,' Tim says.

My mam is smiling. 'Well, hang on a minute – you think I want to be a part of your lying and conniving?'

Jarlath shrugs. 'We're all friends here; I figured you could throw a blind eye?'

'As soon as you're out the door I'll be on to Phil spilling the beans.'

'Ah, I may as well stay so. Sure my swing is near perfect anyway, right, Frank?'

'Practice could only make it worse, Jarlath,' Dad answers mockingly.

Everyone is smiling now. The mood has changed since Jarlath arrived – he has a way of putting everyone at ease.

Mam looks down at her hands, entwined on the table. 'When

you were a guard, Jarlath, how did other people that you've seen deal with this kind of thing?'

At that question, Jarlath steps forward and puts a hand on Mam's shoulder. 'I'll tell you now – you will never, ever get over this. But I promise you it will get easier. Time. It's all time, Kate.'

'I just can't see it,' Mam says, holding his gaze.

Jarlath squeezes her shoulder. 'I know. It's going to be gradual, so gradual that you won't notice it, but the pain will ease.'

My mam nods and looks down. Jarlath looks at both my parents, then at my brothers and Pam. 'Right now you think you will never be truly happy.' My mam looks up at him as he continues. 'I'm telling you that you will be; not in the same way, of course, but you will be. It's just going to take you time – a lot of time, but together you'll get there.' Mam tries to smile and he smiles back. 'You'll get there, honey.'

He turns around and sees Pam hanging on his words – they all are. She smiles at him and he gives her a little wink that makes her feel better than any words could.

30

When the phone rings, John half-thinks about not answering it. He's still not over the jet lag and has just been through a shitty day at the courthouse. All he wants is to relax and watch an old episode of *Seinfeld*. The only reason he picks it up is because the ringing is annoying him and he wants to get rid of whoever it is.

'Hello?' he barks.

'Alright John, it's Brian.'

'Oh, hi Brian – how's it going?' Brian rarely rings him but he doesn't find it at all strange with the day that's in it.

'Grand. I was hoping we could get together and have a chat – me, you and Tim.'

'Yeah of course – when?'

'Now, actually. Is that okay or are you doing anything?'

This is where me and John differ. If I was feeling wrecked and all I wanted to do was crash out and watch *Seinfeld* I'd come up with an excuse as to why we'd have to wait until tomorrow to hook up. Even if I didn't, I'd at the very least be pissed off that I had to go out and I'd hesitate slightly. But John doesn't. He can hear it in Brian's voice that he needs to see him. Brian is like a younger brother to him too, so John doesn't waste a second.

'Of course – now is fine. Where?'

'Is Niamh home tonight?'

'Yeah, she should be in about a half hour,' John says, checking his watch.

'Can we make it our place then?'

'Okay. Right now?'

'Yeah.'

'I'm on my way.'

***

He gets to Brian and Tim's apartment just before half eight. Their place is pretty cool. It's in-between two blocks of offices and stepped back from the street so, despite being close to town, they have no neighbours. There is a handy little lane leading up to the gaff and the pair of them are there when John arrives, both of them looking at Tim's new moped. It's a heap of shit, but Tim is delighted with it.

'Alright John, how's it going?' Tim calls. 'My new moped – what do you think?'

John hesitates. 'It's lovely – I think my granddad had the same one when he was a young fella.'

'Did he?' For a second Tim doesn't realise that John is taking the piss out of him. Catching on, he says, 'Oh fuck – prick.' Then smiles. 'It's cool, though, isn't it? Kind of retro.'

'Flares are retro, man; this is an antique.'

Tim's face looks slightly hurt so John backpedals. 'Ah no – I'm only messing; it's quite cool alright.'

'You reckon?'

'Yeah – I could see you spinning around Dublin with some lash clinging on to you from behind. Real French-movie style.'

Tim has a grin from ear to ear. 'Deadly – I can't wait.'

'Where are you going to get some French lash to go for a spin with?' Brian asks sarcastically.

'Don't worry yourself about it. They'll come to me,' Tim says, looking down proudly at his gammy bike. 'It may not look like much, but I can almost smell the pussy I'm going to get from it.'

'No, I think that's just the smell of your rank-ass bike,' Brian says.

The apartment is open plan, so the kitchen is linked with the living room. John and Tim sit down on the couch while Brian puts on the kettle. 'Sugar or anything, John?'

'Lots of milk – till it's almost cold.' Brian thinks this is weird but says nothing – he figures he'll overdo it for the craic, put in half milk and half tea. Only thing is that's just the way John likes it, so Brian is slightly disappointed when John takes a sip and says, 'Perfect.'

'Jesus, you really do like it cold, don't you?'

'Yeah – it means you can take bigger sips.'

'Why not just have a glass of milk then?'

'I don't really like milk by itself.'

Brian's a bit puzzled, but he lets it alone – there are more important things to talk about than John's odd taste in drinks. He finishes pouring himself a cup and sits down opposite the two lads.

'Listen, thanks for coming out tonight.'

'No problem – mad day what?' John says.

'Sure was.'

'You guys okay?' John asks, taking another sip of the milky tea.

'You know.'

'Yeah.'

'You okay?' Tim asks.

'Ah, the same.'

The three of them are silent for a second, then John pipes up. 'What did you want to see me about?'

'Well, I don't really know how to say this …' Brian hesitates. Tim glances at Brian, not knowing what to expect – Brian hasn't told him the reason for this meeting either – but he can see how much our brother is struggling to find the right words.

'Jesus – what?' Tim snaps.

'That prick didn't get enough,' Brian blurts out. 'He didn't get punished enough – you know what I mean?'

John nods. 'Yeah, I'm so sorry, lads.'

'Don't be sorry, John – it hurts you every bit as much as us,' says Tim.

John shrugs. 'I guess.'

'Listen.' Brian's still trying to get to what he wants to say. 'I can't have this fucker running free after only a year or so.'

'What do you mean?' Tim asks.

'I mean, I don't think I could live with myself if he was out enjoying life while we're left without a brother and Robbie without a dad.'

John puts his cold drink down on the coffee table. 'What are you saying, Brian?'

Brian looks down at his hands, is surprised to see that they are balled into fists. 'I'm not sure yet – but you are the only two I can talk to about this. The way I'm feeling now, I don't know. I'm not asking you to do anything with me, but if something happens when he gets out, will you stick up for me?'

'Stick up for you?' Tim queries.

'Yeah – you know what I mean, say we were together or something?'

Tim and John look at each other with matching expressions of not knowing what the fuck to say. John leans forward towards Brian. 'Listen to me, Brian. I'm so, so sorry for what you are going through, believe me I know how you feel – Chris was the only brother I ever had.'

Brian's nose starts running and he puts his fingers to his eyes to try and stop the tears. 'I know he was, John.'

'It's all still so fresh, and you're right – that prick didn't get enough time, it's a fucking outrage. But there is nothing we can do about it.'

Brian just looks at him and John knows what the look means. 'Brian – you can't.'

I'm surprised Tim is so silent through all this; he's usually way more vocal. He's basically trying to figure out what to think. He can see the hurt and anger in Brian but doesn't know if our brother really means what he is hinting at. Is he just trying to get something out, in the same way that Tim had been right after my death? Tim has in some ways gotten over the idea and he'd assumed that Brian had too, since he had been the one who shot down any talk like that the first time it came up.

Brian isn't just saying it, though. I can see deep down inside of him; there is no doubt in my mind – if somehow he could come face to face with Danny Murray, Brian would try to kill him.

'You don't really mean what you're saying, do you?' John asks.

Brian's not meeting John's gaze. 'I don't know. All I know is that I have never felt like this before – and if this feeling isn't gone in eighteen months then I don't know what I'll do.'

'It will pass, and any time you feel like this I want you to ring me.'

'I feel like this all the time,' Brian admits, wiping his nose.

'Then ring me all the time. Or talk to Tim, we are all here for each other. To get each other through this. But you cannot do anything stupid when Murray gets out; you have to let it go.'

Brian shakes his head. 'Dublin's a small fucking town – what if I bump into him?'

'I don't know. Let's hope that doesn't happen, but even if it does you can't do anything. It would do none of your family any good if you wound up in jail.'

'That's why I asked you if you would stick up for me.'

John feels the strong need to drill some sense into Brian. He becomes more animated as he continues. 'I'm not entertaining this, Brian – we are not in a movie and I'm not somebody's alibi. This is real life and if you do something you will get caught – no matter how many people say they were with you. You are one of the first people the guards would look to if your man got killed.'

Tim finally joins in. 'John's right, Brian – I know how you feel, I kind of feel it too, but no good will come of it.'

Brian looks up at Tim and wipes the tears off his cheek. 'Okay,' he whispers.

Tim continues. 'It's not okay, this is mad talk and I think we all know that it's not in you to murder someone. But if you ever want to talk about it again, like John said, ring him or talk to me and we'll help each other, alright?'

Brian feels no better after talking about it – feels no different, but he decides to let it go.

'Do you agree with us? Do you understand?' John asks.

'Yeah.'

'You're sure?'

'Yeah – thanks lads, sorry about this.'

'That's alright man, any time you feel like this I want you to talk to us, okay?'

'Okay,' he nods.

He's sorry he brought it up with them and knows he never will again. But he also knows that the feeling he's spoken about will not go away. Tim's relieved, taking Brian at his word; John too starts feeling better about the situation and good about himself that he's been able to help.

John smiles at him, 'You promise?'

Brian stares back at John blankly. 'I promise.'

31

When you're a kid you have lots of worries about growing up. I remember hearing horror stories about people's first wet dreams – *Wet Dreams Gone Wrong*. I was about eleven when I first knew what a wet dream was, or kind of knew, anyway. It sounded great at first, but then you'd start to hear horror stories around the schoolyard that so and so's cousin had a wet dream about their mam, or worse yet, their dad.

I was terrified because dreams are something you have no control over. I remember hearing that this guy a few years ahead of me, Gavin Hickey, had his first wet dream about Wizbit. You know, that spongy yellow triangle creature from *The Paul Daniels Magic Show*. I heard that the theme song was playing in the background as your man rolled around with Wizbit:

> *Wizbit grew about 3 feet high.*
> *Ha ha this-a-way,*
> *ha ha that-a-way,*
> *ha ha this-a-way,*
> *my oh my!*

I could never quite look Gavin in the eye after hearing that, even years later when I figured it was probably bullshit. Every time I saw him I'd always have that theme tune playing in my head and think about what a pervert he was.

You soon learn that wet dreams aren't all they're cracked up to be, anyway, because you are beating off long before you have one.

I used to worry about not having as much fun as an adult too. When you're a kid you're always running around playing chasing, playing guns – adults always seemed to be having less craic because they'd just be sitting around a table or something. I asked my mam about it once and she told me in no uncertain terms that being an adult was way better than being a kid. I didn't get it. 'But what about all that "school days are the best days of your life" stuff?' I asked.

'That's completely untrue – being an adult is so much more fun.'

I couldn't see how that would be the case at the time, but I still totally took her word for it. From that moment on, I couldn't wait to be an adult. I wasn't great at being a kid – I hated school and always being told what to do – so the thought of having more fun as an adult sounded great.

She was right too, being an adult was great craic – I loved it.

Danny had the same kind of worries as me when he was young – not the Wizbit thing, of course, but other ones. Like being terrified that one of your parents might die – which of course came true for him. Or how when you're a kid you're afraid that when you grow up you might go to jail – which of course has also come true now. That's all Danny can think about during his first night in Mountjoy – how did it get to this point that he is now a criminal? One of the bad guys. As long as I've known him he's been a bad guy, yet he's still trying to figure out where it all went wrong.

Maybe if his mam hadn't died, he thinks. But not really, he was just unlucky where his punch landed on me. He's been in loads of fights and nothing like that had ever happened. He was a bully in school because of his size, has pushed people around all his life – even in primary school, before his mam died. He looks around the cell. These are the kind of guys that are supposed to be here. His life was supposed to be teed up differently. It should not have come to this. Okay, maybe not Seamus either, but the other three, Christ.

How the fuck did Seamus wind up here, anyway? He's dying to know. He'll ask tomorrow at some point. Even though it's only his first night he can already tell that he's higher up on the pecking order than this guy. Poor bastard. Danny watches him sleep, round belly, mouth wide open – the more he thinks about it, Seamus doesn't look smart enough to be some swindling businessman; he looks more like a regular fuck-up. Danny lets out a little chuckle – just the faintest of ones. The thought of this poor eejit in prison. He's glad he's in the cell with him, at least there is someone worse off. At least Danny has his height and bulk, and he prays that the others will assume that he is a genuine tough guy. But then he thinks you can always spot the real deal against a fake – 'Shit, what am I going to do when that happens?'

Danny starts thinking of tomorrow – his first day among the wolves. How will he spend it? Should he try to talk to someone or keep to himself? What will he do if someone confronts him? Act tough or run away – although where the hell can he run to, anyway? He squirms about, uncomfortable on the skinny floor-level mattress, but that's not why he has trouble sleeping. Rolling back and forth, all the worries of tomorrow fill his brain. I'll stay with him all night, waiting for him to sleep so that I can wake him right back up again.

32

John finishes his cold tea, chats a bit longer with Brian and Tim –
mainly about the hearing and how much they all hated the barrister.
How the hell can they do that job? Worse than the criminals – that
kind of thing. He's anxious enough to leave and really needs to see
Niamh, so stands and hugs the lads goodbye.

Outside, he sits into his car and lets the engine run for a minute
to unfog the windows. I sit with him. I actually taught John how
to drive – well, I kind of did; I was the first person to take him
driving. We drove around a train station car park and I remember
thinking he was pretty good for a first timer, despite nearly loafing
his head off the steering wheel once or twice from lashing on the
break.

As the windows defog, John shuffles through his Spotify. I
can't believe what tune he puts on – Antony and the Johnsons'
'Hope There's Someone'. Christ, it's a beautiful song; I wish they'd
thought to play it at my funeral. He puts it on because he wants to
feel sad, wants to think of me. The way your man sings somehow
makes John feel like it is personal to him. Music has a great way
of doing that sometimes. When he sings about being scared of a
middle place between light and nowhere I feel like he's singing
about me too.

John switches on his headlights as he turns onto the road and the
two of us listen, with John singing along at the top of his voice; I'd
join in with him if I could. Instead I just feel grateful that I knew
him and had him as a best friend. I feel truly lucky.

It's gone ten o'clock when John texts Niamh while driving to let her know that he is on his way home. He's dying to see her; it's been such a long day. He drives to a roundabout where he should turn left in the direction of his home, but at the last second swings right. For some reason Pam has jumped into his head. He doesn't know why he has to see her, he just does.

When he arrives at my old house he walks up as far as the front door before he has second thoughts about going in, realising it's a bit late. He doesn't want to frighten her or wake Robbie, so texts her instead of ringing the doorbell.

Hey Pam I'm outside can I come in?

He's not long waiting when Pam answers the door in her dressing gown. 'John – you okay?'

'I'm fine,' he says as he steps in the hall, 'I just had to see how you are.'

'Thanks, John, I'm glad you're here.'

The two of them sit in the living room and Pamela puts on the gas fire.

'Thanks for calling over.'

'Pam, you look so tired.'

'So do you, John-Boy.'

'Yeah, well, I'm jet-lagged.' He almost says, 'What's your excuse?', but holds off. He knows full well what her excuse is.

The two of them share a smile. Then Pam sighs. 'I can't sleep, John; it's terrible. I just can't sleep without him. And when I do Robbie wakes me up. And I feel like screaming my head off at him.'

John frowns. 'Is there anything I can do? Take Robbie for a little while or something, give you a break?'

'No, it's a lovely offer, though.'

'Seriously, even just for a week?'

'Thanks, John, but as much as the little monster drives me crazy he's the only thing keeping me sane.'

John chuckles. 'That's good, I like that.'

'What?'

'Well that, it's an oxymoron or something isn't it?'

'I think it's just a play on words. Are oxymorons not things like terrible beauty?'

'Exactly – that's the same idea as crazy keeping you sane, that's an oxymoron.'

'You're an oxymoron,' Pam says.

The two of them chuckle.

'Piss off.'

Pam's face has lit up – she looks less tired, somehow. She always loves taking the piss out of John and he knows she does. Maybe that's why he called over. Not to talk about the sentencing or to get her feelings on it – he already knew the answer to that. Just to be there for her, say something stupid and tease each other.

It's after one o'clock when he finally leaves. He feels bad that Niamh is in the house by herself but knows she'll understand. When he finally crawls into bed with his new wife, he warms his feet against her the way Pam used to do with me. Niamh is practically asleep but just whispers to him that she loves him. 'I love you too, baby.' He kisses her on the ear and falls asleep almost straight away.

33

Danny's not fully sleeping; he's just trying to convince himself that he is. Getting up time is looming and he knows it. If he could just get a little sleep before the approaching alarm call at 8.20 a.m., he thinks. His eyelids are heavy, he's just about there. Time for me to swoop into action.

Wake the fuck up!

A little bit of eye movement. All the while he's telling himself that he's just about to drift off. A quiet little whisper in his ear. He can't hear me, but he can feel it. I know he can.

Open your eyes, Danny; you're awake.

His eyes reluctantly oblige me.

I love seeing the disappointment on his face. The failure he feels for not being able to conquer whatever the hell is keeping him up is so evident in his expression. He closes his eyes again quickly but another little whisper – *You're awake, Danny; open those eyes, you are awake* – forces them open again. He looks around the room and through the glass wall. He can just about make out the time on a clock hanging on the wall down the corridor near one of the guard stations. Shit – it's 7.10 a.m. He turns over onto his side but no amount of shuffling about is going to change anything. Now all he can think about is the clock and how even if he does manage to sleep, in just over an hour he'll have to get up.

'Fuck it anyway,' he mutters, as he sits up. He looks around the room and sees that Seamus is awake as well and gawking at him from his bunk. Danny shudders at the sight. 'Nobody sleeps the first night,' Seamus says creepily.

'No, it's not that. I never sleep well – not for ages.'

'Oh.'

'Plus – it's fucking uncomfortable in here,' Danny says, gesturing to the skinny-ass mattress that he's been stuck with.

'You won't sleep the second night either,' Seamus adds. 'I haven't properly slept since I got here.'

Danny's curiosity gets the better of him. 'When was that?'

'Four days ago.'

'Why was that?' He figures just come out with it – fuck it.

'Why are you here?' Seamus asks defensively.

'Manslaughter.'

Straight out with it again; no more bullshit.

Seamus lifts himself up on his left elbow. 'Oh? Car or something?'

'Bar fight.'

Wasn't much of a fight. God, I'm still so embarrassed by that.

'So how about you?' Danny persists.

'It's complicated.'

'Tell 'im, Seamie.'

Wacko is up on the top bunk above Seamus and looks down at the pair of them with a big smile on his face. It's an infectious smile, so Danny joins him with one.

'What?' Danny probes.

Wacko's smile lengthens. 'Poor auld Seamie was caught with a hooker.'

'You go to prison over that?' Danny asks.

'You do when she's only fourteen,' Wacko sneers.

'I didn't know she was fourteen!' Seamus cries in his defence.

'You knew she wasn't fuckin' eighteen!'

'I thought she was sixteen or maybe older.'

'Oh, that's alright so – tell him how they caught you, Shambo.'

'Shut up,' Seamus whimpers.

'Fuckin' eejit started writin' the bitch love letters!'

'Ah Christ,' Danny says with a look of disbelief.

'This clown was bangin' a kid, then sendin' love letters to her bleedin' ma.'

Seamus looks flustered. 'Not to her mam – to the address I had. I didn't know she lived at home.'

Wacko laughs so hard he looks ready to fall off the bunk bed. 'I didn't know she lived at home,' he mimics in the same desperate tone. 'Where else is she gonna bleedin' live? Fuckin' Thailand? Why didn't you text your mate Gary Glitter and find out where she lived?' Danny laughs at that one. 'I'm going to call you Seamie Sparkles from now on,' Wacko declares. Danny cracks up and Wacko is into it. 'Yeah, wha' you reckon Dan – Gary Glitter and Seamie Sparkles together at last! You'd have mothers lockin' up their prams for miles around. Streets will be bare – you'd hear a fuckin' pin drop when these two boys roll into town.'

'At least I'm not a junkie,' Seamus mutters.

Wacko's expression hardens. 'Watch it, kiddy fucker – at least drugs are fun. Then again I suppose you find ridin' kids fun. Pervert – that's your drug, bald twats.'

'I didn't know she was fourteen,' Seamie's voice is breaking a little bit and Wacko draws back.

'Ah, I'm only buzzin' with you Shambles – you know tha'.' Wacko hops down from his bunk and leaps in beside Seamus. 'Come here to me,' he calls out, grabbing Seamus playfully around the neck and wrestling him to his chest.

'Get off me,' Seamus cries.

Wacko looks delighted and Danny, in a strange way, wonders if he might actually like Wacko.

There's a sudden rustling from the other top bunk. 'Shut fuck up all you.'

'Ah good mornin' Bogman – and how'd ya sleep?' Wacko asks.

'Shut fuck up or I beat you.'

'Fine, thank you, although I have a sligh' crick in me neck.'

'Wacko! Shut fuck up.' Bogdasha sits up and gives Wacko and Danny a look that puts the shits up both of them and stops all conversation.

Lying back on his mattress, Danny thinks again about how he can't wait to get the hell out of this cell and into his own. Just a few days. This Bogdasha guy really scares the crap out of him; the other three seem harmless enough, although he still reckons that he can't trust any of them as far as he could throw them.

He just wants to be alone. The whole experience has been so horrible since the conviction. Straight from the courthouse to the prison. Well, not straight. First he had to sit in this heap of shit of a wagon for over two hours. I don't know what they're called, but it's basically a wagon with a bunch of box cells in them for transporting inmates to prison. Slightly inhumane if you ask me but fuck it. He had to sit there for two hours and wait for whatever else was scheduled in the court to finish up. At least the drive to the prison itself wasn't too long, but the wait before leaving felt like he'd been in the wagon for days, stuck sitting on that really uncomfortable plastic seat. He'd never felt so alone in his life and, knowing Danny's history, I'd been surprised that he wasn't falling around the place, bawling his eyes out. He hadn't even done his trademark eyes filling up thing – he just sat there looking at the wall of his box cell, which was about a foot from his nose. There were marks there that past inmates had scratched in. One big mark looked like it was done with a lighter – and Danny couldn't help but wonder how the hell it had been done, as you're cuffed behind your back the entire time you're in there.

Once they finally got moving, his next stop was to an office outside the prison where all his personal belongings were taken.

They finally took his cuffs off and he felt ever so slightly less like a common criminal. He was then brought into the main prison where he first got his whiff of wet cardboard – all his details were taken: Height – 6 foot 4 inches. Weight – 210 pounds. Tattoos – none. Birthmarks – none.

'Sign here.'

He took the pen and noticed that his hands were shaking. He scribbled his name with weak fingers. It didn't look like his signature; it looked as if someone else had written it. He felt as if he was someone else. But then, he was, and he would never be the same man again.

ONE
YEAR
DEAD

34

Danny looks up at all the pictures of Michelle and debates whether or not to take them down. She dumped him a month ago, but he keeps thinking maybe she'll come to her senses. What poor dozy Danny doesn't realise is that dumping him *was* Michelle coming to her senses and even thinking about getting back with him is the furthest thing from her mind. While he's agonising over the photographs, she's watching *Scrubs* repeats, for Christ's sake. You have to laugh at the poor bastard – while he's tormenting himself over her and imagining that somewhere across the city she is looking at his picture and crying too, she's laughing at the curly headed dude who was in *Platoon*.

She stuck with him for the first four months he was inside, but it just got to be too much. For a start it was a bit of a pain in the arse having to visit him, and it was humiliating too. She disliked being associated with the kind of people she'd run into down there. Grandmothers telling her how they sneak drugs in to their grandsons by kissing them during family visits – giving her the best tricks for it. Michelle found it and them disgusting. She felt dirtier and dirtier after every visit.

Not to mention that Danny wrecked her head during each visit. He'd try to make an effort to be upbeat when he'd see her, but she just found him depressing and boring. They'd end up small-talking. It wasn't his fault, to be fair – what the hell are you going to talk about in them shitty little booths? Someone sitting on either side of you, not at all private. Plus the fact that there was nothing to talk about, anyway. Danny didn't want to talk about life inside, but he didn't particularly want to hear about life outside and all he was missing either.

Crappy state to find yourself in. Plus, she was sick of taking his clothes and washing them. There is no big launderette in Mountjoy. You start off with prison-issue clothes and then, after a couple of weeks, if you want to wear your own clothes you get someone from the outside to bring them in and take them out once a week to be washed. Michelle found all that degrading.

If she was being honest with herself, she'd found the entire situation far harder than she'd imagined right from the start and had really wanted to end it after the first month. But she'd been afraid people would think she was a bitch for leaving him there to rot. After four months of it, though, she'd finally had enough: 'Fuck this,' she said, 'fuck this.'

Still, a month after the break-up, Danny continues to look at the photographs. Her beautiful face, her big lips, her white teeth, sallow skin for a girl with blonde hair – although her hair is dyed so that isn't anything too amazing. She is beautiful, though, he thinks. He loves looking at her, even though it causes him pain now. He has gone through the same ritual the last few nights, telling himself that if she doesn't visit that day he'll finally do it – get rid of the photographs once and for all. It's not easy, though. In fact, it feels like the hardest thing in the world. These photos got him through a lot of rough nights at the start of his time in the 'Joy.

He remembers first moving into the cell five months ago. Initially, he'd been half-pleased just to be out of that horrible five-man cell. After sitting alone for five minutes, though, he got an overwhelming feeling of disappointment when he realised how boring his life was going to be for the next eighteen months – how the hell was he going to do it?

The cell is basic: a springy bed, bare blue walls, a TV, a tiny window you can't look out of, a bit of a desk and a jacks in the corner. Nightmare. He wasn't sitting there long that first day when he was called to the office of the governor.

'Danny Murray, my name is Governor Sean Logan.'

'Hello,' Danny said as he sat down in front of the governor's desk. He hadn't a clue what to expect, so his nerves started kicking in.

Logan leaned back in his chair, which was grazing the back wall of his pokey office. 'I don't meet with every inmate on their arrival but you are slightly different from the norm here.'

'How so?'

'Well, you've no previous convictions, you don't know anyone here, you're not a drug user. You're not from their world, Mr Murray. Unfortunately, Danny, you are going to stick out like a sore thumb.'

Brilliant.

Shit, Dan thought. 'Right,' he said. 'Is that why you called me in here, to tell me I'm fucked?'

The governor gave a little laugh. 'I called you in here as I do all prisoners not from their world, in order to let you know what the score is – okay?'

'Okay,' Danny said, relaxing slightly.

'There are four blocks here: A, B, C and D. You are in Block A, which is together with B. D is the green floor opposite you and Block C are the protected cells.'

'Protected how?'

'Those inmates are guilty of sex crimes, mainly, so they need to be protected from the other prisoners.'

Seamus popped into his head; that poor eejit would land up there.

'In your block there is a communal television, a good-sized yard and you can join up to either metalwork or fabric courses if you wish.' Danny nodded at the governor; he seemed like a decent enough bloke, straight talker at least. '8.20 a.m. is alarm call. If you wish to have breakfast you will be called down to collect it by order of whichever tier you are on. You are tier A1 on the ground floor, so will be first called to collect your breakfast and bring it back to your cell.' The image of the jacks in his cell jumped into Danny's head; *guess they don't believe in the expression 'don't shit where you eat'*, he thought grimly.

The governor continued, 'You will have one shower a week. You will earn an allowance of €11.70 a week and there is a small shop where you can buy chocolates, cigarettes, that kind of thing. Dinner is at approximately midday and lockdown is at 7.10. Have you any questions?'

'Visiting?'

'Thirty minutes, once a week. It can be any day from Monday to Saturday, and any time between ten and twelve and two till four. You are allowed to have eight people on your visit list and you are also entitled to one six-minute phone call a day. Phones are beside the fabrics workshop and there are also two in the yard.'

Danny sat there, trying to take it all in. Eight people on the visiting list; he struggled to think of three.

'Now, Danny, on a more personal level.' Danny sat up and could see the governor hesitate, wanting to make sure he'd get his message across clearly. 'Try your best to blend in. That will be impossible at first – you will be noticed, but that's not to say that you can't blend in after a while. I've seen many people in your position over the years, some fit in, some don't. It all depends on the person.'

Danny looked at him blankly.

The same thought as before passed through his mind. *Shit.*

***

As time goes by I feel more and more pathetic. Me and Danny are in the same boat on that front. I'm completely useless. Having awesome superhero powers but not being able to do any of the cool hero stuff. It's like a guy with a big mickey who's impotent. I'd rather have a small stiffy than a big floppy. That's what I feel like being dead. Makes me feel like a big floppy.

Danny saw a big floppy during his first prison shower. Weird too because it was on the skinniest bastard he'd ever seen. Your man was looking at him strangely, too, and Danny got the fear that he would try and use that big thing he was washing on him. The prison shower is something all men fear all their lives, like the way you'll never one hundred per cent swim in the same way in the sea after seeing *Jaws* (in a certain mood, a brush of seaweed off your toes can make you shit yourself).

Danny couldn't believe it. His first ever prison shower and this skinny bastard with the big dick was going to try and fuck him. He started tensing himself up and giving your man dirty looks until it occurred to him that your man seemed even more freaked out than him.

No wonder.

Danny, all muscles, staring at your man's cock, eyeballing him, then looking back to his cock again. The poor skinny lad thought his number was up.

He made a sharp exit and Danny started to calm down. He'd been shaky all week. Logan was right – he had been noticed, and not in a nice way. I think his size helped him, at first; he was twice the size of ninety per cent of the lads in there. He wondered why they were all so small, then figured it was because they were all junkies. There was none of the weightlifting posturing out in the yard, unlike what he'd seen in all the US prison movies or TV shows. Instead, it was just a bunch of skinny scumbags out of it or trying to get out of it.

None of them risked throwing a dig at Danny at first because he looked like he'd be able to kick the shit out of most of them. But they did whip the piss out of him and he had no good comebacks. He also spoke differently to them, so that was enough – he has a pretty standard Dublin accent but to them he sounded highfalutin'. No matter what he'd say they'd just repeat it in an exaggerated posh accent and laugh at him. But the worst thing was that he reacted poorly any time he was confronted, so they copped on quickly that he was not a tough man, just a big man.

He knew all this himself. It was still early days and nothing of any major significance had happened, but if he didn't man up soon he'd have the small bastards taking a pop at him, and if that happened what would the big bastards do?

After a couple of weeks he was still completely friendless – he'd seen Wacko knocking about but there'd been no sign of the other three. Wacko would give him the odd nod, but other than that he acted like he didn't know him. *What a bastard*, Danny thought, but in fairness what did he expect? Danny had changed a bit himself in that he wasn't crying the whole time like he'd been on the outside. Thank fuck for that because they'd really have a field day with him then.

Still, he got slagged constantly. He'd never experienced anything like it before. I don't know if it's ironic, but it's definitely funny – he'd always been the bully not the bullied. *Doesn't feel nice, does it, dickhead?* Although I suppose I can't talk.

As the weeks passed, the slagging off got nastier and more consistent. And Danny standing up for himself and getting more aggressive came too late – they had already made their minds up about him, so getting more in their faces just pissed them off even more. Danny could see it too. *Fuck*, he thought; it was only a matter of time.

That time came almost a month to the day after he first came to live in this shithole. He was sitting in his cell, looking at his plate. Danny's a picky eater, like me. I looked at the food he was struggling to eat and I knew that I wouldn't have liked to eat it if I'd been in his shoes. It wasn't how you imagine prison food. I mean, it looked alright, just not very tasty. In fact, nothing about prison is how you imagine it. The cell doors aren't made of bars, for instance. The cells are fucking awful. No proper windows, a big hefty door closing you off to everything so you can't do that mirror trick where you stick it out through the bars in your cell and look at the dickhead in the one next to you. There's no big boss either – there are one or two main hard men, alright, that nobody fucks with, but there's no gang boss calling all the shots. The prison guards are sound enough and get on okay with the inmates. The other fucked up thing is that there are lady screws as well. I thought for sure it would be all blokes for a male prison and women guards for women prisons, but no. They don't really get any abuse either; nothing major, anyway – not even wolf whistling or anything, but then again they're all pretty rough-looking.

Anyway, the food looked alright – like canteen food – it's just it wasn't for me. Not for Danny either. He's not crazy on mashed potatoes and he had a big wad of them on his plate. He lashed a bunch of salt on them and on the meat, which had fuck all sauce – just dryish mince, not great now at all. I watched his face, looking forward to seeing how he'd do on his first bite. Barely a wince – *Not bad, Dan, prison has hardened you.* As he was eating, one of the tossers a few cells up walked past the open door of his cell and called out, 'Eat up, pussy.'

'Fuck off!' Danny shouted as your man went out of sight.

But he heard him shout back, 'You're fucking dead pussy! You big fat cunt!'

Jesus. He dug into the rest of his food, but all the while he could feel an uneasiness rising in him. That little prick out there, what the fuck?

He polished off his dinner and was making his way back to the kitchen to drop off his plate when he got an almighty belt on the back of the head. Christ! For that second he forgot where he was; all he knew was that his brain was rattled. The daze was just leaving when another guy in front of him grabbed him by the hair and dragged his head downwards, kneeing him in the face.

Danny was still in shock mode, so there was no real pain; he just knew he was getting hit and was being forced to the ground. He regained his footing, grabbed hold of the waist of the person in front of him and ran like a bastard – crashing the guy who kneed him against the wall and headbutting him square in the face. Danny turned around to a kick in the leg from the 'Eat up pussy' guy and a punch in the face off some prick he'd never even seen before.

Danny's big arms threw out wild punches, every third or fourth of them landing. The four fists aimed at his face started blinding him. None of them were particularly sore, but he could see fuck all so couldn't find a good target. I found myself in the surprising position of being half up for him.

By the time the first screw rushed to break it up I couldn't really say that they'd gotten the better of him. The guy he'd headbutted was only just getting up; the other two were standing, alright, but so was Danny. They don't carry batons or anything, so the guard had his work cut out trying to restrain the three men who were still going at it hell for leather.

The fight moved a few feet from the kitchen to the middle of the hall and by this stage all the guards in the area were jumping in to stop it, with everyone in their cells and up on the balconies shouting, cheering and spitting.

A female guard jumped between Danny and the guy he had loafed, who was now foaming at the mouth. The pair of them were tugging at each other's collars and the guard tugging at their arms. The inmates watching all shouted out, 'Lady officer on the floor!' She tripped up in the scuffle and Danny pushed your man away and stopped fighting.

For Danny the fight felt like it had lasted for ten minutes but really it had been less than one minute of pure anger and aggression. All directed at him.

Everything had calmed and he looked at the officer as she got to her feet. His wide-open chin was too much for the guy he'd loafed to turn down, though, so he shot out a sucker punch that cracked Danny in the temple. As soon as it hit he heard a collective 'Ahh' from above, as if to say, 'Ah come on – not cool.'

Danny took a step back, his head spinning. The fight was over and he couldn't figure out what had just happened.

After that incident, the other inmates had a certain amount of respect for him. What he hadn't known during the brawl is that fights are always supposed to stop when a lady officer is in the mix. They'll go on as long as possible no matter how many male guards are involved, but when someone shouts, 'Lady officer on the floor', everyone is supposed to stop dead. He had stopped fighting out of instinct when he saw her hit the ground – though it'd also been because he was so damn tired. But the inmates looked at it as the old school respect thing that has always gone on here. It wasn't like he was Mr Popular after that or anything – it's just that he blended in more.

***

Life in prison has gone slowly for him since then. He's still cacking himself most days but a little less now because he isn't really bothered by anyone. He keeps to himself and thinks a lot of Michelle. He actually looks forward to lockdown – he hates walking around the yard or the main room, I mean he fucking hates it. He despises everyone in there and doesn't want to make friends – fucking scumbags the lot of them. *So this really is where I belong?* is a recurring thought. *I'm like one of these pricks? I suppose to certain people I'm worse, maybe I am worse. Most of these losers are just junkies – I'm a fucking killer.*

During lockdown at least he can just sit on his bed and not have to look at all the horrible bastards all around him. Just sit there, watch TV and jerk off. He's surprised by the things he finds himself wanking to. I've gotten used to seeing all this kind of stuff – I've seen everyone I know naked. I've seen them shit, toss off, scratch their bollocks, wipe their arses, pick their noses and toss off some more. It's not pleasant but I just don't care anymore. Danny beats off about anything nowadays – the slightest thing sets him off. A *Dove* ad or something. The fleeting glimpse of side tit and five seconds later he'll find himself with jocks around the ankles and pulling the belly off himself.

Half the time he wouldn't even be horny or anything; he'd just have a peddle to kill the boredom – thank God for the TV in the room. He'd often wait up until three or four in the morning, praying for something to come on that shows a pair of tits. *American Pie* came on once at about two in the morning and he was so happy you'd think it was his birthday. He has jerked off so much in that room that you can actually smell the jip.

It actually reminds me of when I was a young fella. Nineties' Ireland was a pretty barren place for someone of wanking age, let me tell you. No Internet and most porn was illegal or hard to come by. I remember jerking off to a dirty joke book, for Christ's sake. Pickings were slim. Me and John used to have to get the bus into town, call into Eason's bookstore and flick through *H&E*, which was basically a nudist magazine. It was the best we could get, but it was still pretty grim: some middle-aged chick playing badminton alongside old dudes with balls down to their fucking knees.

Despite his lack of material, Danny enjoyed all the tug jobs he gave himself except the ones he has had about Michelle post-breakup. With these, he'll look at the photos of her, have a peddle and then feel so pathetic he'll want to cry. To his credit, he doesn't. It reminds him of when he first started doing it; how the whole thing had been taboo and he couldn't talk about it with his mates, so didn't know if everyone was at it or not. He suspected they were, but still figured it was wrong, so every time he blew his beans he'd get this sinking feeling in his belly. That's what he gets after a Michelle wank.

Teenagers are so jammy nowadays. Every show or movie about adolescence always has loads about the main lads jerking off. So young lads watching all know it's normal. Proper order too. In my day the guy who tossed off in a movie was always the loser or something. When I think about it, it's kind of funny – back in school there was always one poor bastard in every year who got the name for being a wanker and it would stick with him his entire school career. Getting ridiculed all day by a bunch of kids who can't keep their hands off themselves either. It was a real necessity, though. Jesus Christ, you'd be getting stiffies the whole time and always at the worst possible time – just before you'd have to write on the blackboard or something. Riding a bus was always a nightmare; God forbid you'd drive over train tracks or something – that would really make things pop. You'd rush home to the enjoyment of a wank, but that would always be followed by the horrible downer of the aftermath. Wanks back then were real roller coasters of emotion.

Danny is sick of that feeling, sick of thinking about her, sick of loving her, sick of himself, sick of every fucking thing. *Take the pictures off the wall, rip 'em up and throw them in the bin,* he urges himself. That'd be a first step at least to getting over her. No more pathetic wanks, looking at her smiling face. This time he's going to do it. Really. One by one he takes them down and one by one he puts them in the bin. He lies back on his bed, feeling slightly proud for a moment, then all of a sudden he's scurrying over to the bin with his pants around the ankles, desperate for one last hurrah. Why not?

Tomorrow she'll be gone.

35

John starts unbuckling the belt of his jeans as soon as he reaches the bedroom, so he can get into his relaxing-time tracksuit pants. It had been a handy enough day at work, so he can skip the shower and head straight into chilling in front of the telly. He's just undone the first notch of his belt when the prong of the buckle snaps. 'What the fuck?' *My favourite belt*, he thinks; *my only belt come to think about it*. Standing there with a not-too-bright look on his face, he doesn't notice Niamh step into the bedroom.

'I was trying to think of an interesting way to say this,' she says, her cheeks glowing, 'but since I can't I'm actually just going to come out and say it.'

'Say what?'

Niamh gives him the widest of smiles and says, 'I'm pregnant.'

'What?' John says with a smile on him now to match hers.

'I'm pregnant!'

The words have barely left her mouth and John has her in his arms, swinging her around the room, the both of them laughing hysterically.

'You're pregnant?'

'Yep.'

He gives her a big, happy smooch and asks, 'When did you find out?'

'Just now, before you came home.'

'I can't believe it,' he says, finally putting her down.

'I know, I still have to go to Dr Jordan, but the home kit …' she says, waving the little stick thing.

'Well them yokes are a hundred per cent, aren't they?'

'Well not a hundred, but basically yeah.'

'My God, baby!' He gives her another hug and looks at her. 'I'm going to be a dad; I can't believe it.'

'I know, I'm going to be a mammy.'

'Holy shit.'

The pair of them burst out laughing again.

This is wonderful. I can't believe I'm here for this. One of the few perks of being dead. I'm so delighted for John; he's going to make a deadly parent. Niamh too.

John's beaming. 'This is the happiest news of my life.'

'I know, I can't believe it either.' The smile hasn't left her face.

'Come here, baby, or should I say Mammy?' The two of them burst out laughing again and embrace some more. 'My boys can swim!' John shouts and she gives him a playful little slap on the shoulder, then dives in for another hug.

***

John can't wait to tell his dad. Any time anything of major significance happens, his dad is always the first person he tells – good or bad, he needs Jarlath's opinion or feedback or advice or whatever. We all adore Jarlath, obviously, but he can be a hard man at times and isn't always the easiest to please. He's always expected a lot from John – more so than from anyone else – so I guess John has always looked for his approval as a result.

When he drives up to the house he can see Jarlath in the garden, working hard at something. Not a day goes by that this man wouldn't be working.

'Hey, Dad, what're you at?' John says as he gets out of his car.

Jarlath looks up at John with a grimace on his face. If you didn't know him, you'd think he wanted to kick the shit out of you, but that is just his work face.

'Your mother says she wants a wider driveway, so I'm digging back the grass. I'm going to knock that pillar down, bring it maybe four or five feet in, build it up again, then tarmac the whole thing,' he says as he gestures with his massive hands, all the time looking at what he is planning as if he can see it right there in front of him.

John smiles. 'Well Jesus, Dad, I can give you a hand with this; I can get you a good deal on tarmac as well.'

'Okay, yeah. I was going to talk to you about it, anyway.'

John shuffles his feet. 'Cool …Well, I have something I'd like to talk to you about, as it happens.'

'Oh yeah?'

John can't contain his excitement and he gives his dad that same smile Niamh gave him. 'Me and Niamh are having a baby.'

Jarlath looks him straight in the eye and gives him a delightful little grin. He turns and places the shovel against the wall nice and neat as John waits. He rubs his big mitts off his legs, cleaning them before sticking the right one out for John to grab hold of. They shake hands, smiling at each other for a few seconds before John throws the left arm around Jarlath's shoulder, which he welcomes. Out of only a handful of times that the pair of them have hugged, this one is the longest. They clap each other on the back before going back to just a handshake and Jarlath says in his deep, quiet voice, 'I'm proud of you, lad.'

'Thanks, Dad.'

John is already feeling good, but when he sees a slight shine in his dad's eyes – which he has never seen before – this makes him even happier. Jarlath had a best friend who was killed in a car crash. He had told John that he cried the night he heard about it, but John hadn't seen it. He'd only talked to John about it around the time of my death, so John would know that he understood his pain. But a happy tear, no way – he didn't think it possible.

'Thanks, Dad,' he says again.

'You've made me very happy. Come here, sit down,' Jarlath says as he leads John over to the garden wall. 'My God, Niamh is pregnant, eh?'

'Yep,' says John, the same big smile on him as before.

'Well fair play to her, that girl was born to be a mother.'

'I know; she'll be great.'

Jarlath nods. 'Oh she will, she's a good woman – there's nothing she wouldn't do for you. I still remember the first time I met her.' John knows the story well but lets his dad continue. 'She was to meet you here but you and your mother got delayed some place.'

'Auntie Moira's.'

'Oh that's right! Ha, ha, the old hag.'

John shakes his head, chuckles. 'Jesus, she had us there all night, waiting on the cat to get better. I think in the end it just had a shit or something and was grand.'

'Crazy as a loon, that one. Anyhow, Niamh was to call around and you guys weren't here and didn't she show up anyway. I saw this little young one coming up the driveway and I say to myself: what the hell am I going to talk to this one about? Little slip of a thing, she was.'

'I know, gas the pair of you ended up going on the session.'

'Well, she came in, fair play to her, and I made some sandwiches. All we had in the house was vodka so didn't we start having highballs.'

'I know, sure I rang to let her know we wouldn't be back, but at that stage you guys were well on your way.'

Jarlath starts to giggle. 'Well Jesus, didn't we end up having a great night. When I think of her walking up the driveway all smiles and me wondering what the heck I was going to do and sure enough the two of us turned out to be the best of friends.'

John nods as his dad continues. 'A great talker, she's not afraid to give her opinion – we had some great chats that night. Some arguments too. But nice arguments, she'd always be so pleasant even if she disagreed with you. You were going on and on about her and I thought there is no way she could be as good as you say, but then I met her and I could see what all the fuss was about.'

'Thanks, Dad. She loves you.'

Jarlath waves away John's words. 'She's a great wee girl, that's all, and now she'll have a baby of her own.'

'Yep.'

'Well done *a mac*. You know you've heard this before from every clown who has a baby. How great it is, how it changed their life, how everyone should have one. The words probably don't mean anything because you've heard them so much they've been diluted.'

'Yeah, I suppose.'

Jarlath leans in towards his son as he continues. 'Well, the truth is there are no words to describe what it's like; that's why the words don't mean anything. You have to live it to get it. You know, I wanted to have a little girl when your mother was expecting you. Most guys get all macho, wanting a son, but I wanted a girl to protect. I figured a boy didn't need as much or something, I don't know, sounds silly now. But when you were born you were so tiny I could fit your whole body in one of my hands,' Jarlath says as he stretches out his long fingers. 'I couldn't believe anyone could be so small.' John chuckles a bit. 'But you were perfect. A full head of hair on you. And I wanted to protect you forever. I told myself that I'd never let you out of my sight. I could be a bit of a wild man before you came along, but after that day I said no more. Your mother wouldn't have allowed it, anyway.'

They both laugh.

Jarlath fixes his gaze on his son now, eager to get his point across. 'But I've seen what a fine man you've turned into, from that tiny little baby. You can't understand how proud that makes me. But you will understand soon enough, because now you'll have one of your own. You'll know what I mean when the baby is born; you'd be willing to set yourself on fire for it. And in thirty odd years when I'm long gone you'll know what I mean now when you have a first grandchild of your own to look forward to.'

'Thanks, Dad,' John says, looking down at the ground as they share in a moment of silence. 'Thirty years from now you'll still be kickin' it though.'

'Yeah, maybe, old and grey.'

'Well older and greyer,' John says, joking.

'Funny.'

Jarlath stands up, smiling, and takes hold of the shovel again. 'Now go in and tell your mother.'

John pushes himself away from the garden wall. 'Are you coming?'

'I'll be in in a bit. I just want to finish up this small patch first.'

'Okay, thanks again, Dad.'

When John reaches the front door of the house, he looks back at Jarlath digging up chunks of earth. He watches his big shoulders stretch, the sun shining off the steel of the spade, he watches his dad do what he has done his entire life – make a better home for his family. John smiles and hopes he will be able to do the same.

36

With Michelle's pictures finally gone, Danny takes on a new outlook in life. His cell is bare and he likes it like that. He doesn't want any photos or posters that remind him of what he's missing. Those shitty blue walls look terrible to me, but Danny starts to get used to them, starts to accept them. He even stops watching so much TV. He lies there, looks at the ceiling and thinks about his situation and what he's done. He starts thinking about me.

He has never really done that before. Instead it was all about the predicament he was in and how bad it was for him. Or at least that's what I thought. Perhaps I was too blind to see that I was always in the back of his head; he just didn't have the courage to let himself go there. Now that's all he does. He replays that night over and over, each time wishing he'd acted differently. He thinks of my face, but more so he thinks of Pam's face the day he saw her in the courtroom – contemplating the utter destruction he's clearly brought to her life. He thinks about the guy shouting at him outside the courthouse and the other one pulling him away – Tim and Brian. But when he finally lets himself think about my son, that's when I can feel him going to some dark places.

I gave up my lame haunting techniques, by the way, after the first few months of him being in prison – though I still stay with him most nights. Tonight, he's trying to think if there is any possible thing he can do for my little boy when he gets out. Stupid things are coming into his head, like setting up a trust fund or sending him random gifts. After an hour of this, he realises that there is nothing he can do. Stay away, disappear, kill yourself –

that might be the only thing he'll appreciate one day. It's gone three in the morning when he starts drifting off to sleep with Robbie on his mind.

I watch his eyes getting heavy and let him fall into a deep slumber like I've done each night for the past few months. I think of Robbie too and watch him in his cot. His cute little nose, his sweaty fringe clinging on to his wet forehead, his beautiful mouth, slightly open, dishing out steady, barely audible breaths. I could watch him all night and wish I could protect him forever. He has changed so much already since I died. I miss being there properly for all his little milestones, and will miss so many more.

An almighty dart of pain and anger hits me. At the exact same moment, Danny bursts awake in his cell. Pumping sweat, he nearly falls off his bed. 'Are you there?' I swear he's looking right at me. I always watch him from the back corner wall opposite his pillow and that's exactly where he is looking now. 'Are you there?' He cries again as he jumps to the other side of the cell.

What the fuck? He looks terrified; I'm half-terrified myself. Can he actually see me? He rubs his eyes, hoping he is still asleep in a nightmare. He looks up at the blue nightlight that stays constantly on in all the cells in Mountjoy. He never much liked it before, would prefer sleeping in utter darkness. But he's glad of it now.

A third time he asks, 'Are you there?'

'I'm here.'

And for the first time in five and a half months the nightlight goes dark.

***

'It's really quite common.'

Danny looks blankly at the psychiatric doctor as if your man is the dumbest fucker that ever walked the earth. The med room is not exactly a relaxing setting, anyway, but this bloke isn't helping matters. Dr Brady puts on his best I'm-a-kind-guy grin and says, 'You'd be surprised how common something like this is, actually.'

Grin, grin, pat on the shoulder. Patronising wanker.

'What, talking to ghosts is common? Maybe for Mystic Meg or some fucking gypsy – no sane person ever talks to ghosts.'

'No, no – not a ghost, Danny. It's common to experience all sorts of trauma after going through such an extreme event as you have done. Post-traumatic stress manifests itself in all sorts of ways – it can be voices, reliving the event, feeling like someone else is in the room, etcetera.'

'It's not post-traumatic stress; that thing happened over a year ago, for Christ's sake.'

That thing – *thanks, asshole.*

'The symptoms can start immediately or after a delay of weeks or months even.'

Danny shakes his head, once again eyeing up the doctor. Doctor Brady is way too old to have a step haircut. He suspects that the blond streaks in his hair are highlights too. *I'm going to take advice from this guy?* he thinks as Brady flicks his fringe away from his eyes with a sudden head jerk. 'They usually appear within six months of the traumatic event, but for you, given that being here in prison is a constant burden of stress, it's not surprising that something has finally cracked.'

'What, so my mind is cracked – thanks, Doc, break it to me gently why don't you?'

'No, I didn't mean it like that. Sorry, Danny, what I mean to say is that you are in a very stressful situation – you are alone with your thoughts a lot. The mind can turn on you; it is a very powerful and complex thing. Let me ask you, have you experienced any muscle or back pains?' he asks, bringing his pen to his clipboard.

'I guess – around my shoulders is tense the whole time.' Danny rubs his neck as he speaks.

'Have you experienced diarrhoea?'

'Apart from shitting myself when I first came here, no.'

The Doc lets out a little chuckle and Danny gives him that same blank (I-can't-believe-I-have-to-listen-to-this-idiot) look.

'How about headaches?'

'No.'

'Feelings of panic or fear?'

'Well yeah! I thought there was a fucking dead man in my cell last night; panic and fear were pretty much at the forefront.'

'Right. Well apart from that?'

Danny looks at the doctor. 'You look like Richard from *Richard and Judy* – has anyone ever told you that?'

The doctor frowns. 'I'm sorry?'

'I'm in prison, you do realise that, don't you? I'm not from Sheriff Street or just some junkie who doesn't give a bollocks. I'm surrounded by fucking animals that would sooner piss on me than speak to me. That might decide to kill me for some sort of sport or initiation thing, I don't know. I'm despised here and I am totally alone – so yes, doctor, I am terrified from time to time.'

'Okay, I understand your frustration, but I am only trying to help. I need to ask these questions so I can help you to get better.'

'Look, maybe it was just a fucked-up nightmare or something,' Danny says dismissively.

'I know you don't believe that, Danny. I'm told you were quite terrified when they brought you to the psychiatric ward last night – do you remember that?' Terrified is not the word. He could barely walk.

'Of course I bloody remember.'

I can't believe I've finally haunted him. This is wonderful – I'm the greatest ghost in the world!

'Okay, well you don't want that to happen again and again, do you? You need to talk to me, Danny, so I can help you.'

'What am I supposed to say? I feel like a fucking whack job. I believe that the guy I killed was in my cell last night, for Christ's sake. Now I know that's crazy and if someone told me the same thing I would say they're crazy. I know all this. I know it's not true, but at the same time I know that he was there last night. I know that saying those words makes me sound nuts; it's a horrible feeling believing something and knowing the fact that you believe it makes you crazy. Does this mean I'm losing my mind – am I going to end up some vegetable in one of those padded cells you've got here?'

'No, Danny, I can help you.'

That's what you think.

'How?'

'Tell me what happened last night. What made you scream for help?'

'I just told you,' Danny says, irritated.

'You said you saw a figure in the night after waking up from a nightmare.'

'It wasn't like that,' Danny interrupts. 'It wasn't some figure and it wasn't a nightmare.'

'Tell me then. Tell me what it was,' Doctor Brady says, resting his clipboard on his lap for the first time. This poor eejit does actually want to help. Danny's still not rating him but leans forward, anyway, and looks directly into his eyes.

'I could see his son,' he blurts out.

'In your cell?'

'No. Would you just listen to me?'

The doctor stays silent and gestures for Danny to continue. 'It was in a dream. I knew it was his son because he was standing over the boy, watching him sleep. It was a nice image. It was bright and shining in my dream, but then the image got swallowed up and I was someone else watching myself sleep in my cell, someone who was intent on killing me. I could see through burning red eyes that wanted to rip me apart.' Danny swallows a gulp of nothing, trying to get an ounce of saliva back in his mouth. 'Now I know all that was a dream. It scared the crap out of me and I woke myself up out of it. But then I thought …' He hesitates.

'Please go on,' says Brady.

'It was as if I knew he was in the cell when I woke up. The man I killed. The room just felt different. It was as if the back wall was darker than it should have been. So I called out. And then I heard his voice.'

'What did the voice say?' Brady asks curiously.

'He said, "I'm here."'

The med room is silent for a moment before the doctor pipes up. 'Is that all he said?'

'I just started screaming then.'

'What about the room, Danny? You said the light went out.'

Danny puts his head down; he can't look the doctor in the eyes anymore. 'Everything went dark and that's when I saw it.'

'It?'

'It was as if he was coming out of the walls. He wasn't like a normal man, he was cloaked in the darkness of the room and he was glaring at me. I started pounding on the cell door for help and every time I turned around that shadow figure was still there, glaring at me. It didn't make another sound. That was the most terrifying thing about it. I heard him in my head when I first woke, but when I saw him he just glared at me. I'd whip my head away again or close my eyes, but every time I turned to face him, there he was. Motionless.'

'You heard the voice in your head?' the doctor says straightly.

'Oh, here we go. Not in my head. Not like that, I'm not hearing voices. But yeah. Fuck. Yeah, it was in my head. So maybe I am going crazy.'

'Danny, please. It's not a question of crazy. This really does sound like it might be as simple as an extremely vivid dream. It sounds very similar to sleepwalking. You could be up at your cell door but still be in a state of unconsciousness, which would account for seeing the figure at the wall.'

'Sleepwalking?' Danny says, unconvinced.

'Yes,' says the doctor, smiling. 'Or night terrors. Waking dreams can be bizarre and frightening. Hypnopompic hallucinations are a very common neurological phenomenon that occurs if you are at the in-between state where you're neither fully awake nor fully asleep. Hallucinations of realistic images like dark figures or hearing voices will often be experienced. Even other senses, like touch, can be stimulated. They are essentially dreams experienced while you are awake. But the important thing to remember, Danny, is that this type of thing really is quite normal.'

Danny shuffles his bum in his seat, relaxing ever so slightly, wanting to believe the doctor.

'Now,' says Brady, looking pleased with himself. 'I'd like to understand a little more of what you are dealing with. Can you tell me what you remember about the night you hit ...' he raises up his clipboard again and flicks through the pages, 'Christopher Cosgrave?'

Danny shudders. 'Christ, even just hearing his name ... I don't want to talk about that night.'

'Danny, if I'm to help you deal with the trauma you've experienced we need to explore this. Rather than avoiding the trauma and any reminder of it, I want you to recall and process the emotions and sensations you felt during the original event.'

'And why is that?' asks a sceptical Danny.

'Well, in addition to offering an outlet for emotions you've been bottling up, by letting it out you will also help restore your sense of control and reduce the powerful hold the memory of the trauma has on your life.'

Danny slaps his palm down on the table. Doctor Brady raises an eyebrow in response. 'But that's just it. I haven't been bottling it up, it's all I've been thinking about. When I don't think about that night or his family nothing happens; when I do think about them I'm hearing voices and shitting myself in a dark room that is meant to be a bright room. I'm fucked.'

This is honestly the happiest I've been since I became a ghost.

Doctor Brady's tone remains neutral, soothing. 'Well, there is a difference between playing something in your mind over and over and actually talking about it to someone and trying to come up with some sort of closure.'

'What if I don't want closure? Jesus Christ, I killed a decent, innocent family man. He deserves more than my closure. His family deserves more.'

'So what are you saying? You want to keep having visions? Waking up in the middle of the –'

'Of course I don't!' Danny interrupts. 'But I don't want to forget about them either.'

'Having closure doesn't mean you forget, Danny; it just means that you can come to terms with it – deal with things in a better, healthier manner.'

Danny shakes his head. 'I don't deserve that.'

'Maybe not, but you are still alive and if you want to have any kind of a life you will have to face and overcome these issues, and it should be possible to find a way of achieving this that is respectful to Christopher Cosgrave's memory but also lets you move on with your own life.'

This is such bullshit; it's not some wacky dream or post-traumatic stress. I'm fucking haunting him and all the talking in the world about it won't make a damn bit of difference. *Wooo motha fucka! Wooo.*

37

'Come on, Robbie, this way,' Pam says, smiling to him. 'Grab my hand.' For Robbie's third birthday Pamela wants to start a tradition. Robbie follows along, kicking blades of grass and pebbles, not paying much attention.

'Where, Mama?'

'I told you, we're going to visit Daddy.' They walk to where my gravestone stands. It's the one place I haven't gone to with Pam prior to this. I haven't been back here since my funeral and I can barely remember that; I was crying so much that it's all a blur. But today is different; today, I decide to accompany them. It actually isn't as bad as I thought. Depressing as hell, don't get me wrong, but you know – when was the last time I wasn't depressed?

'Where is he, Mama?'

'Well he's right here … this is …' she struggles to find the right way of saying it. 'This is Daddy's garden and this is where he lives under the ground, helping the flowers and grass to grow. And where he watches over you, helping you to grow.'

Robbie looks down at the grass, confused. 'Can he see me?'

Pamela doesn't believe it, but she looks down at Robbie, smiles and says, 'Yes, he can see you.'

Robbie waves at the ground, 'Hi, Dadda.'

Hey, buddy. If only Mammy knew that I can see you, that I'll never leave you. That I'll always be with you.

'Good boy.'

Pamela's eyes fill up with tears and she wishes to Christ that things weren't the way they are. How could everything have gone so wrong?

I'm sorry, baby.

'I like Dadda's garden,' Robbie declares.

'You do? Good. Would you like to come back here?' Robbie nods his head. 'Well we can come back here any time you like. I wanted to bring you on your birthday because I know your dad would want to see you.'

'Where is he?'

'I told you, honey, he's here. You can't see him, but he's watching over you and wishing you a happy birthday and he's very sorry he can't share it with you.'

The first of many birthdays I'll miss. Fuck it, anyway – I can only imagine this getting harder.

Pam takes another minute and watches Robbie run his finger along the engraving of my name on the headstone. He doesn't know what it spells, of course; he just likes the feeling of the hollowed-out letters on the cold granite.

'Okay, Robbie, let's go – we'll come back soon.' Robbie looks kind of sad to leave. I like being here with them and don't want him to go either. Pam takes his little hand and leads him away, down onto the path towards the gate entrance into the car park. I stay behind and watch them walk away, but just before my gravestone is out of view to them, my little boy turns and waves goodbye.

***

Our house is full for his birthday party. Going to a kid's birthday party was the last thing Brian and Tim felt like doing. They'd been on the piss the night before, so stepping out to the back garden and a bunch of screaming kids on a bouncy castle was the last thing they needed. Still, fair play to them, they showed up.

'Hi, guys, thanks so much for coming.'

Actually, scratch that – Orla is the last thing they need. Thanks for coming, she says; it's not even her gaff.

'Jesus Christ – he's my bleedin' nephew,' both the lads think. 'Hi, Orla,' they say in unison.

'How have you been keeping?' As soon as Tim says that, Brian shoots him the stink eye and Tim knows that he's made a mistake. Don't get her started, the stink eye tells him.

But it's too late.

Orla sighs. 'Oh, you know me, Tim, never a dull moment. You've heard I've taken up dance?'

'Right,' says Tim.

Brian takes a look around, spots Pam. 'I'll leave you two to it, I just need to say hello to Pam.' Tim gives him a look like he might actually belt him.

'You should come to one of our shows,' Orla suggests.

'You reckon?'

'You'd love it. They're really cool – not what you'd expect at all from a modern dance troupe.'

'Oh no,' Tim says, meaning it as an involuntary fearful exclamation, but Orla hears it as a question.

'No, not at all. This next one we're doing for example is all to Bob Dylan music!'

'Cool.'

'Yeah, it's called "The Lives of Bob Dylan" and it's going to be a medley of his music from the sixties right up to when he went electric.'

Tim remains mute.

'And of course all the hippy vibe. And all through the expression of dance; there's no dialogue.'

'Very good,' Tim mutters.

Orla looks so excited that Tim begins to feel bad about his short answers. He decides to show some interest, 'Eh, who do you play in it?'

'Well, there aren't really parts – we have a bunch of Bob Dylans to show his different styles, and I play fans and stuff along the way, but for the final number the whole cast is Bob, so I get to play him at the end.'

Tim doesn't overly listen to her answer – he's eyeing up some chocolate donuts on the table – but hears enough to say, 'Oh, that's cool.'

'Cheers. I'll Facebook you when it's on, be good to all hook up you know?'

'Yeah definitely,' Tim says with a fake conviction that surprises me with how genuine it sounds. Now, though, a look of pain emerges on his face as he struggles to find something to say. Poor bastard. He hates small talk. I did too. I mean, I fucking hated it. I was terrible at it as well. I often felt sorry for whatever poor prick was stuck small-talking with me because I'd give them nothing. I'd rather have awkward silences and have the conversation end quickly than the more socially acceptable bore-the-tits-off-each-other-type chats that could go on forever. It used to always be the weather that everyone small-talked about, which was bad enough, but at least the weather changed from time to time. When the recession hit, small talk reached an all-time low because nothing changed for years. I felt such joy when it ended, because I didn't have to listen to any more of the same damn conversation every time I met some new fucking dummy:

'Oh it's very quiet out there, isn't it?'

'Yes.'

'Everywhere's the same.'

'I know.'

'I blame the radio.'

'Do you?'

'It's all doom and gloom. People are afraid to spend money.'

'……'

'It's the same all over. Do you know something? I think it's worse it's getting, not better.'

'Shut the fuck up! Will you shut the fuck up, you dozy bastard! Do you think I haven't heard those stupid points before over and over again? That you are the first person to come up with those ridiculous boring views? What's more I don't give a shit about your musings on whether or not it's the same all over or whose fault it is. If you think it's getting better or worse, who the fuck are you? You know nothing, piss off you fucking wanker!'

Just once I would have liked to have said that. Anyway, at least in death I don't have to make small talk.

Tim mentions something about it being a nice day, then sees my parents arrive. 'There's my folks,' he says and calls out, 'Hi guys!' with a big wave. He nearly knocks my dad over with a hug.

'Hey, Tim, how are ya?' Dad says with a smile.

'Great. Hi, Mam.' And he gives her a kiss.

'Hi, Tim,' my mam says happily, not quite understanding why he is so enthusiastic to see them. Then she turns to Orla. 'How are you, sweetheart?' Tim grimaces as Orla looks about to start in on something again, 'Oh, you know me, I can't complain. As a matter of fact …'

'Hi, folks!' Pam interrupts with big hellos and hugs for my parents.

Thank Christ for that, Tim thinks. 'Hi, Pam, you look lovely,' he says.

'Thanks, Tim! You look like shit.'

Tim laughs and tells everyone that he has been up all night. 'Burning the candle at both ends,' my dad says as he ruffles Tim's hair as if he was a kid. 'Young lads, they never learn.'

I don't know how many times I heard him say those exact words to me.

The day is a success. Brian gets stuck in despite his hangover – throwing kids in and out of the bouncy castle and all that, children up on shoulders and stuff. So much so, in fact, that when one of the neighbourhood kids leaves, Brian overhears him ask his mother, 'Can we get that clown again for my birthday?' Little bollocks. There's the usual puke in the bouncy castle incident that has all the kids screaming and nearly makes Pam puke herself as she cleans it up. It's the mixed-in Monster Munch that really adds to the stink of the vomit – a completely new kind of horrible, but to Pam's credit, she powers through.

It's good to see my parents happy for once. They spend most of the time playing with or watching Robbie. He's such a lovely little boy, very gentle and calm – always with a slight grin on his face. He kicks a ball back and forth to my dad as my mam cheers every time his foot hits the leather. 'Very good!' she encourages. Robbie bursts out laughing, kicking it again as my dad does an over-exaggerated dive, as if he's a goalkeeper struggling to make a save. I know it hurts them, in a way, to play with him, as he reminds them both so much of me. He looks just like me – the same milk-chocolate eyes matching his wispy, light-brown hair. He purses his full lips any time he concentrates on something, just like I used to do. He even has the same egg-shaped belly I had at that age.

When Brian takes him to go on the bouncy castle, my parents stay sitting on the grass and smile at one another, each knowing what the other is thinking.

'He's a right little man,' Dad says.

'He just breaks my heart he's so lovely,' says my mam. 'Can you believe he's three already?'

'I know, hard to believe.'

'Do you remember when Chris rang us after he was born? He was so happy that he had a boy. He said he didn't mind if it was a girl or a boy, but I knew deep down he wanted a son.'

That's true, but only because I felt I wouldn't know what to do with a girl. It's all boys in my family, so the idea of a little girl kind of scared me.

'He did, he was over the moon. He kept bragging that he was going to be the soundest dad in the world. I believed him too, and he did turn out to be a fantastic father.' My dad gets hit with a wave of anguish. His face goes red and he grits his teeth. Mam reaches out and puts her hand on top of his.

'It's okay, honey.'

He grabs her hand tightly and glares ahead.

I can feel the ball of anger and sorrow in my dad's stomach; the not knowing what to do, the feeling of pain, of loss, feeling like somehow he has failed, let me down. Knowing that Danny Murray is alive and well and will soon enough be back on the streets living his life. How unfair it all is, feeling inadequate, like he should be able to do something. He worries for my boy and what his life will be like without a dad. He's sorry for me and all that I will miss, and he feels sorry for himself because he simply misses me.

'He looks so like him,' he finally says.

'I've never seen anything like it – he's the absolute spit of him,' my mam says with a smile.

'He was a great man for kicking the ball around too. He should be here to do it with him.'

Mam nods. 'Yes, he should.'

'What's it going to be like for Robbie without his father?'

My mam takes a minute and looks at Robbie as she speaks, 'Christopher was a wonderful, wonderful dad and nothing will change that. But look at him in Brian's arms – how safe he is. Or when he's with Tim, how much he laughs. Nobody can make him laugh like Tim can. And when I look at him when he's with you, that's when I truly know that everything will be alright in his life. The love and generosity you show him is already beginning to shape him. You are the best man I know and our three boys were so lucky to have you growing up, and now Robbie has you too.'

Dad gives her a bewildered look. 'I wasn't all that.'

'You were more. Robbie has no shortage of positive male role models in his life – you made sure of that.'

Dad smiles. 'Well, I think you had something to do with how the lads turned out as well, you know.'

She laughs. 'I sure did, and I'll keep little Robbie on the straight and narrow too.'

'I worry that's all …'

'I know, but don't. Not about Robbie, anyway; he'll be fine. He has nothing but love around him. And that's it.'

My dad looks back at my mam. 'I know he does.'

They watch Robbie laughing hysterically as Brian passes him down from the bouncy castle and into Tim's arms. Tim purposely falls flat on his back as he raises Robbie above him. Robbie laughs even louder as he stretches out his whole body, arms and legs straight, his fists clenched to form the perfect Superman pose.

38

'Alrigh' bud.'

Danny hears the words but doesn't bother looking up. He often sits alone on one of the few benches in the courtyard of Mountjoy. Nobody has said hello to him the entire time he's been in prison, so naturally he assumes it isn't directed at him. 'Bud! What's the craic?' This time it's a little louder and closer, so he glances up to see Wacko standing there, looking at him with a shit-eating grin that Steve Guttenberg would be proud of.

'Alright,' Danny says back.

'Wacko, remember me?'

'Yeah, course. The holding cell.'

'Yeah, Johnner, isn't it?'

'Danny.'

'Yeah. Do you have a smoke?'

'No, sorry.'

Danny has an uneasy feeling – something isn't right. This guy hasn't acknowledged his existence in months and now he's being all buddy-buddy. He sits down beside him on the bench, causing Danny to shift slightly in his seat.

'Fuckin' freezin', isn't it?' says Wacko.

Danny looks up at the clouds, obstructed slightly by the huge meshing draped from one end of the high walls to the other to stop locals from lashing sliotars filled with drugs over the walls with hurley sticks.

'It's cold enough, alright,' he answers.

Wacko leans uncomfortably close. 'Here, I've a question for ya.'

'What?' Danny asks as he looks behind him, half expecting someone to jump on him.

'Are you nuts?'

'What?'

'Are you nuts?'

Danny scowls, 'No, I heard you; I just don't understand the question.'

'Pretty fuckin' simple question.'

'Am I nuts?'

'Righ'.'

'Why, what did I do?'

'What did you do?'

'What the fuck is going on here?' Danny says, agitated now.

'Relax, man. I just heard you went crazy. Went fuckin' nuts. That they brought you down to the psych ward kickin' and screamin' about dragons and magic demons and all that shit.'

'Dragons and demons! What the fuck? No, for Christ's sake.'

Wacko elbows him. 'That's what they're sayin', lad. I said you must have been off your head on acid.'

'No, nothing like that.'

'They brought you in, though; I know that much for a fact.'

'Yeah, they brought me in, but it wasn't for no magic shit or dragons.'

'What then?'

Danny looks away, spits on the ground. 'What the fuck is it to you?'

Wacko seems surprised by the tone. 'Just being friendly.'

'By asking me if I'm crazy?'

'It's as good a thing to talk about in this shithole as anythin' else.'

Danny gives him a weary look. But the guy has a point and it's the first time anyone has shown any interest in him since he's arrived.

'Suppose you're right.'

'I've ended up there meself a few times, but I'm always off me fuckin' head,' he says as he searches his pockets and takes out a smoke. Danny thinks about commenting on how a second ago he'd tried to scab one off him but thinks better of it.

'Here, do you want one?' Wacko offers.

'Thanks,' Danny says as Wacko moves in so close that Danny can smell his stale breath. He studies Wacko's face and notices that he is way older than he looks. Because he is skinny, wears tracksuits and acts like such an eejit, he'd assumed that he was in his twenties. But looking at his lined face now, he realises that this fucker is closer to forty.

He whispers, 'If you want me to sort you out with any shit let me know.'

'Like what kind of shit?' Danny whispers.

'Any shit. Smoke, smack, that acid shit you like – come to me.'

Danny shakes his head. 'I'm not into acid. I told you that.'

Wacko smiles at him and moves his face away. 'Yeah, whatever. You're a fuckin' header, I saw you fightin' those wankers when you first got here and I know you're into droppin' acid by yourself and shit. You come to me and I'll hook you up.'

Fuck it, Danny decides, no point explaining anything to this guy; may as well just go along with it. 'Alright, thanks man. I'm staying the fuck away from acid after the last time, though. Bad, bad trip.'

'Ah ha, I knew it,' Wacko says with a look of vindication.

'But weed, can you get me weed?' With that Wacko takes a look around and cautiously reaches into his pocket, taking out a pre-rolled joint.

'Fuck yeah,' Wacko says as they smile at each other. 'Well, hash.'

'Just as good.'

'Here, come down here so.' Wacko gets up and Danny follows him to the corner of the courtyard where he sparks up the joint, keeping it hidden in his hand. He takes a bunch of pulls, nearly finishing the thing, before handing it to Danny. 'Watch it, now,' he warns. Danny looks around and carefully takes a few quick tokes himself. 'Fuckin' good, isn't it?'

Danny is about to say yes but coughs out a laugh instead, which delights Wacko. 'Ah ha, told you,' he smiles.

'Cheers man, this is good. Fucking powerful.'

Wacko gives him a devilish grin. 'It's dipped in opium, so it really fucks you up.'

Danny's eyes widen. 'Holy shit.'

Wacko starts walking away, so Danny follows. 'Where we going?'

'Pool.'

'For a swim?' Danny asks, astonished. For a second he wonders how he could have gone six months in this place and missed the fact that it has a swimming pool.

Wacko looks back at Danny, laughing, and gives him a you-poor-clueless-bastard wrap around the shoulders. 'No, not a swim, you gobshite. A game of pool.'

Danny blinks and he's standing with a pool cue in his hand.

'What colour am I?' is met by a blank stare. Wacko starts laughing at him as Danny grows more frustrated. 'What colour am I?' he repeats.

'Just hit the fuckin' ball, you plank,' Wacko cries.

Danny looks down at the table and realises that the game hasn't begun yet and it is his break. 'Oh fuck.' He starts laughing himself. 'I thought … I thought we had already started.'

'Yeah, yeah, I know. Just fuckin' break, will ya?'

He lines up his shot for ages then lashes into it, scuffing the side of the white ball, which somehow manages to miss everything else on the table.

Wacko pisses himself again and says, 'Here, watch this.' He struts to the table; it's clear that he genuinely believes he's going to blast the triangle of balls into oblivion and pocket at least five of them. He does look the part, to be fair. Once ready, he strikes down forcefully on the cue, but manages to miss every ball as well. 'What the fuck!' he says, looking at the pool cue as if it is somehow to blame. He puts some chalk on it, then hunches over to retake his shot, this time lightly breaking up the bunch.

'Your go.'

It's the longest game of pool ever. One is as bad as the other. The longer they play the more they start to get on with each other. When either one of them finally pots something it's met with 'good shot' compliments and all that. But, God, they are shite. I expected this of Danny, but I'm surprised at Wacko.

'What's your favourite sport?' Wacko asks, handing Danny the pool cue.

'Don't know; rugby, I suppose.'

'Yeah, yeah – fuckin' tough sport man. Them pricks really hit each other.'

'What's yours?' Danny asks as he misses another sitter.

'Football. I support Arsenal, like.' He goes on and on about football and Danny can't keep up. He doesn't follow it, anyway, but trying to decipher all this football talk while off his face on an opium-hash concoction is impossible. All he can do is nod, smile and throw in the odd Roy Keane in Saipan comment.

'What do you reckon the shittest sports are?' Danny asks to try and get away from the football talk.

'Don't know. Fencin' or some shit.'

'Well at least that has swords.'

'Yeah suppose. Runnin's pretty shit.'

'I was thinking more along the lines of the one where they make the horse dance around in a square.'

'Wha'?'

'You know, it's in the Olympics. The horse kind of walks around in a square and they give him points.'

'What the fuck are you on about? That's the fuckin' circus you're thinkin' of. The Olympics,' Wacko says with a big smile. 'You're fuckin' mad.'

'No, no. Seriously, it is a sport – they have them walking around kind of skipping.'

Wacko bursts out laughing. 'They warm them up before the races, you gobshite!'

'No, Christ. I know the difference, I'm telling you it's a sport ... what's it fucking called?' *Dressage*, and I agree – totally shit.

Wacko can't stop smiling. 'Whatever, man, your shot.' Danny takes the cue as Wacko falls into deep thought for a moment before saying, 'Sumo is pretty shite.'

'Sumo wrestling?'

'Yeah, did you ever see it? The chinks are gas, two fat blokes giving each other wedgies and they make a sport out of it.'

'I never thought of it like that, you're fuckin' spot on,' Danny says, grinning.

'It's disgustin'.'

Danny smiles at Wacko and hands back the cue. This has been by far the best day he's had since being locked up. Since way before that, even. Maybe since the night he met me. The crazy laced hash that Wacko gave him has definitely helped, but mainly it's down to Wacko himself.

'Why do they call you Wacko anyway?' Danny wants to know.

'Have a guess,' Wacko says standing up straight.

'Because you're a wacko?'

'That's what everyone says. It's 'cos I used to love Michael Jackson. Would show up to school with only the one glove and the whole lot,' Wacko says as he lashes into another shot, this time potting the 6 ball.

'Brilliant,' Danny declares. This guy is brilliant, he decides; his face now sore as his smile muscles are not used to the exercise.

39

Pam's feeling pretty good this morning as it's such a sunny day. The past few years the summers have been terrible and this one is an exception only in that it has been beyond terrible. Instead, it has been absolutely catastrophic. It has rained every day. Most years you'd open up the blinds in the morning with the hope that it would be sunny – don't get me wrong; usually it would still be raining, but at least you had hope. This year, though, even the hope has gone. So this morning Pam opened up the blinds expecting to see the same grey sky, but instead the sun glistened off everything. To make matters even better it's a Saturday, which means that she can do something nice with Robbie. Get him out of the house.

She decides to take him to a fun fair for kids at the local leisure centre.

The place is packed when she arrives, kids screaming and going mental. I hated this shit when I was alive, but it looks pretty appealing to me now. Well, not appealing, exactly; I just wish that I could be here properly. Be one of the dads getting involved in tug-of-wars and the three-legged races. Last time I was at one of these things I laughed my ass off at all those fools actively participating – now I just wish that I was one of them. Happy assholes. The state of them, falling over each other, their bellies exposed when they hit the ground. Laughing as they pull their T-shirts back down to cover their guts. Worse still are the fit dads. The ones who keep themselves in shape. Taking everything so seriously, trying their best and being visibly peeved if they don't win.

As I scan the crowd, I feel myself getting more and more pissed off – at least, until I notice how happy Pam looks. I haven't seen her this happy since before I died. She's grinning from ear to ear. Any time one of these dummies falls over during the three-legged race she bursts out laughing. She cheers mad for whatever team she decides to support in the tug-of-war, then laughs at them if they lose. Everyone here is having fun and Pam feels it and is soaking it up. I can feel it too – and slowly I let my hatred and jealousy go and enjoy being there with my family.

Robbie wants to try everything. The bouncy slides, of course – up and down, up and down; Pam smiling and waving with every go. He's drawn to any game that has a ball, constantly skipping the queue to get his next go. He also gets his face painted as Spider-Man – although the kid that paints him is only about thirteen and does a shit job, if you ask me. He looks more like a basketball than Spider-Man. There are obstacle courses, wet sponge games, and Robbie has to try them all. He's too small for a lot of them, but Pam always manages to find a way to make him feel like he's taken part.

After several activities, Pam kneels down beside Robbie to give him a juice as she cracks open a can of diet coke for herself. Pam always orders diet coke instead of normal coke – as if it makes a damn bit of difference. We'd be at the cinema and she'd order the large nachos with cheese, the giant popcorn with extra butter, and a diet coke. As Robbie takes a sip from his juice, she bites into a hot dog she's just bought off a sweaty-looking van chef. Ketchup oozes out all over her hands and she's about to start looking for a tissue in her handbag when it begins to piss from the heavens without any warning.

Shelter is a good bit away and gathering everything up proves difficult as she doesn't want to get rid of the hot dog. It's too tasty and she's starving. She can't just grab Robbie either because she'll get ketchup all over him – plus her hands are full, anyway, between the handbag, hot dog and can of diet coke. In the end, she picks him up with her right arm, but it's precarious, so she only makes it a few steps before putting him down to reposition him as all the while people scurry past, rushing for shelter.

A man stops and says, 'Here, let me help you.' Before she has a chance to answer he has picked up Robbie and is jogging slowly towards the nearby canopy. Her first reaction is of slight annoyance at your man's presumption and she feels awkward that a stranger has picked up her kid. At the same time, she's grateful for the help.

I don't like the dickhead.

By the time she gets under the canopy she's drenched. She looks damn good soaking wet in her summer clothes. The have-a-go hero hadn't noticed just how good-looking she was when he first offered his help. He notices now.

'I believe this is yours,' he says, flashing his pearly white teeth and putting Robbie on the ground. Robbie can't get out of his arms quick enough; he didn't appreciate being thrown about the place without any warning. He shoots your man a dirty look and takes a step away to watch the rain bounce off the grass outside the cover of the canopy.

'Thanks,' Pam replies and glances down at Robbie, making sure he doesn't wander back out into the rain. As she glances down, your man looks at her tits. Quick as a flash, eyes back in polite position by the time Pam looks back at him. I actually can't blame him on this one – it was more reflex than anything else.

'I'm Ger,' he says, holding out his hand.

'Pam,' she responds, shaking his hand.

'Where the hell did that come from?' he says, referring to the rain.

'I know, serves me right for not bringing a coat.' There's something different in how she's speaking to him. There is an air of flirtation about it; she's looking right into Ger's eyes and her smile has a sexier tilt to it than her usual big happy grin. Ger picks up on it too and holds her gaze.

'No, what you're wearing looks good,' he says with a laugh.

This line hurts – he's clearly taking the conversation to another level. Her T-shirt is welded on to her from the rain so you can see the exact shape of her tits and this stranger is making light of it. What's worse is that Pam is into it.

'Oh, thanks very much, I'm drowned here,' she says, looking down at herself, pretending she isn't aware of what Ger means.

Pam is getting embarrassed, holding the hot dog; she thinks it makes her look unattractive, so she glances around for a bin.

'What're you looking for?' Ger asks.

'I need to dump this thing – it's as wet as me.' He gives a sly little grin and almost says something provocative, then thinks twice about it. Instead he just says, 'Here, give it to me.' He takes it and disappears into the huddled-up crowd.

I can feel the knots forming in Pam's stomach. She has such a mix of emotions as she waits for him to return. She liked the look of him straight away and recognised how he was looking at her. While they were talking she didn't think of me once; all she could think about was that your man was a big ride.

'Now!' he says on his return. 'Hot dog gone, will there be anything else I can help you with today?'

Tosser.

'Stick around; I'll call you when I need you,' she answers, smiling.

'Well maybe I should give you my number so?'

Pam's flustered; she wasn't expecting that. He notices and draws back, 'Oh sorry, not to worry.' Looking down at Robbie, 'Of course, you're married.' Pam says nothing for a while; she just looks out on the rain and Ger starts to feel a little uncomfortable. He has nowhere to go and is stuck beside this supposedly married chick, who he now realises he can't score with. He can't just piss off either because then he'd look a right wanker.

'Really bucketing down,' he says lamely, trying to break the uncomfortable silence.

'Sure is.'

Now she is thinking of me – *finally!* – and thinking about what to say to Ger. She starts to regret not telling him that she isn't married anymore. Even if it just meant staying talking to him, to keep him interested. It felt nice, having someone look at her like that again; it didn't have to go anywhere, but for the first time in a long time she has enjoyed the feeling of being desired. But it's too late to say anything now. She can't just blurt it out. The awkwardness between them is growing – she can see Ger's reddening complexion from the corner of her eye.

Ger can feel his cheeks burning, which makes him more em-barrassed, thus turning his face even redder. *Fuck this*, he thinks, *haven't taken a redner in years.* He'd started off so smooth too, he thought; and he really liked the look of this girl. Standing so close now he can smell her T-shirt, the rain mixed with her own odour. She smells amazing; it makes him want her more, but it also makes him want to get the hell out of there because he made such an ass out of himself.

'I'm actually not married anymore.'

Like a hollow-point bullet straight through my fucking heart.

'Oh?' Confidence back, redner fading. He notices that she is still wearing a ring but decides not to mention it. 'Sorry to hear that.'

'Thanks.'

Pam turns to him with a smile and he can see again her massive eyes.

'So who's this little fella?' he asks. Yep, his confidence is indeed back now. Mentioning the son is a smooth move; seem interested and a nice guy at the same time. *Ger: King of the Kids!* The prick.

'This is Robbie, say hello, Robbie.' Robbie has zero interest. He's too busy watching the rain hit the muddy puddles to care about some old dude talking to his mam. All he can think about is how much he wants to jump in those puddles. Stick his hand in them and feel the gooey brown stuff from the ground.

'Hiya, Robbie.'

Still no response, which suits Ger. He gives Pam an isn't-he-cute look before saying, 'Well, if you won't take my number will you at least let me buy you a new hot dog to replace the drowned one?'

She thinks on this for a moment, as she is still hungry, but decides that she doesn't want to be scoffing her face in front of him. 'No, no – I'm good, thanks, the rain mixed with soggy bread has turned me off the idea.'

'Fair enough, it was fairly manky when you handed it to me alright.'

'Oh yeah, thanks for that.'

'Well, I wouldn't have taken it if I'd known how much ketchup was on it.'

Pam laughs so he continues, 'Fucking covered me it did.'

'Sorry about that – it got me too, if that makes you feel any better.'

'Not really, look at my sleeve.' Sure enough there is a bit on it. 'This is a new shirt!'

'Oh well – small price to pay for helping out a lady.'

'You're right there.'

The rain starts easing off and people begin to leave the confines of the canopy. Pam and Ger remain inside, though, as they continue talking. Eventually Pam says she better get Robbie back home and he asks again if he can call her.

'Give me your number,' she says, not giving much up. Cool bitch, he thinks. And she walks off with his number in her pocket and their possible future in her hands.

Her mind is racing the entire way home; she doesn't listen to a single word Robbie is saying (which is a lot). He keeps mentioning all the different things he did: when he kicked the ball, how he threw the wet sponge through the hole. All she thinks about is Ger's smile, his tall frame and wide shoulders, how he made her laugh, how he looked at her. His green eyes. Would she ring him? Part of her knows she won't – can't. But why not? Because she's not ready yet. It's been over a year, is that long enough? Silent tears begin to fall as she drives; deep down, she knows that she isn't ready. She feels bad to even think about it: *poor Chris – I'm letting him down. How could I even think about stuff like this?*

But when she gets home she doesn't throw out the number. She puts it in a drawer and, for her, in a way, that's as good as calling. It means she's deciding that there is a possibility she will call in the future, however remote that is. She's giving herself permission to have a choice. It's a first step in a long line of steps to eventually moving on.

SIXTEEN
MONTHS
DEAD

40

I never saw a dead body outside of the relative comfort of a funeral home. Nicely laid out, best suit on, make-up, hair combed. All prim and proper in the coffin, all very tasteful. Mourners gathered around, candles burning. Well, I've seen myself dead but that doesn't count – I was literally going insane at the time.

This time is different. To see someone dead. Away from the controlled environment of a funeral home everything is far from tasteful. There's a smell of shit and piss and an unflattering expression on his face. Even still, you can tell it was a kind face. A face that I had liked and I find myself feeling a bit sorry for Danny that he won't have a dad when he gets out of prison.

Danny Senior lay half on the couch, half on the floor, for almost a week before he was found. The neighbour from across the street noticed that his car was left out on the road and eventually got suspicious because Senior would never leave his car on the road for more than a day or two. After him not answering his phone or doorbell, fair play to the neighbour, he decided to take action. He found an open window at the back of the house, brought his ladder and climbed up and in. Even though he was upstairs he got the stench straight away. Fuck. *Prepare yourself*, he thought, as he walked slowly down the stairs and into the front room. There poor Senior lay, face bloated and turned dark purple. The neighbour nearly vomited. He didn't, though; he composed himself, went into the kitchen and calmly picked up the telephone.

Senior's probably floating around here somewhere, wondering what's going on. Poor bastard. Pity we haven't met now that he's dead. I stood over his body just as he passed away, half expecting that we would meet because of our connection or something, but no. Nothing. Another fucking disappointment in a long line of them. He hadn't been in the best of health the past few years, anyway – always one thing or another wrong with the fucker. Typical shit from a widower with no wife to look after him and so let himself go. Never eating right, gaff not that clean. Still, he was a good man and didn't deserve to end up like this – to die of old age at only sixty-four.

In the moments leading up to his death, he had sat there, looking at an empty bottle of Paddy's, wondering how he was going to get another drink. It was too late to walk down to the pub. The best bet, he thought, would be to sleep on the couch, wake up and hit the early-house with all the other alcoholic losers. He was so depressed. He felt awful, his whole body didn't feel right but, as with a lot of men (especially of his generation), he didn't bother his hole going to the doctor.

Not my generation, though – the slightest little ache and I'd be on to Pam complaining and probably head down to the doctor for a prescription. I rarely heard my dad complaining about pain – and if he did you could be sure it was bad, whatever it was. There should be a happy balance, though – the last time I went to the doctor's I truly regretted it. I had a rash on my mickey that I knew in my heart was only eczema, but because it was on my balls I was overly sensitive about it. Also on the cream for eczema they say you're not supposed to put it on your balls so I figured he might have special stuff to prescribe.

I didn't go to my usual doctor as it was too embarrassing an affliction and I wanted a stranger to check me out. Terrible move on my part. The doctor was this crusty old man with yellow teeth. Maybe it's a personal hang-up I have, but I believe the person treating your health should at the very least look healthy themselves – and that definitely was not the case with this guy. He put me up on the table and I had to pull down my pants and spread my legs, stirrup style. Very emasculating. It looked like I was about to give birth. My poor mickey didn't know what to think and fucking shrivelled back up into my belly, terrified. It would have been humiliating enough without my dick looking like an acorn – that made it all the worse.

I lay there with him looking down on me and as he reached out his hand I realised he wasn't wearing any rubber gloves! His nails were mad long and the horrible bastard did a scratch-scratch between my balls and ass with his index finger, flaking off the dry skin. All I could do in response was turn my face away in shame and disgust. How many other asses had he scratched that day? He didn't wash his hands after he was finished with me, I know that much. Turns out it was eczema and he told me to use the exact cream that I already had. When I said about the *not to use on sensitive skin* warning that's on the label he told me not to mind that. Perfect. Utterly humiliated for nothing. I never showered as vigorously as I did when I got home; I practically gave myself a skin-peel I scrubbed so hard.

Who knows, maybe after that experience I would have been like the old-timers, always making a fuss about going to the doctor's. Maybe that kind of shit used to happen all the time back in the day and that's why they hate doctors.

Whatever the reason, it's a pity Danny Senior didn't go. As his time approached, he felt pain in his neck, his throat. His chest had been aching on and off for a while and he was constantly out of breath. Always having dizzy and nauseous spells. But he'd just put that down to the drink. Put it all down to the drink, really. He was so mad at himself for falling off the wagon, but he couldn't help it. Not after what had happened. He knew deep down that it was killing him, but he always brushed that thought aside. He spent his nights thinking how he'd failed in life and how he'd let his son down. He'd cry at the thought of where his boy was stuck. Blamed himself and was so worried for him that he couldn't eat. The drink didn't even help him forget. It hadn't helped after his wife died either, so what made him think it would be any different this time? Most of his time was just spent feeling mad and disappointed in himself. The only thing that kept him going was the thought of his son getting out of prison. Then he'd sober up, he'd reassured himself; then he could be happy again. Be a good supportive father. He just had to get through these next nine months and the drink would be his crutch. As bad as it was, he needed it. Who could blame him?

That night, the empty bottle of whiskey faded as he drifted off to sleep, the weight of the world on his frail shoulders. Forty-five minutes later his broken heart stopped working altogether. There was no big sudden shock of pain that woke him up – in that respect, at least, it was a peaceful death, even if his last sight was of a symbol that he had come to associate with everything he hated about himself.

41

'Danny? Danny?' Governor Logan looks at Danny's blank face and tries again, 'Danny, are you okay? Do you understand what I've just told you?' Logan decides not to press it any further; of course he understands.

They sit in silence in the governor's office before Danny finally speaks. 'Okay, thanks,' he says quietly, then stands up to walk out of the office.

'Wait, Danny. I know it can't be easy this happening while you're in here. I'm truly sorry for your loss.'

Danny doesn't turn around or say anything; he just stares at the door, waiting for permission to leave. Logan gets up and walks over to him, trying to think of something comforting to say. Nothing appropriate comes to mind. Instead, he places a hand on his shoulder and opens the door, giving one of the guards a nod as Danny takes determined strides back to his cell.

He sits in his cell, staring vacantly at the wall. A half hour passes and he finally lets out a sob. *Please no* is all he keeps saying over and over in his head. *Please no.* He received none of the particulars from Logan; or maybe he did, he thinks, but he can't remember anything past the first line: 'I'm so sorry to have to tell you, but your father has died.'

It's all his fault and he knows it. Now he has two lost lives to be held accountable for and one of them is the only person in the world that he loved who loved him back. He's now more alone than ever.

A ball of self-hatred forms in his stomach for what he has done to his dad.

He thinks of the last time they spoke, when his dad came to visit only two weeks ago. At the time Danny recognised that his dad looked like shit – he was clearly back on the drink full time – but he hadn't pushed it, not wanting to hurt his old man's feelings.

Danny always hated the initial stages of any visit. He'd walk out and have to stand against the wall before the visitor sat down. There'd be up to six other inmates at a time talking to their own families or whatever, half of them trying to smuggle drugs in. It always took a while to adjust to the no-privacy element of the room too. Small talk at first, but by the end of the half hour he always wanted more. That day, in particular, he had wanted his dad to stay longer; he desperately wanted to stave off the loneliness for just a while longer.

'I better head off, son,' his dad had said, rising from his chair.

'Hang about, sure the guard hasn't called us yet.'

'He's about to. I always hate the rushed goodbyes.'

'Just another minute,' Danny said, smiling.

'Of course.' Senior smiled back at his son but couldn't hide the sadness in his eyes as he lowered himself back onto the chair. He got like this every time they had to part.

'I'm fine, Dad. I'm doing okay. Considering everything, I'm going to be out soon enough. Sooner than I deserve, really.'

'Well, I'm living for that day.'

'How are you holding up?' Danny asked.

'You know, good days and bad.'

'I know; I'm sorry, Dad.'

'I know you are, it's not your fault,' he said out of habit and politeness.

'Well, it is actually. It's all my fault.'

'None of that. I'm my own man. We all have our demons. I'm going to be tip-top by the time you get out, don't you worry about that.' They smiled at each other and Danny believed him. He would be fine, and once free Danny could go about making amends for what he'd put him through. Be a better son.

'I hope so.'

He didn't mean it in any negative way, but Senior took his comment to be slightly patronising. That maybe he wouldn't be able to get off the drink. Triggered by memories of past judgemental arguments and mixed with the bit of whiskey still in his system, he snapped back at him:

'If I say I'll do something I will.'

'I know.'

'I don't need you of all people judging me, okay?'

'Jesus Christ, Dad, who's judging who?' Just then the guard called out that time was up and both of them were left hurt and angry.

'Listen, don't leave like this,' Danny said. 'I didn't mean to judge; I'm just looking forward to getting out, that's all.'

'Fair enough, sorry,' Senior mumbled. He still had a bit of a bold head on him but was calming quickly. 'Sorry, son, see you soon.'

'Yeah, see you.'

Danny plays their last meeting over and over in his head. With each recollection, his dad grows more and more angry with him and their little misunderstanding escalates in Danny's head until it is an out-and-out fight. Maybe it wasn't as bad as all that, he finally allows himself to think. But what does it matter, anyway? What does anything matter?

42

Wacko sits at the edge of the pool table and focuses on the bin. He has one peanut left to throw and wants it to count. The last three he has missed. Left eye closed, he has the target in his sights, confident he'll make the shot. Pulling back his arm he fires, missing by about four feet. Shite! As he tries to figure out how he could have missed, he notices Danny standing against the wall, watching him.

'Alrigh' Danny, don't know how I missed that. Think it stuck to me finger last minute.'

Danny says nothing and Wacko's too stoned to notice the dead expression in his eyes. 'What's up, man?'

'My dad died.'

Wacko looks stunned – he wasn't expecting that.

'When?'

'I don't know. I just found out today.'

'Ah, that's terrible. Was he old?'

'No.'

Danny needs some sort of comfort. There is nobody else he can talk to. Ever since the game of pool they have been friendly, getting stoned a few times together. It's bleak, he knows, but as shit as he suspects Wacko will be at this kind of thing, he's all he's got.

'He was only sixty-four.'

Wacko's silent. He's so baked that it makes the situation seem even heavier than it is and he just wants to get the fuck out of there. Danny picks up on this and realises he hasn't a friend in the world – why should Wacko give a shit? He turns to walk away.

Wacko looks at Danny's hung shoulders and before he can stop himself calls after him. 'Hang on, man; let's take a stroll.'

The two of them stand in the corner of the yard as Wacko rolls a joint very conspicuously. He dare not look up at Danny – he's afraid he'll be crying or something. His heart does go out to him, though. What a place to get that kind of news. He finishes skinning up, takes a few tokes, then hands it to Danny. 'Here you go, buddy, this is good shit.'

Danny inhales long and deep, feels his lungs fill, before letting out a giant cloud of smoke. Again. Again. He keeps smoking until he feels nothing. Wacko lets him at it; he can smoke the whole thing if he wants. Danny starts coughing and Wacko pats his back. Tears start to roll down his face – at first from the cough but slowly they turn into actual tears and in no time he's full-on hunched over, coughing and crying at the top of his voice.

Wacko doesn't know where to look. He scans the yard to see who's watching. No one he knows well. Thank fuck for that. 'There, there, man. It's alrigh'… just, you know …'

Danny catches his breath. 'Sorry.'

'Understandable, man,' Wacko says, patting Danny's back. 'No worries.'

'Fuck,' Danny splutters, 'what am I going to do?' He looks at Wacko with pleading eyes, praying that somehow this man – this fucking waster of a man – could come up with something that will help. Something profound. Wacko looks like he wants to deliver as well, which gives Danny hope.

Finally, he speaks. 'I don't know, man.'

Brilliant.

Danny gathers himself – the effects of the drugs are strong. It's that same crazy shit that Wacko always smokes. Blows your fucking head off. He says nothing more and walks away. He drifts into the main hall, down the stained red corridors of A block and into his cell. He is alone. No point pretending any different. No one can help him. Proper order too, he thinks. What good is he to anyone? His mind flickers, the walls move on him and he thinks that I'm sitting beside him.

I am.

'I'm sorry,' he says.

I know you are.

'My dad's dead.'

I know. I was with him when he died.

'I killed you both.' He looks around the room again. The walls are changing colour. 'Who's there!' he screams, then looks at the ground, confused, as if he's forgotten where he is for a second.

'I'm sorry,' he whispers again.

Can you see me?

'I know you can hear me. Can you forgive me?'

No.

'I wish you could forgive me.'

I do too.

'If you can forgive me maybe everything will be alright.'

What do you mean?

'But things will never be alright.'

Maybe they can be.

'Can you forgive me?'

No. I don't know. I don't think so.

'If you can forgive me maybe everything will be alright.' Danny slumps down on his bed, the walls spinning all around him. Too fast for him to keep his eyes open. He closes them to stop the ache in his brain but the insides of his eyelids are spinning just as fast. He grabs his forehead and shouts, 'Make it stop!' Turning on his side, he grits his teeth and wishes that he could sleep to get away from the pain – even for a little while.

It's okay, Danny, calm down.

His body moves to its back and he winces once more.

Calm down, Danny, it's okay.

His breathing relaxes a bit, his eyes remaining closed. His hands move from his forehead to his chest as he calms. The pained expression is still on his face as he drifts off to sleep.

I stay beside him, wondering what the fuck just happened. After over a year of trying to wake up the bastard, have I for once helped him go to sleep? His mind is so scrambled I can't tell if he heard me again or if he was just off his head.

Can I forgive him? Probably not. But still, as I look at this man I have hated for the past sixteen months, I wonder how I feel about him now.

Maybe he isn't so bad after all.

43

John is a fairly open guy, so holding off on telling everyone that they are expecting a baby hasn't suited him. Still, Niamh made him promise not to tell any of the lads until at least three months – but now that they are well beyond it he's looking forward to getting to the pub and breaking the news. If I was around he would have told me alright and he half thought of ringing Davey early on, but in the end he didn't bother. He knew Davey would be happy for him, definitely, but ultimately not really give that much of a bollocks.

Me and Pam didn't do that wait three months thing. We were too excited when we found out that we were going to have a baby. I figured we may as well tell everybody because if the worst happened and it didn't work out we'd end up letting everyone know then, anyway, so as to have shoulders to cry on. So what's the idea with holding off? I never quite understood it, but it's a common enough thing, I guess, and Niamh hadn't wanted to take any chances.

It's a great time for them, anyway, and they're totally embracing it, loving every minute. Apart from crippling foot cramps and being exhausted the whole time, Niamh's the happiest she's ever been. Pamela was like that too when she was preggers. I think that's why Robbie turned out to be such a lovely, placid and easy person. There was zero stress in the lead-up to his birth.

Although, saying that, he was a couple of days early, which we weren't expecting at all, so that did make us a little anxious right at the end. It also meant that I made the terrible mistake of watching one of the *Alien* movies the night before. I had it in my head that he'd be a couple of weeks overdue, so it didn't occur to me that watching little aliens burst out of people's stomachs might be a bad idea so close to your wife giving birth.

It was.

There's a suction yoke that they sometimes use to help the baby come out during the 'Push! Push!' bit. It temporarily elongates the crown of the head so that it looks the exact same shape as the alien's head in those movies. Couple that with the fact that the little fucker is blue. Nobody ever told me that. He came out with a blue, alien head on him and a scrunched-up angry face – he looked hideous. I screamed so loud that the doctor started laughing at me. I was screaming louder than Pam.

Then the doc threw him to the midwife, who seemed to flip him from hand to hand, snipping this and snipping that. Robbie looked so damn slippery that I got worried and told the midwife to be careful. She just laughed at me like the doctor had. As if to say, 'Don't worry, dipshit, I've done this before.' She was right too. In two minutes flat she had him cleaned, powdered and resting in his own little heated spot in the delivery room.

His crying had stopped by the time I went over to him. Pamela was still in the horrors at that stage, giving birth to the placenta. That's another thing I didn't know about. The placenta – just when you think it's over they have to push this fucking thing out. I glanced back and thought, *poor Pam*, but turned back around to study the face of my new little boy. It was perfect. He still had a little frown on him and a single tear remained. It rolled down the left side of his tiny round cheek and I wiped it away before it travelled any further. I made a silent promise to him then that I would always be there to wipe away his tears. It was a promise I could keep for just two years, but it had been one that I'd cherished each time I kept it.

I loved his cry. It never bothered me, not once. I loved being the person to stop the tears, to make him feel better. It made me feel better. It made me feel like a man.

He's crying now.

Not over anything serious. It's just that his nose is all stuffed up and he can't get to sleep. Pamela is with him. Like she always is. Calming him, making him feel better. Her everlasting patience and soothing voice are working. She is so strong. How did I not see her strength when I was alive? She always impressed me, don't get me wrong. But the way she handles everything now, especially with Robbie, mystifies me.

She hasn't been out in ages. She could do with a night out but doesn't even see it herself. Doesn't care about it. All she cares about is him. Still, I know she'd enjoy herself if she was with the lads now. They're all down in the local, where John is finally after breaking his big news.

'That's fantastic. Do you know who the father is?' Davey says, all thrilled. Fanny laughs and gives John a slap 'n' grab high five.

'Congrats, my man, that's super news.'

John beams. 'Thanks.'

'What are you going to call him? Or her?'

'Don't know yet. Well, if it's a boy I want to call him Chris, actually.'

Fanny looks into his pint and says quietly, 'That would be nice.'

'Yeah except Niamh doesn't like the name – never did.'

'Really, why the fuck not?' asks Davey, slightly annoyed.

'Ah, there was some kid in her primary school who they all called Pissy Chrissy for whatever reason and it turned her off the name … guess he smelt like piss or something.'

Davey chuckles. 'Fair enough.'

This sucks for me. Some knobhead from Niamh's class has robbed me of a namesake just because he couldn't hold his piss? I would have loved them to name their child after me – I'd be remembered for the rest of that guy's life. I guess I can understand it, though. For some reason the name associations you develop from school days stay with you, no matter who comes along after. If there was a kid in school called Philip that you hated, then you can be sure you'll hate that name for the rest of your life. It's like how I'd never been mad about the name Pam, as there was a frizzy-haired teacher's pet who used to always rat on me in my class with that name. Even Pam couldn't change my dislike for the name and she's my wife.

Fred arrives from the bar with a big smile on his face and pint in hand. 'What's the story, lads?'

'Alright, Fred, guess what?' Davey says.

'What?'

'John's not gay!'

'No way, since when? Does Niamh know?'

'She does now,' John says, taking out his phone and showing Fred the picture of the baby scan.

It takes Fred, the dummy, a minute to figure out what it is, then he says, 'No way! She's preggers? Congratulations, man. Do you know if it's a boy or girl?'

'Nope, find out on the day.'

I can't wait for him to find out. The namesake thing doesn't matter, anyway, because I can see her. I can see my best friend's little girl growing inside Niamh; her tiny fingers have already started to develop. Soon she'll have her own set of unique prints. Then her skeleton will begin to harden; she'll grow eyebrows and eyelids, her wrinkled skin will start to smooth out. Next she'll be able to open her eyes and follow light before her lungs develop enough for air. Then comes the most beautiful and amazing thing of all.

Then comes life.

TWO
YEARS
DEAD

44

I can go anywhere – anywhere within my own world, that is. Past, present. I'm beginning to appreciate that more now than I ever did.

I can go back to when I asked Pam to marry me. It's even more perfect than I remembered it in life. We were on a boat off the coast of Sicily that broke down in the middle of the sea. Everyone else on board was panicking that it would never start again, while the tough-looking ferryman worked on the engine. But me and Pam didn't give a shit. Instead we looked at it as getting a free couple of hours on our boat trip, so headed up to the top deck where no one else was – for some reason no one else wanted to go up top and instead were all huddled downstairs and indoors. We couldn't believe it – maybe being from Ireland meant that getting some time in the sun was more important to us, I guess; anyway, there was no way we were missing a minute of it.

As we were sprawled out on the floor, sunbathing, holding hands, hugging and laughing, I toyed with the ring in my pocket. I had planned on asking her at the restaurant later that evening. But as we sunned ourselves on top of the boat, I realised that this place was perfect. We were in our own little world.

I can hear the waves soothingly brush against the boat, the mumble of quiet voices downstairs. I can see Pam's beautiful happy face, rounder then than now. The fair skin of her cheeks slightly burned, light-brown freckles forming on her arms. I can smell her unique sent; not perfume, just her. God, the waves are so soothing. The gentle rock of the boat – let them take forever to fix it. I can look into her huge golden eyes and get lost in them; I can hold her hand as I did then. Watch her roll over onto her belly and listen to her happy giggle. She wouldn't be expecting what I'd say next. 'I always want to remember this day.'

'I know, me too. It's deadly, isn't it?'

'It is. But I always want to remember it as the day I asked you to marry me.'

And then she says something I will never forget. She says, 'What?'

I reach into my pocket and take out the ring, make sure she knows I mean business. Standing her up, I stay kneeling. I hold out the ring.

'Will you marry me?'

We both burst out laughing as she jumps on me, kisses me and says, 'Of course, yes!'

I can cradle her in this embrace for eternity. Even if it is just a memory, I can hold her here and never let her go. When all this really happened, the boat was fixed pretty soon after and we were sent on our way back to the real world. But not where I am now. Now it's better, the boat will never be fixed and I can cling on to this moment. We can stay in this happy, loving place, wrapped in each other's arms forever.

***

I blink and I've missed another Christmas. Not quite as bleak as the last one, but it was still pretty shit. My family were definitely starting to come around a bit, but Christmas was still depressing for all of them. My own house still looked like Ebenezer lived there, no lights or candles in the window or anything. Pam better pick up the pace next year. She had a tree up, alright, but that's it.

Brian and Tim talked about me at Christmas more than they have at any other time of the year, I guess because they're pissed more at Christmas. Every time my name is mentioned there is a darkness in Brian that nobody can see but him and me. He holds it deep down. He's become good at hiding it. My parents watched *Back to the Future* again, this time the first one, and everybody went on the piss for New Year's. Nothing new about it except maybe a number.

John had to work a fair bit through the holiday and watching him dig his shovel into the icy ground was fun. Not because it was a pain in the ass for him but because he did it with a smile on his face. I think of how I watched him at work during the months after my death – how he turned his face from the other workers when his eyes filled, how lonely and sad he felt, and how he thought he'd never get over it. As much as I like being missed, I like happy John more. He gets progressively better with each month. The wedding and honeymoon helped, though obviously the sentencing had been a bit of a setback – fucking dickhead of a judge – but other than that things have been on the up and up and he was looking forward to the coming year and what lies ahead.

***

I go back to the first time my parents took me camping around Ireland. It was before the lads were born, so it was just the three of us. My dad borrowed this heap of shit tent off one of his mates. It was blue, yellow and brown. The blue and yellow were the colour of the canvas. The brown was something that had grown on it over time. My dad – like a lot of dads, I think – would get a bit into 'Angry Dad' mode on holidays. Especially on camping holidays, as there was nothing but shit jobs for him to do. The setting up of the tent being the first one. It was nothing like today where they just pop up – these bastards, you'd need a degree in engineering to master.

Mam had taken me to the playground as my dad put the finishing touches to the tent, which at the time we thought looked fantastic and were so proud of ourselves for erecting. It was only on the way back, when we saw it from a distance, that my mam and I realised how bad it was. Surrounded by huge caravans, luxurious trailer tents, fancy German back-packer tents, stood this filthy, gaudy yoke. The two of us looked at each other and my mam said, shocked, 'Christ, we look like tinkers.' I burst out laughing and said the same thing to Dad when we reached the tent – he was none too impressed after all his hard work.

The trip was great, though. We went to the Ulster Museum where I saw a painting by Jack B. Yeats. It freaked me out a bit because my granddad had just passed away and the solitary man depicted in the painting reminded me of him. It shows a lonely figure walking between this world and the next, trying to arrive at something he may never be able to reach. My dad told me that the man was on his way to heaven because of the bright white towering colours on the horizon. Like a white Emerald City. But I didn't think that. What I did think I couldn't quite understand. Now I see that the huge white mountains scared me as I thought they told of a glacial future of isolation and loneliness for the traveller. They scare me still as the painting is now etched in my mind, the man no longer reminding me of my granddad but of myself. He is moving – in what Yeats called *On Through the Silent Lands* – heading for one last bridge to cross, to go to a place he might not want to get to. What that bridge represents, for him or me, I'm not sure.

I wasn't right after seeing it. Cried with the worry I felt at the thought of my beautiful granddad all alone, frozen in an icy world of nothingness. I wonder now how close this could have been to the truth. Is he lost like me? Cold and abandoned. Forever condemned to a silent place, searching for a reason for his own existence and dreaming of a future where he can cease to be. Or has he found peace? I need to believe that he has. That, in the end, Yeats' scene is just a painting, a master's interpretation of something I don't fully understand, and that there is, in fact, hope for us all.

My dad was able to give me hope that day by wiping away my tears and assuring me that everything would be alright, that his father had found a world which offered him more than this one ever could. I believed him then. I want to believe him now. My mam gave me a hug that I can still feel. She picked me up and told me that Granddad loved me and was with me always; then I blew my nose into her tissue. Afterwards, Dad took me and Mam golfing (well, pitch and putt) to take my mind off it. Mam hates golf but knew I liked the idea of it, so went along to make me happy. Because that's what mothers do. It was both of our first times playing and the pair of us were useless, but we were equally useless, so laughed together and complimented one another every time we hit the ball past ten feet. Pretty soon I had forgotten all about the image that had so deeply affected me.

The next day Dad took me fishing. Something every dad should do with his son. He brought me to one of those places where it's specially set up for catching fish. A fiver to stand beside a foaming river with such an abundance of trout and salmon you could almost pluck them from the water with your hands. It was great for the confidence – I thought I was the best fisherman since Captain Birdseye. I remember looking at my dad, wondering how he knew so much. Was there nothing he couldn't do? I still look at him like that. We took our fish back to Mam, who cooked them on the barbecue. I hated fish at the time so of course didn't eat it, but she made me a burger and I loved the fact that they were eating what we'd caught. Made me feel like a grown-up.

At night they slept side by side, their outside shoulders touching the canvas of the tent as I was wedged in at the top, basically acting as their pillow. But I didn't mind – it was only in later years that we found it funny and joked about it. At the time, I felt like I was on an adventure. They made me feel like we were equals, like I wasn't just a kid; we were all in this together. One night, it rained so much that I woke up to a pack of almond slices floating past me. That tent really was a heap of shit.

***

I sat with Danny through the days, weeks, months after his dad's death. I travelled back and forth to my family, as well as to past memories that no longer felt distant. I waited with John in the hospital to find out if his daughter was going to be alright – were the complications serious? I shared his delight when the doctor informed him that mother and baby were both doing fine. I cried with him when he saw his little girl for the first time. I stayed with my brother Brian late into the night as he contemplated what he'd do now that the eighteen-month deadline was looming. I watched my son turn four, marvelled at how much he has changed since I left. I'm with Pam always. I'm with everyone I care about all the time.

***

I sit with Danny three weeks before he is set to be released. I watch him take the drawstring cord out of the waistband of his tracksuit pants and wrap it around his neck and I hope that he won't go through with it. Why I want him to live, I have no idea. After all, this is what I wanted from the start: him to be dead. Like me. Well, I suppose that's not entirely true. I do have an idea why I don't want him to go through with it – I like him.

Sure, he can be a dick, but there is goodness in him too, even if it has taken me a long time to see that. He's just a mixed-up guy, insecure and stupid. I will never forgive him for what he took from me, but I don't overly blame him anymore – he didn't mean to kill me, he's just a big, thick, ignorant fucker.

And he's super mixed up now. The weight of his dad's death in particular has really messed him up. Thoughts of Robbie too. He hasn't spoken to anyone in the past few months, hardly ever left his cell. He had seen Dr Brady a few times after their first session, but once he started agreeing with Brady that his vision was nothing more than a weird night-terror dream he was able to move on from it. To be fair to Wacko he made a bit of an effort with Danny after he broke down in front of him. In a weird way he was the only man keeping him somewhat grounded, but once Wacko got released there was nobody.

'You'll be alrigh', bud,' Wacko had said the last time they spoke. They were sitting outside on the same bench on which he'd been when he first approached him. Danny squinted through the cold March sun but didn't say anything. He knew he wouldn't be alright.

'Four months, man. That's fuckin' nothin'.'

'I know,' muttered Danny.

'Trust me. I've fuckin' been there. This place is a kip, but once you're out, man. Ah it's deadly then. You'll be grand.'

'I don't have anyone when I get out, though.'

Danny wouldn't usually be this upfront with Wacko. But that day he didn't feel like pulling his punches, he wanted to be honest. Plus, he was feeling extra emotional because he was going to miss his only friend in there. Maybe his only friend anywhere.

'Ah don't be sayin' tha'.'

'It's true,' confirmed Danny.

Wacko felt a little awkward then. He hated when Danny got too

serious on him. He liked him, sure, but he saw Danny more as a
lost puppy type of guy. Or maybe a lost Saint Bernard. Either way,
some poor soul that he couldn't help throw a bone to every now and
again. He was a nice guy, Wacko, but he'd been through a hell of a
lot himself in his life and finding much sympathy for what seemed
like the norm just wasn't in him. He didn't have a mam or dad
either, but you didn't hear him whinging about it.

'Anyway, man, I better leg it,' he said as he pulled on the last
drag of his smoke. 'Need to gather up some shit. Chin up though,
mate.'

'Yeah, cheers, man,' Danny said as he clapped hands with
Wacko. 'Been cool knowing you.'

'You too, Danny. Four months, mate. Fuckin' nothin'.'

As he stood up and walked away, Danny called out after him,
'Hey, Wacko! You on Facebook or anything? Stay in touch like,
when I'm out.'

Wacko turned around. 'Na, man. I don't do any of tha' shit.'

And then he was gone.

Brilliant.

Danny would have smiled at Wacko's total blasé farewell if it
hadn't made him feel more alone than ever.

Without him, he became further isolated to the point where
he never slept anymore and the sharp stab of anxiety in his gut
was so overwhelming at times that he felt like vomiting. The closer
he came to release, the worse it got. He couldn't eat; his stomach
would wake him up every night. Between that, nightmares (on the
rare times that he did manage to sneak a few minutes of sleep) and
me, he hadn't slept properly in two years. The thought of getting
out of prison just scared him now. He had nothing on the outside
but a whole bunch of fears he'd have to face. Nobody was waiting
for him and there was nothing but a cold, empty and run-down

house full of his father's demons to live in. At least in prison he could hide.

He has been toying with the idea of suicide for quite some time. Pretty much since the week of his dad's death. Telling himself that the world would be better off without him – that my family would be better off; he would finally give them some closure. It made him feel like a better person. If he could at least think about doing it, then maybe that meant he wasn't such a bad guy.

At first, he'd dismissed the thought as some sort of grieving process. Unfortunately the thought festered. Why shouldn't he do it? It would make people happier and at the same time end the constant battles he was having in his head. In some way, it might even make up for what he did. The more he thought about it, the more it seemed like the only reasonable thing to do, until it became the only thing he thought about.

He had originally planned on hanging himself the night before his release but got sick of waiting – why put off the inevitable? It's not like he was having so much fun in prison that he felt he should squeeze the last three weeks in, then goodbye world. No, he thought, may as well get to it. He went to write a suicide note and the fact that he had no one to address it to confirmed that he was doing the right thing. He was about to put the pen down when the words suddenly began to flow:

To Robert Cosgrave,

This is a very strange letter to write and one where I don't really know how to begin. To say I'm sorry I'm sure would mean nothing to you or maybe even anger you further I don't know. I am sorry, more than you know. I realise you are just a boy and perhaps will never read this but this note is for your mother too. Maybe she can tell you about it one day and the gesture I am about to make. I figure with me not in the world anymore maybe you and your mam will at least think I got justice. It's what I think anyway. Because of my actions my dad died too, I think it was a broken heart. So you see I lost my dad too and for the same reason, me. I never wrote a will so this is going to be it as well. Maybe it's not a legal document but these are my wishes. My father owned his house and left everything to me, I want to leave it to you and your mother Pamela Cosgrave. It's all I have and hope it goes some way to letting you know the pain I feel for what I have done to you and your family. I wish there was a stronger word for sorry, I feel stupid writing it. I hope giving up my own life will say it better than the word.

I don't know how to sign off. I hope you have a good life.

Danny Murray

He put the pen down and sat for a moment on the bed. The next part had been all worked out for weeks. Taking his chair he put it against the wall under the small window that's high up in his cell. He pulled the cord from his trackie pants and made a noose on one end. The window has flat bars tight against the glass but at the bottom of one of those bars, where it meets the concrete, is a tiny gap no bigger than the width of a pencil.

Standing on the chair he slid the other end of the cord into this small space and tied the cord to it with six knots to make sure it would hold. Crouched awkwardly, he fitted his head through the noose.

Standing in that awkward position with knees bent, head touching the window, he allows himself a final thought about the whole situation. This is the only thing to do. He is surprisingly calm as he kicks his legs free, but then the back of his head cracks off the wall and the cord tightens around his neck, leaving him hanging there, twitching in pain.

45

Ger looks through the book section in the supermarket, hoping he won't bump into anyone he knows. *Where is he, the little bollocks*, he thinks. Scanning the shelves, he spots him. With a quick glance over his shoulder, he grabs the Justin Bieber biography and throws it in his basket. As he walks down the aisle, he turns directly into Pam's vision. Both are taken by surprise and straight away he takes a redner, thinking about what's in his basket, and then the notion strikes him that the last two redners he's had in God knows how many years were in front of this one. She must think he's an awful nervous bastard.

'Pam,' he says, 'hi.' There are women he's had sex with whose names he doesn't remember, but there is something about Pam, and he's delighted with himself that he remembered it right away.

'Ger, how are you?'

The fact that she remembers his name gives him a little boost, but he's very much aware that she never phoned him and he's also concentrating on trying to hold the basket in such a way that she can't see into it. Pam notices that he seems mightily embarrassed and doesn't really know what to say.

'I'm good, thanks.' He decides just to bite the bullet; he's sure she's seen the book and besides it's something to say. 'It's for my niece, it's her birthday and she's a big fan.'

'What?' Obviously Pam hasn't looked in his basket and has absolutely no fucking idea what your man is on about.

He lifts up the basket. 'Bieber.'

She looks in and bursts out laughing at his picture on the cover.

She always found Justin Bieber funny because he's the head of Orla. That always tickled my funny bone too, there's a bit of a lesbian vibe off both of them. Ger mistakes her laugh, thinking she doesn't believe him. 'Honestly, Jesus, I'm no fan.'

'I know, I believe you,' she says with a huge smile that makes him smile back.

'Christ, of all the people to bump into when buying this.' He has a shy laugh and Pam likes it.

'Don't worry, your secret is safe with me.'

'Thanks.'

'So what music do you like then, if not the Biebs?'

'All stuff, really.' He looks to the music bio section on the rack and sees *The Beatles* right beside Justin. 'These guys, of course,' he says, pointing. 'They're no Justin Bieber now, but they're still pretty good.'

Pam gives a little chuckle. 'Amazing band, I adore John Lennon.'

'McCartney is a legend too.'

'Ah he is yeah, but he's nothing really without *The Beatles*, is he?

'You reckon?'

'For sure, have you seen him lately? It's like he's turned into Shakin Stevens' cool uncle or something.'

'Ah that's a bit harsh,' he laughs. 'What about the Frog Song?'

'The Frog Song? Jesus – everyone brings up that one in the "How shite McCartney is since Lennon split" conversation.'

Ger gets defensive. 'It's a good tune.'

'Okay, I'll give you that – I did love it when I was a kid.'

'"Live and Let Die"?'

'Two songs in forty years.'

'Shit, that's not great. Still he was a Beatle – that makes him a legend.'

'You're right there,' she says, smiling. *This guy is cool*, she thinks.

'Where's your little fella?'

'Robbie? He's at crèche. I'm collecting him now, actually; just had to pick up a few things.'

'Cool.'

'I never asked you have you kids of your own?'

'Me, no.'

'Oh, were you at the fun fair with your niece then?'

'No, I was working.'

'Really?' Pam looks at him – he doesn't seem like the type to be working at one of those things. Ger picks up on her surprise and smiles, 'Yep, that's my job.'

'You're a carney?'

'I'm no fucking carney!'

'Sorry,' she says, trying to hide her laugh.

'I hire out the bouncy castles.'

'Oh right.'

Ger can tell she isn't too impressed, so wants to clarify. 'Well, I'm an architect, really, but when the whole country went to shit I'd very little work on so I got into the bouncy castle business.'

Pam raises an eyebrow. 'As you do.'

'Well, I've a mate who's a bit of a wheeler-dealer-type bloke who started renting out one, then asked me to come in on it. And I've been doing it ever since. Believe it or not, we do alright – you should check out our website for the next time Robbie has a birthday party.'

'I definitely will,' she says with a little more respect in her voice. 'What are you called?'

'Mister Bouncy,' he says with a wry smile.

Pam pisses herself laughing, 'You're Mister Bouncy?'

'I'm Mister Bouncy,' and laughs with Pam.

As they continue talking, Ger listens enough so he can make comments back, but all he keeps thinking about is what a lash she is and how much he'd love to kiss her. And then hopefully bang her, of course, but in this moment all he wants to do is kiss her. It's hard for me to watch. I've seen Pam flirt with guys over the years, but it was always in more of a jokey kind of way, never in a way that made me jealous. This is proper flirting; she likes this dude. He's a tall fucker too, which pisses me off because I wasn't that tall. I think this guy is slightly better-looking than me too. I had nice hair, but you could tell that one day I'd be bald. Not this prick, fucking hair like Michael Landon.

Pam enjoys talking to him. He's more handsome than she remembered and his deep voice seems almost soothing. There's also a nervousness about him that she finds endearing. It's not like he's all over the place or anything; he's keeping his cool and being funny, but she can tell that he's trying to impress her. And it's working, even though Ger keeps thinking about what a fool he is making of himself. He's trying to crack gags and realises that he's being over-animated, but she seems to be enjoying it so he keeps it up. He doesn't want her to leave.

He is also very aware of the elephant in the room – the fact that he had asked her to call him and she never did. This whole time he's trying to decide whether or not to mention it. And if so, how? Should he make a joke out of it, should he simply ask her to call him again? He's no dummy either, he can tell that she likes him, but then again he thought that the last time. Pam is thinking about that too. She's embarrassed she didn't call him; well, not so much embarrassed, but she feels bad and knows he must be thinking about it. She wants to explain why she didn't call. How her heart had been ripped out of her chest, how her loneliness and despair are only outweighed by her longing for a person she will never see again. That although she craves the human contact of a man, the very thought of the act makes her overwhelmed with grief and guilt.

The mad thing is I actually want her to give this guy a shot. The idea of her fucking him makes me want to puke, but seeing how miserable she is makes me feel even worse; her feeling guilty for wanting to move on. I want her to be with someone else, though I have no idea how I'm supposed to watch. The riding will be harrowing enough but it's the pillow talk that's really going to hurt.

Let's say she ends up with this guy. At some point he's going to ask who she loved more. All blokes are insecure babies when it comes right down to it. Whether she means it or not, she'll have to say him, no guy would accept anything else and when she does, I don't know how I'll be able to handle it. Fuck me, if I'm not in heaven by then I suppose I'll know that I'm in hell. But I do want her to be happy, more than anything that's what I want. And if it's torture to watch her with another man, well then that's just the way it has to be.

But all that is a long way off, anyway. Sure, she likes him, but she's still terrified that he'll bring up the calling him thing again. The longer they talk the more convinced she is that he will ask her out, so she racks her brain trying to come up with different excuses. She decides that before he has the chance to broach it she'll end the conversation and head off.

'Listen, great seeing you again but I really better go. I'm running a bit late.'

Ger can't help but look disappointed. 'Sure, great seeing you too.' He does want to ask her out but decides against it and simply says, 'Hope I bump into you again.'

She smiles and walks away from him for the second time.

As she leaves, Ger wonders what it is about her that makes him so flustered. He's only met her twice but both times he has gotten on better with her than he has with any woman he can remember. He's mad at himself for not getting a date. A single mother should be easy to get a date with, but not this one. She seems so confident to him, so out of his league. Maybe he could never score with her, he thinks. Or maybe she is just super friendly and the sexy vibe she was giving off is just her natural personality. Maybe all blokes fall in love with this chick and she's oblivious to it. Like the way all guys think good-looking waitresses fancy them because they are so friendly. This girl probably can't help it, didn't mean to be so flirty. But then again she did laugh at all his jokes and stayed chatting for ages. Maybe she does fancy him, he thinks. Maybe he does have a shot and why the hell is he leaving it up to chance?

'Pam!' he calls. 'Do you shop here …' He's about to say 'often' but thinks it's too clichéd, so stops himself at the last second. '… much?'

Big difference.

She turns and smiles, giving the slightest of nods as she keeps walking. He is aware that, having done this, he looks way less cool. That in one fell swoop he has just negated any coolness he has shown in the past twenty minutes. At this point, though, he doesn't care; at least he knows that he will see her again. He'll make sure of it.

46

Danny feels like his eyes are going to pop out of their sockets. Everything has gone red and the ringing in his ears is deafening. He kicks out, which jerks the cord further up his neck, and he can literally feel the life being squeezed out of him. He begins to lose focus on the room and his thoughts are not about his life or the fact that in a matter of minutes he won't have one anymore – like I said before, none of the life-flashing-before-your-eyes shit. All he thinks about is the physical pain and discomfort he is going through. He kicks out again and this time it's even more excruciating than before. His forehead burns; he can feel every hair on his head tingle as the oxygen struggles to flow past the rope wrapped tightly around his thick neck. His thoughts turn to Robbie and he is once again glad that he will be dead soon. He takes a breath that goes nowhere and as the last scrap of oxygen leaves his brain he passes out.

I'm helpless once again. My mind is rattled – I am willing the man who killed me to live. What is the point in his death? Life is too precious a thing to throw away. I know that now, only too well. His death would serve no purpose – would it make my family any happier? Not really. They might be glad he's dead, alright, but it won't change how they feel day to day – it won't bring me back.

Watching him passed out and strangling to death, I yell at him.

Wake up!

I've screamed at him like this many times before but always for my own amusement. To keep him up at night, to try and torture him.

Wake up, Danny!

This time, though, it's no joke – I want him to hear me now more than ever.

Life is precious, Danny, wake up!

I have woken him up in the past when he was asleep. I know I have. Can I wake him up when he is unconscious and when his life depends on it?

Life is precious, Danny, don't give it up for me. Wake up, Danny, wake up!

I can see behind his eyelids; he is trying to stir, trying to wake.

Life is precious, Danny!

His eyelashes flicker but he can't open his eyes – he's too far gone. He's lost. I know he's lost but still I give it one more shot, pleading with him not to give up, to wake up. He can hear me, I think, but he can't respond.

Wake up!

His leg kicks out for a third time – one last attempt by his body to cling on to existence. The fierceness of the twitch forces his whole body forward and his fifteen-stone frame is almost too much for the cord. It stretches further and moves up past his Adam's apple to around his jaw line. He drops slightly so the tops of his toes are touching the ground. The noose isn't a good one and the shift in position makes just enough room for air to rush back to his brain.

His eyes spasm open, just for a second, then close again. His tongue is beginning to stick out as he coughs and grabs hold of the cord with his fingernails as best he can. On the tips of his toes he can relieve the slightest bit of tension from the vice grip around his neck. It won't be enough. He squints his eyes open again, darting them around the room, then reaches his leg out to his bed, but slips and feels the ferocious tightening surging through his entire body. He can't fail again. His head is getting lighter – in a matter of seconds he will pass out again. He spots the chair he scuffed away at the beginning of all this. It's still standing just a few feet from him. Keeping his right foot scraping the ground to balance himself, he stretches out his left leg, digs his heel into the chair as hard as he can and pulls it towards him.

When the chair is close enough, he puts his left foot on the seat and transfers his weight to it. Then he drags his right leg on top of it too and feels an immense amount of pressure lifting from his neck. His tongue is retracting as he claws his fingers between his neck and the cord. He gets the tiniest of gaps, just a few millimetres, but it's enough. He takes a deep breath and the gravity of the situation hits.

He is going to live and he is glad.

He stays in that position for a few moments, gathering his strength before tackling the knots. They have all tightened so much that they are a bastard to undo – the fact that he is so weak doesn't help. He just wants to be free.

It takes a full fifteen minutes until he is able to untie the first, then slowly, one by one, the rest follow until finally he is able to slip his head out, get down off the chair and collapse onto the bed.

He turns over onto his back, rubbing his neck. Soft tears roll down his temples as he stares up at the ceiling, his lips mouthing the same four barely audible words over and over. I can see the faintest of smiles as he whispers again to himself, 'Life is precious, Danny.'

47

His remaining time in prison goes by in a daze. He manages to conceal the bruising around his neck by wearing his hoody zipped right up as far as it will go and walking around with his chin down. He isn't worried about the inmates noticing; they take no notice of him, anyway. But the guards. They'd have sent him back down to Dr Brady and God knows what else. He doesn't need that. He just needs to get through the last few weeks peacefully, before trying to figure out what the hell he will do on his release.

When that day arrives, he stands outside on the busy street and can't help but do the customary look up to the sky thing that you see in every movie when someone gets out of prison. He does it on purpose, wants to experience the cliché. It feels good. He has to admit that to himself. Christ in heaven, it feels good. Wacko was right; that place really was a kip.

He has survived the most boring place on the planet. Only just. But he survived nonetheless, and with each step he takes away from Mountjoy, the feeling of relief grows. The burden he wears in his heart remains, however, stuck tightly inside his chest. It's telling him to try. To do better. Not to be such a prick all the time. And to somehow figure out a way to help Robbie and Pam.

He takes the bus home. There'd of course been nobody to meet him when he walked out into freedom, but it was the way he wanted it. Still, it was a lonely feeling. He's thinking along those lines when he notices a young man on the bus, standing close to the driver. A father, clearly, his little boy asleep in the pram beside him. The child is close to the age Robbie had been when I was taken from him. Danny just sits and stares. A flash of him wrapping the noose around his own neck leaps into his head, which makes him feel nauseous. He did the right thing, though, he thinks. It's better that he is alive. He'll just have to prove it.

***

People look at him funny. They treat him differently too. His dad was well known in the neighbourhood, so, by default, Danny is well known too. It's an old enough estate and the same people have been living in it for years. Every time Danny had visited his old man – before all the shit hit the fan – the neighbours had always been friendly, saying how lovely it was to see him and all that. Now, they act like they hate him.

The house also acts like it hates him. Not one damn thing works in the place. The heating is bollocksed, or at least he can't figure it out. None of the doors close properly; all the locks are finicky. There is crap everywhere. He always knew his dad was a bit of a hoarder, but he didn't quite realise to what extent until now. Shit pops out of every drawer he opens with the same enthusiasm as a jack-in-the-box. It's all worthless junk. Stuff like ribbons, which he can't figure out why his dad owned, and about a million measuring tapes, newspapers from decades ago. Still, he can't bring himself to throw any of it out.

The solitude of the house is tough. Prison was lonely, but at least he could use the walls as an excuse for his loneliness. On the outside, though, he can't hide from it. None of his so-called mates reached out, nor he to them for that matter. He rang Michelle once but she didn't even answer. Never rang him back either. His message, he thought, had been a good one.

'Hi Michelle. I just wanted to let you know that I'm out and that I'm okay. I understand why you had to end things. You did the right thing. Anyway, no need to call me back or anything, just wanted to let you know. Give us a bell if you want to chat. Okay. Talk to you.'

Perfect, he'd thought. No pressure. Down to earth. Quite cool, if anything.

But there'd been nothing from her. Not a word. He knew he said the no need to call back thing, but fucking hell, he didn't mean it.

What in God's name is he still doing here? His nights are still sleepless. He hates the gaff and the more contempt the neighbours show him, the more he begins to despise them back. They don't want him here. Michelle doesn't want him here. He doesn't even want himself here. Why not leave? Sell the house and sail off into the sunset. Head off to London or someplace where nobody knows who the hell he is.

He has a thought then, which gives him a feeling close to happiness. It's the first time he's felt good about anything in over two years. He had promised Robbie and Pam in his suicide note that he would give them the house. He failed at the suicide, but he won't fail at that part of the note.

Excited by this feeling, he sets to work straight away.

He knows Pam won't want to deal with him so gets it all done through a solicitor. Just as well, he's terrible with forms and all that, so the solicitor does all the grunt work on getting the deeds ready to be handed over. The whole thing only takes a week.

Only problem is when Pam gets the call from the solicitor to explain the situation she hangs up the phone. She's fucking sick to her stomach and wants nothing to do with the place.

'It's probably worth a lot of money, Pam,' Orla points out.

'Fuck him! Does he think that will make everything better?'

'Of course not.'

'It's hard enough knowing that he's out of jail but now he's trying to do what? Help poor old me? The fucking nerve of the prick, I'd fucking love to kill him.' She's not crying, she's furious.

'I suppose you're right.'

'I don't get it. I just want him out of our life – I don't want help from him, the arrogant bastard, we don't need his help. It's his fault everything is so horrible. All of it's his fault. He has destroyed my life, he's ruined everything.' Now she's crying.

Orla feels like her heart will explode. She can't stand to see her best friend like this. Just as things were turning around too. All she wants to do is take Pam's pain away but knows there is no way of doing that. 'I'm so sorry, darling. You poor thing, Christ I wish there was something I could do.'

'There's nothing anyone can do. I'm trying to get through each day the best I can, then I get some call out of the blue. You should have heard the asshole on the other end of the line – as if he was giving me this amazing news.' Orla stays silent. 'What does this Murray prick think anyway – I don't understand what he's trying to do? He's going to support us now, is that it?'

'I don't know, sweetheart, maybe he's just trying to say sorry.'

'He's not. The sick son of a bitch is probably getting off on this. He's killed my husband so, what, now he's my protector? I feel fucking violated.'

Orla puts an arm around her, trying to fight back her own tears as she comforts her friend.

***

Danny wasn't thinking, all right – of course none of that was his intention, he just wanted to say sorry but went about it all wrong. Still, there is probably no right way. He was going to devastate Pam no matter what. The very mention of his name terrifies her. Owning his house all of a sudden was only going to upset her all the more.

Dosey bastard. Still, despite the setback he decides that he won't give up. He'll put off leaving the country, sell the house himself, get the money together and then figure out how to give it to Pam.

Another problem is Pam isn't the only one who doesn't want his shitty house. No one is biting. To be fair, the house isn't that shit, it's just that his dad left it in a bit of a state. He figures he'll do it up and drop the price.

It's a big job doing up a house if you're on your own. A terrible job. Danny isn't much of a handy man either, so I get a kick out of watching him work. The painting part is fine but a monkey could paint a wall. It's the little things that have gone unnoticed over the years that trouble him. Among others, the hot press door has to be lifted, the bathroom hot water tap doesn't work for some reason, there's missing skirting in the kitchen, the kitchen itself is in bits. Every room needs something. And that's not even mentioning all the shit he has to throw out.

He has none of the right tools, the poor bastard, or the know-how. He's on Google every five minutes, checking how to fix this, how to fix that. A million little things that the right man with the right tools would probably get done in a day take Danny three months.

Men today are crap. I was the same. As a kid I'd look at my dad in awe as he'd tackle electrics, carpentry, engines. Whatever the fuck. He built our garage, our patio. But it was no big deal, everyone's dad did that kind of shit. I remember asking how he was able to do so much and he told me that it comes with age, that by the time I was a dad I'd be able to do it all too. I was delighted. The older I got I kept waiting for this day to come when I could do all that cool stuff. Except it never arrived. So disappointing.

***

When he finally gets a buyer he can't believe it. Ironically, it's a couple in their thirties with one child. They've a daughter, but still, he feels strange about it. He meets them only once on their first viewing and thinks they somehow know about him and what he has done. That they study him with a morbid curiosity – as if to show their daughter what a bad man looks like. He's wrong, of course. They don't know shit about him. But he feels that way about most people he comes across, like somehow they all know. As if his experiences before and during prison are now so etched in his face that they are as obvious as if he were wearing a badge.

Three months of fucking about with hammers and screwdrivers, paintbrushes and step ladders has finally paid off. €420,000. Fucking sweet. It does cross his mind to keep the lot, travel around the world and live it up. I can't blame him for entertaining the thought; after all, you can't help what pops into your head. Entertain it is all he does, though. He doesn't see it as his money. He takes €10,000 off the top for himself and justifies it as covering all the work and effort he's put into getting the house ready. That's just what he tells himself, though; truth is that he hasn't a penny and heading to England with €10,000 is a lot better than going there with nothing.

With the easy part over, he gives a sigh of relief. How to get Pam to take the money will be the tricky bit.

48

Tim has been worried about Brian the past few months. Well, the past six months, really, but the last few in particular. Brian just isn't himself. He's well aware that Danny Murray is out of prison and puts a lot of Brian's behaviour down to that. They used to be able to talk about everything, but that isn't the case anymore and the way that Brian has become quieter with each passing week really makes Tim anxious. But any time he brings it up, Brian just shrugs it off and says he's grand.

The more he watches Brian the more convinced he becomes that Brian is suffering from depression. Tim knows fuck all about depression but he figures this must be it. Once he comes to this conclusion, he starts worrying about what he's heard people with depression do – he starts worrying that Brian might try to top himself. He can't figure out a way of approaching the subject. Guys are funny like that, even two as close as Brian and Tim – there's no way in hell he can ask him if he's suffering from depression. First of all, he doesn't want to insult him, but even if he does say something Brian would only laugh at him and he doesn't want that either. Best to keep his mouth shut, Tim decides, and just keep an eye on him. Go for pints and stuff, try to cheer him up.

Brian isn't depressed; he's angry. That anger festering inside him grows stronger and stronger as the days pass. He's furious that Danny Murray is out of prison, running free while his brother is dead. It's funny because I'm kind of over it, whereas he's gotten worse. I'm still heartbroken about not being a part of everyone's life – Pam and Robbie's most of all. But I've accepted it. The same way as people with terminal cancer end up accepting their fate. They go through all the emotions first: denial, anger, bargaining, depression, and then they accept it. Just like if you put a scratch on your beloved car or shit yourself instead of farting – the emotions all come in the same order.

I've come to terms with it, kind of. Being dead is all I've known for over two years now, although I don't really look at myself like that anymore – I'm alive in some fashion. I exist. I watch over the people I love.

But Brian is stuck way back in anger. Stage two. He's never really been able to move on. He goes about his business, but the pain that makes him hate is lodged deep down in his underbelly. Danny getting out of prison just sets it free.

He has thought long and hard in the months since Danny's release and has finally decided to do something. He wants Danny to hurt; he wants him dead.

It's surprisingly easy to find out where people live. Brian googles Danny Murray and at first finds fuck all – a bunch of Facebook guys and some Gaelic footballer, but none are the one he wants. He's known the area that Danny hails from since the hearing, though, so tries Danny Murray Castleknock, and lo and behold up pops the obituary of Danny Senior, picture and all, survived by son, along with address. Easy. He does a slight double take as he's a bit surprised to see that his old man is dead, but decides not to dwell on it.

He drives out to the address and watches Danny at the house taking down the For Sale sign. He almost jumps out of the car right then and there at the sight of him; that big galoot strutting back into his house, all proud as punch after selling his gaff. Fucking wanker. *Laugh it up now, you piece of shit.* He pulls on the handle of the car and steps out, but when he looks up Danny has gone back inside. *Kick the door in. No. I still have time*, he thinks. *Not much time. God knows where this guy is off to with the house sold for himself.*

Brian studies the house for a long while, contemplating what to do next. He just wants it over, wants to feel something other than this hatred. He just wants to move on. He has been a little hasty driving over here without a plan. *Catch your breath*, he thinks, as he sits back into his car. He closes his eyes but instead of a plan entering his brain he sees me. It's a random thought. Something that he hasn't thought about in a long time. Usually he avoids thinking of me because it goes straight to my funeral, or worse, to the man who killed me. Strange that a happy memory enters his head now – although he hadn't been happy at the time, the incident has since entered into our own family folklore and Brian's memory forever.

He was only five when I woke him up in the middle of the night by lightly shaking him, 'Brian … Brian … wake up, buddy,' I whispered in my crackly, not-quite-broken, fourteen-year-old voice.

Brian opened his gooey eyes and saw me smiling down at him. 'What?' he asked.

'It's your birthday! Happy birthday!'

'It's my birthday?' he asked.

'Run in to Mam and Dad to get all your pressies!'

And so he did. At the time I'd thought it was the funniest thing ever – watching the poor little bastard waking Mam and Dad up a good four months before his birthday and demanding his presents.

Brian sat in his car outside Danny's house and smiled at the thought of it. It was terrible, for sure. But he could see the funny side of it now.

I actually felt awful after my little prank. Brian cried all night and Mam and Dad gave me such a bollocking. Poor fella. I can still see his face. The little chubby cheeks on him drenched with tears. I ended up crying myself that night for hurting him so much. I don't know what I was thinking – that one really backfired.

The next day, or rather later that day, after we'd all gotten up properly, I made it up to him. I said I was sorry, that I'd just got the dates mixed up, but that I would treat today like it was his actual birthday. I took him to the cinema to see *Toy Story*. He loved it; I did too, deadly film. I got him all the junk food we could carry. When we went to buy the ice cream, I made the mistake of asking him which size he wanted, 'Small, medium or large?' Should have known never to ask a five-year-old such a stupid question; of course he got the large. He was half-frightened of the cone when it was handed to him as the height of it covered the length of his torso. Before the trailers had even finished, the ice cream had covered the length of him.

For the next few years I'd always try and do something for him on 'fake birthday'. It would usually just be a small pressie like a colouring book, or I'd let him decide what to put on the telly or something. It lasted until Tim got a little older and started asking why he didn't get a second birthday too. I let it fizzle out after that. We did resurrect it a bit as adults, though, for the craic. I'd send him a happy fake birthday text, or if we happened to be together I'd mock-fuss over him.

Sitting in the car, Brian remembers me a few years back, laughing as I jumped up from the table to make sure he didn't have to get his own beer out of the fridge in our folks' house. 'Not on fake birthday, little man!' I declared. 'Allow me.' Brian burst out laughing as he nodded his approval of me handing him the bottle.

He grips the steering wheel tightly as the smile leaves his face. He turns his eyes towards Danny's house. He'll come back tonight. Surely Murray will still be here tonight. The sign was only just taken down, after all. He glares at the front door one last time before turning the key in the ignition and driving away.

49

A cheque for €410,000 would be a hell of a lot harder to turn down than a shitty gaff, Danny figured. He knows Pam wouldn't want to see him, but he won't go through the solicitor either this time. Instead he'll try to be as honest as he can with her. He still has the suicide note and maybe, just maybe, she will believe it's genuine, he thinks, as he puts it and the cheque in an envelope along with a short message.

A day later, Pam opens up the letter without thinking. She sees that it's a handwritten address so is a little curious and hopes it will be something nice. She spots that there is a little note, along with what looks like a letter. But it's the cheque that draws her eye and particularly the name that is signed to it. Her first reaction is to scream, but she clamps her mouth shut and breathes heavily out her nose. Rage runs up her spine and she wants to kick the glass screen of the front door, but instead she just stomps and grits her teeth. She becomes frozen in the same spot staring at the wall before slowly allowing herself to look down at the note that accompanies the cheque. With her hands trembling, she reads Danny's words:

I know you may never believe me and could never forgive me. But I am truly sorry for what I have done to you and your family. Every day I am tortured with what I have done to you. The letter with this was a suicide note. It was genuine but the rope slipped and I lived. You may not believe that either but it's true. Please take this cheque as a tiny apology. I don't mean it as anything else but to say sorry. I understand you probably want to throw it in my face but I hope you don't. I am leaving the country and you will never see or hear from me again.

I am so sorry. With all my heart I am so sorry.
D. Murray

She feels empty after reading it. Doesn't know how to take it. The
rage has left her and is replaced with pain. That indescribable pain
she feels every time she thinks of the brutality of my death and how
I was taken from her. The kind of pain that makes her want to sink
into the floor and disappear. But she doesn't. She calmly puts the
three pieces of paper on the counter, gathers up Robbie's things to
take him to crèche, then drives to work.

50

We had a rich old granduncle who lived in America and every time he'd visit home he'd always bring us cool toys and things that you couldn't get in Ireland. One year he brought us a baseball bat that Brian and Tim played with all summer; then they put it in the broom cupboard and forgot all about it. There it sat in the very same place collecting dust for fifteen years. Little did it or we know, in all that time, that one day it would have a rendezvous with the back of Danny Murray's skull.

Brian comes across it again by accident when he swings by my folks' place after watching Danny take down the For Sale sign. He knows that he is going to do something terrible tonight and just needs to see my parents – his parents. As always, you wouldn't be long talking to my mam without her giving you a job, so before he knows it he's headed to the cupboard to get the brush to sweep the kitchen floor. The bat stops him dead in his tracks. I suppose he's seen it many times in the last fifteen years – we all have, I guess – but took no notice of it. It was like it belonged there, was part of the furniture. He notices it this time, though. It's not a full-size baseball bat; it's kid-sized, so only about sixty centimetres in length, but it's made of solid ash, so it's hard as fuck and exactly what Brian needs. He takes out the brush, sweeps the floor meticulously, spends some time chatting before saying his goodbyes, and makes sure to conceal the bat in his coat as he leaves.

He doesn't talk much to Tim when he gets back to the flat. Tim has made dinner, which is a rare thing, but he has done it as a nice gesture for his brother, to try and perk him up or something.

It's chilli with rice and Tim is well chuffed with himself. Normally when he'd cook it would be pizza, steak or hot dogs, but this time he's actually gone to a bit of effort and got the recipe off Mam. A simple enough dinner but he knew Brian liked it.

'What do you think – is it like Mam's?' Tim asks when they're sitting at the kitchen table.

'What?' Brian asks, staring at his plate.

'The chilli, do you like it?'

'Oh, yeah, thanks – it's good.'

Tim is totally disappointed at Brian's reaction. He expected much more praise and gratitude. His initial feeling of being pissed off quickly fades, though, at the thought that it's all down to this depression thing again.

Fuck it, Tim decides – something has to be said. It's better to have this all out in the open.

'Shit, Brian, are you alright, man? You're not saying anything.'

'Yeah.'

'You're acting all depressed, what the hell is wrong with you?'

Brian frowns. 'Nothing is fucking wrong with me.'

'You're not yourself, man. I'm getting worried about you.'

With that Brian puts down his knife and fork, stands and abruptly leaves the apartment.

***

By the time he gets to Danny's house all he feels is hate. He parks outside and stews on that hate, trying to feel something different. Trying to convince himself that it is wrong for him to be here.

A half hour passes and still he feels no fear, no concern about the consequences. He just feels utter contempt for the man in the house across the street. With a deep breath, he gets out of the car and marches up the driveway, clutching the baseball bat with blind determination. He rings the doorbell, waits. Now the adrenaline starts to kick in. *Holy shit.* Half excitement, half panic – completely terrified.

It feels like an eternity since he rang the doorbell. Maybe nobody is home? The house has been sold, after all. Maybe he's not here? Brian is about to turn away and run when he hears someone coming to the door. He readies himself and for the first time feels doubt. All doubt. It consumes him – what the fuck is he doing?

Before he can answer the question he is staring Danny straight in the face and raising up the bat to strike down with as much force as he can muster. Danny instinctively turns his body away from the blow but to no avail, as the bat comes crashing down on the crown of his head with a loud crack.

***

Brian storming out of the apartment is well out of character and it really upsets Tim. He didn't even finish his dinner, which Tim knows is one of his favourites. Maybe it isn't as nice as Mam's but it's close enough and Brian always finishes his dinner. Perhaps he was a bit out of line telling Brian he wasn't himself, but it's not like he attacked him or anything. He just told him that he was worried about him.

Because Brian's that bit older, Tim still treats him like the big brother to a certain extent and looks up to him – he hates to upset him and if ever they have an argument Tim would always be the one to apologise first. He hopes he hasn't pissed him off too much, but at the same time knows that he said nothing wrong.

He wants to help Brian any way he can, but doesn't know what to do. He's never had to deal with depression and doesn't know the first thing about it. But this has gone on long enough – now he's driving off to God knows where for no reason at all? Bollocks to that, Tim decides – *I'm going to nip this shit in the bud.*

He did a search for depression on the computer a couple of

weeks ago and came across a page with a lot of useful information. A bit too much information, actually, and that's why he only
glanced at it. Not tonight, though; he'll read the whole fucking lot.
When he sits at the computer he can't remember the name of the
site, so clicks on the history button. He freezes when he sees what's
at the top of the recently viewed list. There the name stands, as if in
bold writing: DANNY MURRAY. Over and over, there are vari-
ous searches of that name. He clicks on the top one. Danny Murray
Senior's obituary appears, along with all his information.

Suddenly it all makes sense. The conversation Brian had with
him and John after the sentencing, how introverted Brian has
become over the past few months and particularly the past few days.
The past few hours. He isn't depressed. The snappiness, the not
talking – it's not depression; it's something worse.

Tim looks at the address on the screen – the search is only from
earlier today and Brian has just stormed out for no apparent reason.
This address could be the reason. He hopes he is wrong but still
hastily grabs the keys to his bike and runs out the door.

By the time Tim turns his banger of a bike onto Danny's road
he figures that he has totally overreacted. Surely Brian wouldn't
do something this drastic. He continues driving slowly up towards
Danny's address to be sure. Looking out for Brian's car, he allows
himself to smile when he can't see it. But this is followed shortly by
a deep sinking feeling when he does.

No.

Fuck no.

It is parked at the end of the road not far from Danny's house.
Tim presses on the gas so hard he practically does a wheelie. He
looks in the car window as he passes – no Brian. Then he looks up at
the house and sees his big brother beating the life out of someone.

***

The sound the bat makes off Danny's head gives Brian a shock. It's way louder than he expected. So loud, in fact, that it stops him dead in his tracks as Danny slumps to the floor. Brian thinks for a second that he's after killing him with one blow. Danny, on the other hand, doesn't know what the fuck has just hit him. It doesn't even feel sore, he just feels like he's paralysed. He somehow finds the strength to turn over onto his back and look up at his attacker, who is glaring down at him. Brian swings down again as Danny raises his arms for protection. The bat catches him right on the elbow, which is actually more painful than the smack on the head. As Danny lets out an almighty yelp, Brian has a clear target of his temple and swings with ferocity.

This time it's Brian who doesn't know what's hit him. Before the bat lands Tim tackles him around the waist and takes him to the floor, screaming, 'Stop!'

As the three of them lie side by side in the narrow hall Tim pleads again but this time gently, 'Stop, Brian. No more.' Looking into Tim's eyes, the fight in Brian vanishes. The anger fades as he gives in to the grief. Danny lies still. It has all happened so fast that he's only now realising who these people are. When he does, he wishes the bat had killed him. Out of breath and sitting up, the three of them look at each other, nobody knowing what to say.

It is Danny who goes to speak first; but when he opens his mouth he can't; instead he begins to cry. Neither of the guys knows what to do, what to say. Tim gives Brian a let's get the fuck out of here nod and the two of them get up to leave.

'Wait,' Danny croaks.

They continue walking out the door. Danny raises himself to his knees and calls again, 'Please, wait.'

The two lads stop in the driveway and turn to hear what he has to say. Danny can feel the blood running down his neck as he holds on to his elbow. He has the legs to stand, but feels that it's more appropriate to stay kneeling. 'I'm sorry,' he whispers as he chokes on the tears. 'I'm sorry.' This time louder, more definite. He wants to say something else, something better, but can't think what that could be. The guys stay still; they can tell that he wants to say more. He looks at them again through the haze of his tears: 'I'm so ... I'm so sorry.'

Neither of my brothers knows what to say. Tim is about to say, 'Fuck you', but just can't bring himself to do it. He can see the passion in Danny and understands that he means the apology with all his heart. He can't forgive him but telling him to go fuck himself isn't right either. Brian and Tim look at each other again, then simply walk away.

51

Pam hasn't spoken to anyone about the cheque. She lay awake all night, thinking about what to do with it. She was hurt, at first, by its unexpected arrival, but after much thought she admits to herself that it would help, that's for sure. It is a lot of money. Why the hell shouldn't herself and Robbie have it? By morning, she has decided. They deserve it.

She doesn't go into work and instead asks my parents to call over so she can fill them in and also to see if they can mind Robbie later – let her get out of the house for a bit.

Mam's delighted that she's taking the money. She had heard about the initial offer of the house and although she didn't say anything at the time, she'd been disappointed when Pam didn't accept it. My dad has mixed feelings, but overall he's glad too. He justifies it by looking at it as if they have just won a civil case against him.

Reading the letters Danny sent helps them. They see now that he isn't the monster that they built him up to be in their heads. Is it fair that he is a free man while their son lies in the ground? No, of course not. They'd still prefer that he never saw the light of day again, but his apology – it means something. His attempted suicide means that their tragedy has affected him as well. That I mean something to him and will be with him till the day he dies.

Once Pam leaves for the day, my parents read over the letters again, together. Neither speaks afterwards; they're too tired to be angry anymore. It will fester up again in the future and fade again, as these things do, but right now they just feel relief. That somehow the whole ordeal is over – not in the manner that they would have liked it to end, but still, it is over. They don't need to speak. They can tell each other things without speaking; they both feel the same. Instead my dad leans in and kisses my mam on the cheek, which makes her smile.

***

Pam is grateful to be out of the house, not working and not minding Robbie. The letters have helped her too. What happened was a terrible accident, but it was an accident. Danny didn't mean to kill me. Maybe Pam's just tired from the whole thing too; after all, it has consumed her for over two years. The anger, the hatred, the worry – she too needs closure, and this – the cheque, him leaving the country – this is it.

She has a nice day, all things considered. She takes a walk on the beach, watches young families play in the warm October sun. Thinks how the weather will be shifting again and how things are changing. Robbie's first day of school. He looked so grown up in his uniform. How can he be in school already? What has happened to the last two years?

She takes a drive into town and does a little shopping for herself – buys a teapot that she thinks looks cool and a quirky-looking handbag. She almost feels content, driving back to the house, swinging by the supermarket first to pick up some bits and pieces. She's going to ask my folks to stay for dinner.

It's not like Ger is stalking the place or anything – it's just that if ever he needs a big shop, he'll make sure to do it in this one rather than Aldi, which is about five minutes closer to his house. Still, he's been shopping here for the best part of four fucking months and is beginning to think that he'll never bump into Pam again. But today's the day. Unfortunately he's in the toilet-roll section when they cross paths, so for the third time in a row he takes a redner when he sees her. Only three redners in about twenty years and they're all in front of this one – he almost has to laugh at the thought. Then it flashes into his head that maybe she just thinks that's his complexion, which calms him a bit.

'Hello, Pam,' he says quietly. She saw him as she approached, so isn't taken off guard.

'Hello, Ger.'

'Are you okay?' he asks. 'You look a little …' He doesn't know what, so leaves the sentence unfinished.

'I'm okay – how are you?'

'I'm good. I …'

He's about to try to crack some joke but he can see that there is something about her demeanour. She's more serious – looking straight at him. She seems calm but delicate. He doesn't want to bullshit with her. 'I … Listen, the truth is I've been shopping here in the hope that I'd bump into you.' She stays looking at him calmly and he gets a little flustered, 'Em, I'd like to take you out basically so …'

'Oh.' Pam bows her head, not knowing what else to say.

'I know you said you're not married anymore, so let me just take you to dinner and you never know – I think we'd have a real nice time.'

'You've really caught me on a funny day.'

'Just my luck,' he says and Pam smiles, so he continues, 'I've been coming here for fucking months and I catch you on a funny day. Wonderful.'

She laughs slightly. 'Well, being honest, all my days are a little funny, I guess.'

'Oh yeah?'

Pam nods, then starts to fill up. It's just becoming too much for her and the last thing she needs is to burst out crying in front of this guy, who is practically a stranger. 'I'm sorry,' she says and considers turning to run but doesn't want to cause a big scene. She has her basket in her hand and doesn't know what to do with it so looks around anxiously.

'Pam, what is it?'

'I have to get out of here.'

'Okay.' Ger takes the basket from her hand and puts it in his trolley. Then gently takes her by the arm and leads her out the door.

Pam glances back and says, 'What about the shopping?'

'Who cares?' he says gallantly.

By the time they are outside Pam has gathered herself.

'Here, sit down over here.' Ger says and brings her to the red-bricked wall that surrounds the car park. 'Are you okay?'

'Jesus, I'm sorry.' She almost starts laughing.

'Don't be. It's not the worst reaction I've got after asking some-one out.' Now she really laughs and he smiles. 'What is it, Pam, is there anything I can do?'

'I'm afraid not. You see … well, when I said that I'm not married, it's true. I'm not married, but it's only because my husband died.'

'Jesus.'

'He was killed.'

'What? Holy shit, Pam, I'm sorry.'

'Over two years now, but it's still so fresh and today, well, yesterday something happened that's kind of knocked me again.'

This poor asshole, he wasn't expecting that. All of a sudden this beautiful, mysterious woman has a shitload of baggage. It would be priceless if it wasn't so damn sad. To be fair to the fucker, though – he is genuinely concerned. He feels something for Pam and this revelation doesn't change it.

They stay on the wall for the best part of an hour. She tells him everything. He listens and offers the best advice he can, which is basically fuck all, but he listens and by the end of it he feels more for her than he ever did. She jokes with him at the end, after he hears the entire sob story, 'So you still want to go out with me?'

'I'd love to.'

'The thing is, Ger, you're great. I just don't think I'm ready.'

'That's fine. Just take my number and whenever you want – even if it's just for a chat – give me a call.'

'I already have your number.'

'You do?' This makes him happy, knowing that she's kept it after all this time.

'Yes.'

'Well, in case you can't find it.' He writes it out again on a small piece of paper he had in his back pocket and hands it to her.

'Thanks. I better go,' Pam says, standing.

'Okay.'

'Thanks for listening to me rant on. I hope I haven't completely depressed you.'

'No. I'm glad to have seen you again.'

And with that, for the third time, he watches her walk away.

52

Danny said something in his prison cell that's stayed with me. That if I could forgive him maybe everything would be alright. I'm not sure if I forgive him, exactly, but I did not want him to die when Brian called to his door. I've become close to him. I know everything there is to know about him. He's not just any person to me. In a weird way, he's like family or something – we are connected.

Things are changing for me now. Everything is becoming more abstract. So maybe Danny was right. If I can forgive him, maybe I can move on. Will everything be okay? I'm not sure if I even want to move on anymore. I want to stay with Robbie and Pam, no matter how painful it is not to be able to touch them, to speak to them, to tell them how much I love them.

But no matter what happens, if I fade away completely, I'll always be there. I can see that now – the best part of me is with them. With my brothers, my parents, with John. They often think *what would Chris do?* Like I'm their conscience or something. Whether I would or wouldn't have done it in life doesn't matter. It's what my loved ones go by. That's how I'm helping them, by being in their thoughts. I remain alive in their hearts. In Robbie's heart. He'll never know me but I am there, helping him make the right decisions. Of course, sometimes he won't listen – he'll fuck up, do good, do bad, worry, survive, laugh, mess up – but that's okay too. That's life.

Pam is the only one who's still completely clear to me now. I am still with them all but I can let them go. I can leave John with his new family. Him and Niamh doting over every tiny thing their little girl, Sarah, does. The care he takes in handling her and the pride he feels showing her off to everyone he meets. He will be happy, and that little child is the luckiest girl in the world.

Brian and Tim will stay the same. They have always been the one constant in each other's lives – and they will always be there for one another. Their friendship that I perhaps envied slightly in life is something I am so grateful for now. They'll move on from this, they've already begun to. Tim patting Brian on the back for what he did and Brian thanking Tim for stopping him from going any further.

I'm pulling away from my parents too, though I can still see how happy they look when they're playing with Robbie. How happy Robbie is around them. He never stops laughing. I was extremely lucky to have them as my parents and now that is being passed on to my boy. Despite all that's happened, what a happy child he is. What a wonderful job they're all doing.

Danny can move on too, I think. I see him standing by his father's gravestone, saying goodbye. Promising that he will be a better man, that he will do something good with his life. That he will make him proud.

But Pam. I can't let Pam go. Or maybe she can't let me go. I'm with her all the time. Completely. I've never loved or wanted her more than I do now. I watched her cry herself to sleep the night after meeting Ger. I think of the many nights she's gone to sleep like that. The many nights I have lain beside her without her knowing. She believes I'm completely gone, that there's nothing left – if only she knew that I'm here for her in everything she does. That I watched her for days as she walked around aimlessly, lost, back to square one, as bad as she had been during the first weeks of my death. How I long to help her.

Until it suddenly feels as if she is slipping away from me.

At first, I can't help but fight it, with all my soul clinging on to her like a last breath clings to life. But then a calmness follows. I can see her.

Through the haze I can still see her. I can see her sitting on the couch in our living room. I can see her crying. I can see her turning over in her hand the small piece of paper given to her outside the supermarket. I can see her wiping away her tears. I can see her picking up the phone and dialling his number.

ACKNOWLEDGEMENTS

The final task of writing any book is to say thank you to people. This is something I have been looking forward to ever since getting a publishing deal. For me, I must start at the beginning. Carol Ryan, this book could not have been written without you. Thank you for your constant input, for being my first editor, for your help, your guidance. But above all else, thank you for your unrelenting support and for never once making me feel like I went on about this story too much. Despite the fact that it has been all I have been going on about for years. You are my world, my love. The greatest achievement of my life was meeting you.

I had many early readers who gave me encouragement and told me that I was on the right track. Eamonn Shaikh, Stephen Ryan, Linda Ryan, Miriam Ní Fhathaigh, Joan and Eddie Gallen, Paraic O'Muircheartaigh, Rose and Donie Fitzpatrick, and Ed Flannery to name just a few. A particular mention to Jillian Bolger and Derek Landy for taking the time to work on early edits – their input was invaluable. Thank you to the former governor of Mountjoy Prison, John Lonergan, and to prison officer Terry Powell for the access and time you granted me. Huge sections of this book could not have been completed without it and without seeing first-hand the inner workings of the prison. The Irish Writers Centre is a wonderful resource for writers; thank you for the Novel Fair win and the vote of confidence you've given me.

I grew up in a house full of storytelling. Thank you to my mam, Catherine, for telling most of them and for giving me a love of music, movies and books. I would not be a writer if it wasn't for you. Thank you for your influence, for pushing me and for always believing in me. The enthusiasm you showed for this book or anything else I do is a constant lifeline that I am so lucky to be able to grab hold of. Thank you to the best man I know – my dad, Michael. Your artistic mind is an everlasting source of inspiration and ideas from which I am so grateful to be able to constantly draw. The support and guidance you give me in everything is as important to me as air; I could not live or succeed in anything without it. My brother, Mark, yours is a shoulder that I cry on, lean on and am lifted up by. I could not have written this book without having you as a role model. I wish there was a stronger word than *support*, because that word does not come close to conveying what you have shown me throughout my entire life, this book being no exception.

I heard that Maeve Binchy once told a concerned writer that editors were a necessary evil that all writers must endure. Well mine was a necessary good. Thank you Noel O'Regan for your keen eye and dedication to the craft of writing. I will be forever grateful for your tireless effort and the input you put into this book to help make it a better one. Wendy Logue also put in countless hours to the edit of this book making sure no stone was left unturned, and it is all the better for it. Thank you so much to Deirdre Roberts at Mercier Press for first believing in this story. The whole team has been a joy to work with. Thank you Patrick O'Donoghue for getting behind this book, Alice Coleman for her wonderful design, and also to my proofreader, Monica Strina.

And finally to my daughter, Bonnie; thank you for being a dream come true and for giving me one final push to make the dream of this book come true too.

ABOUT THE AUTHOR

As well as being a writer, Kealan Ryan also works as an actor and film producer. He wrote and starred in the feature film *Lift*, which has won multiple international awards. *The Middle Place* was a winner of the Irish Writers Centre Novel Fair and is his first novel. He lives in north Dublin with his wife and daughter.